PRAISE FOR BETTE NOVELS

SPARE CHANGE

"Skillfully written, *Spare Change* clearly demonstrates Crosby's ability to engage her readers' rapt attention from beginning to end. A thoroughly entertaining work of immense literary merit."

—*Midwest Book Review*

"Love, loss and unexpected gifts . . . Told from multiple points of view, this tale seeped from the pages and wrapped itself around my heart."

—*Caffeinated Reviewer*

"More than anything, *Spare Change* is a heartwarming book, which is simultaneously intriguing and just plain fun."

—*Seattle Post Intelligencer*

PASSING THROUGH PERFECT

"Well-written and engaging."

—*Kirkus Reviews*

"Crosby's characters take on heartbreak and oppression with dignity, courage, and a shaken but still strong faith in a better tomorrow."

—*Indie Reader Magazine*

THE TWELFTH CHILD

"Crosby's unique style of writing is timeless and her character building is inspirational."

—*Layered Pages*

"Crosby draws her characters with an emotional depth that compels the reader to care about their challenges, to root for their success, and to appreciate their bravery."

—Gayle Swift, author of *ABC, Adoption & Me*

"Crosby's talent lies in not only telling a good compelling story but also in telling it from a unique perspective . . . characters stay with you because they are simply too endearing to go away."

—*Reader Views*

BABY GIRL

"Crosby weaves this story together in a manner that feels like a huge patchwork quilt. All the pieces and tears come together to make something beautiful."

—Michele Randall, *Readers' Favorite*

"Crosby is a true storyteller, delving into the emotions, relationships, and human dynamics—the cracks which break us, and ultimately make us stronger."

—J. D. Collins, Top 1000 Reviewer

SILVER THREADS

"*Silver Threads* is an amazing story of love, loss, family and second chances that will simply stir your soul."

—*Jersey Girl Book Reviews*

"Crosby's books are filled with love of family and carry the theme of a sweetness for life . . . you are pulled in by the story line and the characters."

—*Silver's Reviews*

"In *Silver Threads*, Crosby flawlessly merges the element of fantasy without interrupting the beauty of a solid love story . . . sure to stay with you beyond the last page."

—Lisa McCombs, *Readers' Favorite*

CRACKS IN THE SIDEWALK

"Crosby has penned a multidimensional scenario that should be read not only for entertainment but also to see how much love, gentleness, and humanity matter."

—Gisela Hausmann, *Readers' Favorite*

The
Summer
of New
Beginnings

ALSO BY BETTE LEE CROSBY

Wyattsville Series

Spare Change
Jubilee's Journey
Passing Through Perfect
The Regrets of Cyrus Dodd
Beyond the Carousel

Memory House Series

Memory House
The Loft
What the Heart Remembers
Baby Girl
Silver Threads

Serendipity Series

The Twelfth Child
Previously Loved Treasures

Stand-Alone Titles

Cracks in the Sidewalk
What Matters Most
Wishing for Wonderful
Blueberry Hill
Life in the Land of IS: The Amazing True Story of Lani Deauville
Esther's Gift: A Kindle Worlds Novella

The
Summer
of New
Beginnings

A MAGNOLIA GROVE NOVEL

Bette Lee Crosby

LAKE UNION
PUBLISHING

Text copyright © 2018 by Bette Lee Crosby
All rights reserved.

Published by Lake Union Publishing, Seattle

www.apub.com

Amazon, the Amazon logo, and Lake Union Publishing are trademarks of Amazon.com, Inc., or its affiliates.

ISBN-13: 9781503901247
ISBN-10: 1503901246

Cover design by Laura Klynstra

Printed in the United States of America

For my husband, Richard.
You have always believed that I can fly.
You are my rock and my inspiration.

Coming to Magnolia Grove

When Lila married George Briggs, she believed they would settle into a lovely little house, raise a family, and live happily ever after. She was partly right.

On a Sunday afternoon, when the summer sun was high in the sky and the air sweet with the scent of magnolia blossoms, she and George went for a drive in the country. They started out looking for a farm stand with fresh strawberries and bushel baskets of peaches, but the moment they entered Magnolia Grove, their fate was sealed.

"Let's stop for a soda," Lila suggested as they cruised along Main Street.

They settled at a sidewalk table, ordered ice-cream sodas, and sat for nearly an hour. Lila was taken with the people she watched come and go—families mostly, some with toddlers, others with teenagers, all of them laughing and happy. The thing that impressed her was the way people greeted one another, stopping to pass the time of day and waving to neighbors on the far side of the street.

"This is such a friendly town, isn't it?" she said, a sparkle in her eye.

George nodded. "Would you like to ride around and see the rest of the place?"

Of course she answered yes.

It was a tiny little town, one you could drive through from end to end in mere minutes, but they were in no hurry. First George circled the lake with its gathering of tiny bungalows at the far end, then he turned toward the residential area. They passed by houses that varied in size and style, yards planted with flowers, and tricycles left waiting on the front porch or walkway. At the end of Carson Street, Lila spotted a bunch of balloons bobbing in the breeze.

"Let's see what's down there," she said.

George obligingly turned, and as they drew closer, he saw the sign that read MODEL HOMES. An arrow pointed toward Baker Street.

"Shall we take a look?" he said, and turned in that direction.

Halfway down the street was a cluster of brand-new Cape Cod houses, five of them in a row. Each one was alike and yet a bit different: the doors a different color, window boxes on some, shutters on others—small changes that gave each home its personality.

Seeing the smile that had settled on Lila's face, George pulled to the curb and parked. Hand in hand, they went from house to house, taking everything in, weighing the yellow countertop against the more basic beige one, peeking into closets and imagining a time when they would need a house of this size for the family they would one day have.

Lila fell in love with the house that had a brick-lined walkway, black shutters at the windows, and a young magnolia tree planted in the side yard.

"Oh, George, this is the perfect place to raise a family," she said.

He agreed. That same day they put a deposit on the house, and they moved in two months later. Before Christmas arrived, Lila had women friends up and down the street, and George was a regular at the men's Thursday-night poker game.

Tracy was born the following summer, and Meghan came along a year later.

With two beautiful girls and a husband she adored, Lila knew all the happiness she had foreseen on the afternoon they drove into Magnolia Grove had come to pass.

That held true until that terrible year Meghan was preparing to leave for the Grady College of Journalism. That summer, the beautiful life Lila had built came crashing down around her.

The Darkest Day

Lila always said Meghan was born with words already forming in her head. When Meghan was barely eleven years old, she used her allowance to buy a black-and-white composition book. On the first page, she wrote "The Private Thoughts of Meghan Briggs" in loopy handwriting and used a smiley face to dot the *i* in her name. Then she drew a flowery border around the words, turned to the second page, and began scribbling thoughts about her desire to have summer sandals the color of a daffodil and how she was drawn to a boy named Marcus. Before the notebook was filled, Meghan knew exactly what she wanted to do with her life. She wanted to be a writer—a journalist or novelist, perhaps.

When she announced this intention, Lila saw the determination in her daughter's face and gave a proud smile. "You surely are like your daddy."

In Meghan's senior year of high school, she applied to the Grady College of Journalism at the University of Georgia in Athens and was accepted. That winter she filled two notebooks with thoughts of going off to Athens and following in the footsteps of Mr. Henry W. Grady himself.

On graduation day, as she walked across the stage to receive her diploma, she glanced out at the audience and smiled. They were all there, all the people she loved: her daddy, wearing a smile that stretched the full width of his face, and her mama, sitting proudly beside him. On his other side, her older sister, Tracy, was looking down at her cupped hands, probably texting Dominic, her boyfriend of the day.

The early-morning forecast had threatened rain, but a gentle breeze pushed the clouds aside. By ten o'clock the sky was a blanket of blue with sunlight dappling the grass. When they gathered for photographs after the ceremony, Meghan was all smiles.

Two days later, everything changed.

The storm that had threatened for days finally rolled through and soaked the ground. The temperature rose to ninety-seven that afternoon, and the air turned so muggy you had to work at breathing. Meghan and her daddy were sitting on the front porch, lazily pushing back and forth in the swing.

"You excited about leaving?" he asked.

"I sure am."

Of course Meghan was ready. She'd been ready for a long time. Before the end of her junior year, she had recommendation letters from three teachers, her soccer coach, and the pastor at Good Shepherd Church. Her dream had become a reality when she'd been accepted to the Grady College of Journalism, and now, in seven short weeks, she would be leaving for Athens.

George Briggs reached across and took his daughter's hand in his.

"I'm awfully proud of you," he said, "but I'm going to miss having my little helper."

"I'm not gone yet," she replied. "I can help out until the middle of August. Maybe by then you can get somebody . . ."

Five years earlier, when George had had his first heart attack, he'd resigned his job as a stockbroker and bought the *Snip 'N' Save* magazine. He'd viewed owning it as a less stressful way to make a living. In the beginning, it was a simple thing to produce the weekly eight-page booklet with front-to-back coupons for savings on everything from a car to a package of toilet paper. But in five years, George's keen business acumen couldn't help shining through and had caused the magazine to grow to the point where it was now forty-eight pages and at times went as high as sixty-four.

The room that was once a den was now the office of the *Snip 'N' Save*. It was in the rear of the house behind the dining room. There was space for two desks but little else. Finding a person to work in such an environment was rather unlikely.

"Maybe Mom or Tracy could help," Meghan suggested.

Her daddy turned with a smile. "You know how your mama is with computers."

With Lila there was plenty of cause for concern. Although she was a whiz in the kitchen, when it came to computers, she was at a loss. Something as simple as multiple attachments threw her into a tizzy. She'd download an advertising order, then find it impossible to locate in the computer. Staring at the screen helplessly, she'd mumble, "It's gone. Simply gone."

Tracy had her job at the bank, and when she wasn't working, she was generally off with Dominic. College was not and had never been part of Tracy's agenda, and neither was working alongside her daddy at the *Snip 'N' Save*.

"Don't worry," George said, then gave Meghan's hand an affectionate squeeze. "I may decide to cut back to thirty-two pages and just turn people away once the issue is sold out."

She laughed. "Daddy, you know you're never going to turn anyone away."

Accepting that she was right, he laughed along with her.

Despite the heat and beads of sweat trickling down their backs, they sat and talked for nearly an hour. Then Lila called for them to come inside where it was cool and have a dish of ice cream. Afterward, Meghan headed for her bedroom where once again she looked through the Grady brochures that she'd read a hundred times before. George took the June issue of *Businessweek* and settled in the living room. Lila puttered around the kitchen until almost eleven, then went in to wake

George. She'd looked in on him earlier, but he'd fallen asleep in the chair as he so often did.

She shook his arm and said, "Honey, it's time for bed."

Moments later, the most horrifying scream ever heard echoed through the house. It wound its way up the staircase, beneath closed doors, and into the far corners of every room. Meghan bolted from the bed and took the stairs two at a time. Following the sound of Lila's cries, she headed for the living room.

"What happened?"

Lila was sitting on the floor, her head buried in George's lap. Sobbing hysterically, she could barely gather enough strength to speak.

"Your daddy . . . ," she said, the tears making her breath hitch, and then her words fell away.

Although Meghan's shirt was still wet with perspiration from the heat of the day, she shivered with the icy thought left hanging in the air. She knelt beside her daddy, took his limp hand in hers, and understood the reality of what was.

"Oh, Daddy," she cried, and dropped her head onto his arm.

When Tracy was with Dominic, she inevitably turned off her cell phone. If she was snuggled into his arms, the only thing she cared about was the feel of his mouth pressed hungrily against hers. The rest of the world could wait.

By the time he dropped her off in front of the house, the ambulance had come and gone, taking George with it. There were still two cars parked in the driveway. The black sedan belonged to Dr. Elliott, who'd given Lila a sedative to calm her. In front of the sedan was a patrol car. Two officers had arrived on the heels of the ambulance and stayed even after the medics carried George's body out.

Tracy rushed in, breathless. "What's going on?"

Lila was lying on the sofa with a damp cloth folded across her forehead, but she popped up the moment she heard Tracy's voice.

"Where were you?" she said angrily. "We've been calling for hours!"

"With Dominic," Tracy replied, then she went back to asking what was wrong.

"It's Daddy," Meghan said tearfully. "We think he had another heart attack."

"Is he okay?"

Even as she asked the question, Tracy knew the answer. It was visible in the slump of Meghan's shoulders and the glassy look in her mama's eyes. She dropped onto the sofa beside Lila and gave a sorrowful sigh.

"Oh, Mama, I'm so sorry. I should've been here. If I'd known . . ."

Meghan looked across at her sister. "You couldn't have done anything anyway. Daddy was gone when Mama found him."

In the wee hours of the morning, Lila fell asleep on the sofa with Tracy curled into a ball beside her. Meghan took the afghan from the back of the chair, spread it across the two of them, then turned off the light and went into the *Snip 'N' Save* office.

In here she could still feel her daddy. She could leaf through the organized clutter on his desk and make herself believe she would find him sitting there the next morning. There was a measure of comfort in running her fingers across his keyboard, in scooting down in his chair and bracing her stretched-out legs against the back of the desk as he did.

She sat for a while. Then, without thinking, she moved the mouse and clicked on the e-mail icon. Three new ads had come in. Meghan downloaded them, sorted them into folders, and then clicked on his calendar.

Next week's *Snip 'N' Save* was already at the printer; the following week's issue was scheduled for release on Friday. The three ads that had come in were the last of what was booked. She clicked on the Adobe icon and opened InDesign, then slid each of the ads into place and closed the file.

Long after Meghan powered off the computer, she remained in the office thinking about her daddy and wondering what he'd want her to do. Oddly enough, the answer she came up with wasn't anything like what George would have wanted.

Lila

I didn't just lose the love of my life; I lost my best friend. My heart feels like it's broken into a million tiny little pieces. I think about how I'm going to move through life without George, and it seems like a task so far beyond me. Just the idea of it makes me feel like I'm suffocating. If I can't even force my own breath in and out of my chest, how am I ever going to be able to care for my two girls?

I look at Meghan and know the pain in her heart is as great as mine. She and her daddy were born of the same soul. They were alike in a thousand ways, ways that I don't even understand. When her heart was broken, it was George, not me, who could comfort her. With him gone, what is she going to do? I hope she will turn to me, but the thing is, I'm not like George; I don't have the way with words he had.

I think back on that terrible summer when Clancy disappeared from our backyard and remember how George's broad shoulders carried the agony of it.

Clancy was Meghan's dog, a gift from her daddy on her tenth birthday. George and I had argued about it, me saying she didn't need a dog and him saying that was exactly what she needed. "Meghan keeps to herself too much," he said. "Having a dog will help bring her out of her shell." He was right. She loved that dog more than you'd imagine possible. When I heard the school bus rumbling down Baker Street, I knew seconds later she'd come barreling through the kitchen door and head for the backyard to check on Clancy.

The day he went missing, I was busy making cookies for the church bake sale, and he was underfoot, so I opened the screen door and let him out. He was five at the time and knew to stay in the backyard.

Meghan came in from school and headed for the backyard. When Clancy wasn't there, she went through the house calling his name, checking the closets and looking under the beds. Once she realized he was nowhere to be found, she ran into the street calling his name. By then, huge tears were rolling down her cheeks.

I panicked and called George to come home from work. That night he and Meghan scoured the neighborhood for miles in every direction. Long after dark, they continued, going from street to street, calling out Clancy's name. It was almost midnight when they finally returned home empty-handed. According to George, they'd gone all the way around the lake and searched the wooded lot behind the ballpark.

As he was telling me of all the places they'd looked, I kept thinking, I should have gone outside to check that the gate was closed.

We went through months of heartache and anguish. Every evening Meghan and George went out at the same time they would have walked Clancy—only instead of walking the dog, they went up and down the streets calling his name. They looked like two sad shadows stuck together. Back then you could almost see the heavy cloud of sorrow hanging over our house. In the still of night, George and I would be lying side by side in the bed and we'd hear Meghan's mournful sobs. That just about tore holes in my heart.

Clancy was never found. It was as if he had simply disappeared from the face of the earth. I knew we'd never see that dog again, and I suspect George knew it also, but as long as Meghan held out hope, he was there for her. There's no replacement for a daddy who will do things like that.

I'm not nearly as worried about Tracy. Yes, I know she will miss her dad, but she's a free spirit. She goes where the fun is. She'll mourn for a while, *then move on. Up until now I was that way myself, but now . . . I doubt such a thing is possible.*

Birth and death change a woman. Birth fills a woman with the joy of life, and death takes back all that was given.

When Tracy was born, I went from being a young woman with few cares to being a mother—a woman responsible for another life.

She was our firstborn, and she clung to me from the day we brought her home from the hospital, but with Meghan it was different. When she was colicky or teething, the only one who could soothe her was George. On nights when I could barely keep my eyes open, he'd take her in his arms and walk the floor until she finally quieted.

There are times when I wonder if Meghan remembers those nights, if perhaps that was when she and George formed this unique bond they had.

Last night I saw her sitting in George's office. Hunched over in the chair as he used to do, she looked like a shadow he'd left behind. I stuck my head in the door and suggested maybe it was time for her to go to bed.

She said, "I can't, Mama. I've got to do this. The Snip 'N' Save *is the only part of Daddy I've got left."*

I swear I could almost hear my heart cracking open when she said that. I wanted to say this wasn't your daddy—he was a thousand other things, but not this. The thing is, I could tell by the look in her eyes that she wasn't going to believe that any more than she believed I checked the back gate that day.

Meghan doesn't give her trust easily; you've got to earn it. George did, and now it's up to me.

I pray that I am up to the task, but the sad truth is I don't know if I am. George would know, *I tell myself.* George would know, *but George isn't here. That thought comes back to me a thousand times a day, and each time it leaves another hole in my heart.*

Perhaps I'm feeling sorry for myself, and right now that's a luxury I can't afford. I'm a mother with two girls depending on me; I've got to stay strong for them. I'll do whatever is necessary to keep our family together and give my girls a chance at the kind of happiness I've known.

A Changing Life

On the day of George's funeral, the friends and neighbors Lila had known for twenty-five years were gathered together. They sat side by side in the pews of the Good Shepherd Church. One by one they came to her, hugged her, and promised to be there if she needed something.

"Anything at all," they'd say, then move on to make way for the next person.

After Alice Watkins hugged Lila and promised to be there come what may, she took Meghan by her skinny little shoulders, held her close, and whispered how she had to be strong for her mama.

"I will," Meghan replied tearfully. "I know it's what Daddy would have wanted."

At the cemetery, Tracy leaned heavily on her mama's arm, but Meghan stood next to George's sister, Phoebe, both of them with the same blonde hair and the same narrow Briggs nose. A gust of wind came by, and for a moment, Meghan fluttered like a leaf that was about to blow away.

That night the three women gathered at the kitchen table, sipping cold cups of coffee and absently toying with food that remained untouched. The question circling the table was, "What now?" George had been the backbone of the family, and without him they were like a ship without a rudder.

Lila's first thought was to close down the *Snip 'N' Save* and sell the house.

"The *Snip 'N' Save* makes money," she said, "but not that much. If we close it down and sell the house, we could manage to get along on our savings and the money from your daddy's insurance."

A look of astonishment swept over Meghan's face. "Close the *Snip 'N' Save* down? Completely?"

"Yes, completely."

"I agree with Mama," Tracy said. "It's more work than it's worth, and none of us want to take on the responsibility."

"Daddy put his heart and soul into building the *Snip 'N' Save*," Meghan countered. "Closing it down makes it feel like he never existed."

Lila gave a disheartened sigh. "It's not what I want to do, but I don't believe we have any other choice."

Tracy nodded. "I've got my job at the bank, and Mama's hopeless at the computer. She's never even opened that design program."

"There are still six weeks before I leave for college. I could teach you how to—"

Lila was already shaking her head. "I've got you girls to worry about. There's no way I can take on that computer."

"I absolutely am not going to quit my job at the bank. Mr. Pelosi likes me. He hinted that I'm in line for a promotion to head teller."

Meghan sat there with her brows pinched into a knotted line. "I was thinking I could put InDesign on my laptop, do the layouts in my dorm, and send the finished magazine back for you and Mama to take it from there."

Now Tracy and Lila were both shaking their heads.

"You're the only one familiar with the business operation," Tracy said, "and I don't see any way you can handle the whole thing from Athens."

"Maybe Aunt Phoebe could help."

"Phoebe?" Lila gave an even more emphatic shake of her head. "Two years ago George asked if she'd like to go in on the business, and she said no. She told him she was retired and planned on staying retired."

"Oh." Meghan's face fell.

The three of them sat there with no one saying anything for a long while, then Tracy offered a suggestion.

"How about instead of closing the *Snip 'N' Save*, we sell it? That way Dad's business would still be intact, and we wouldn't have to worry about running it."

Lila gave a broad smile and turned to Meghan. "That sounds good, don't you think?"

Meghan gave an almost imperceptible shrug. "We'd still want to keep it operational until we found a buyer."

She stayed quiet for a few minutes, thinking through everything. Finally, she came up with an answer.

"I'll wait a year before starting at Grady," she said grimly. "That way I can keep the *Snip 'N' Save* up and rolling until we find a buyer."

Lila hesitated a moment.

"I guess that would work," she finally said. "You wouldn't actually be giving up school, just postponing it for a year."

Meghan didn't say her heart was already there; it had been there for years. She'd filled seventy-six composition books with words. Now she yearned for the knowledge of how to rearrange them, of how to turn them from rambling thoughts into meaningful stories that people would read and then days later discover still lingering at the far edges of their brains.

But her heart was also with her daddy, and Meghan knew the truth. She was the only one who understood the business, knew how to work the design program, understood scheduling, and was familiar with the customers. No one told her to give up her dreams; the thought was her own.

"I could help out," Lila offered. "Not on the computer but maybe typing letters or doing a bit of filing."

Meghan didn't have the heart to tell her mama everything was done electronically. There was no filing or letters to be typed. Rather than explain, she gave a smile of appreciation.

"Thanks, Mama. That would be really helpful."

Tracy's face lit up. "See, there was nothing to worry about after all. Everything will work out perfectly."

Once it was decided, there was nothing more to be said.

The next morning, Meghan sent an e-mail to the director of admissions at the journalism school. She apologized for having to drop out of the upcoming semester and assured him that it was a temporary thing. A year, perhaps, but certainly no more.

That night she wrote about the decision in her journal. Although a single sentence could have told the story, she filled four pages, and every one of them was stained with droplets of tears. On the last page she wrote, "I believe this is what Daddy would want me to do," and closed the book. Ignoring the blank pages in the back, she tied a slender ribbon around the notebook, then slid it into the storage box under her bed. It was the box that held all her other journals, but this was the only one left unfinished.

The following day Meghan moved her few belongings in the office from the small desk with the laptop to the larger one with the desktop computer and monitor you could read from across the room. George's chair was bigger than hers—too big, actually—but she pushed a cushion behind her back and settled into it. She signed on with his password and scrolled through his e-mail.

Although you could see no physical change, she had in fact become her daddy.

Meghan procrastinated for almost two weeks before she could bring herself to type up a description of the business and offer it for sale on Craigslist. It seemed that letting go of the *Snip 'N' Save* was almost like letting go of her daddy. Even when she finally did get around to listing it, she didn't use any of the words she'd once used to describe the magazine. In place of *exciting new venture* and *unique opportunity*, phrases like *long hours* and *complex scheduling* somehow seemed more appropriate.

Not surprisingly, month after month went by, and there was not a single inquiry. No one even called to ask the price of such an offering. The few times "Unknown" did pop up on the caller ID, Meghan refused to answer the phone.

Although nothing was resolved, the problem of what to do with the *Snip 'N' Save* seemed to disappear. Lila never asked questions, and Tracy seemed not to care one way or the other, so when the listing expired, Meghan didn't bother renewing it.

As the weeks came and went, Meghan spent most of her time in the office. On occasion, and it was indeed an occasion, she would go into town and call on the customers who needed a slight nudge.

"I know you'll want to be in the Founder's Day issue," she'd say, sounding exactly like George.

After a few months, the handful of customers who'd at first been skeptical of working with her came around and began placing ads. By then Meghan had comfortably settled into the job and no longer entertained any thoughts of selling the *Snip 'N' Save*. It simply wasn't the right time, she reasoned, knowing full well there would probably never be a right time.

Meghan

Tracy and Mama don't see things the way Daddy did. Mama thinks I ought to be studying something more useful like nursing or teaching, and Tracy claims that college is a total waste of time. Why bother, she said, when you're eventually going to get married and stay home anyway?

Daddy understood how much going to Grady meant to me. He was the one who patted me on the back and said being a journalist was a profession to be proud of. He understood about the words stuck in my head and how I ache to put them on paper.

I remember the day Daddy took me to visit Grady, and looking back I can honestly say that was the best day of my life. We rode together in the car, and when I talked about how I was planning to follow in the footsteps of Henry W. Grady himself, Daddy smiled and said he had no doubt that I could do it.

"If you put your mind to something and stick with it, you'll make it happen," he said.

That's how Daddy was; he believed in me the same as I believed in him.

Grady was my dream, but seeing the Snip 'N' Save *flourish was Daddy's, and I'm not going to let it die along with him. He'd want me to keep it alive, and that's exactly what I'm going to do.*

Not leaving for Grady was the hardest decision I've ever made. It felt like I was giving up on something I'd worked so hard to get, but I did it because I couldn't let Mama sell the Snip 'N' Save *to some stranger. It's the last piece of Daddy I have left.*

Somehow, someway, I'll make this work. I have to, because it's the only way I can hold on to that piece of Daddy. He's part of the Snip 'N' Save *just as the* Snip 'N' Save *was part of him.*

Mama and Tracy might not agree, but I know I'm doing the right thing. At night when I go into the office and sit in Daddy's chair, I can almost feel him watching over me and smiling. Now if that's not a sure sign, then I don't know what is.

The Wild Child

Piece by piece, the Briggs family slid into what was rapidly becoming the new normal. Every Tuesday Lila made a chicken noodle casserole, and Aunt Phoebe came to dinner. More often than not, Tracy failed to show up. She spent most of her evenings with Dominic and came home far later than she'd ever dared when their daddy was alive.

On the first Tuesday of October, Phoebe came to dinner. Where she'd made light of Tracy not being there on previous occasions, this time it rankled her.

"Does she not remember that I'm her daddy's sister?" Phoebe asked pointedly.

"Well, of course she remembers," Lila said, "but she's young and wants to be out having a good time." Glancing at Meghan, she added, "Young people should be out kicking up their heels."

Phoebe's dubious expression was reminiscent of her brother's.

"I'm all for having fun, but if a young person is running amok . . ."

She left the remainder of that thought hanging ominously in the air and reminded Lila that this was the fifth Tuesday in a row Tracy had missed dinner. Dismissing the thought with a flick of her fingers, Lila promised that Tracy would most certainly join them the following week. The tone of their conversation unnerved Meghan and set her to wondering what her daddy would have done.

Long after Phoebe was gone and her mama sound asleep, Meghan lay awake waiting to hear the growl of Dominic's car as he whizzed by to drop Tracy off. When she finally heard him rumbling down the street, she slipped out of her room and into her sister's.

Tracy tiptoed in carrying her shoes. She made her way up the staircase quietly, then crept inside her room, clicked the door shut, and snapped on the light. That's when she saw Meghan standing there and gasped.

"Good grief, you scared the life out of me!"

Dropping her shoes onto the floor of her closet, she turned back. "What are you doing here?"

"Waiting for you," Meghan replied in a disapproving voice.

"Why?"

"I'll tell you why after you tell me why your skirt is inside out."

Tracy glanced down and laughed. "Oh, jeez. It's a good thing you're the one who saw it and not Mama."

"Do you have any idea what you're doing?"

"Oh, pleeease. It's late, and I'm tired. Do I have to listen to you preach?"

"It's not preaching if you love somebody and don't want to see them get hurt. Aunt Phoebe said no man is ever going to respect you if you don't respect yourself."

Tracy put up a hand as if to stop Meghan. "Wait a minute, this is Dominic we're talking about. Dominic doesn't put a lot of stock in this respect stuff, but he's crazy about me. If I asked him to do handstands in the middle of the street, he'd do it. That's how wild he is about me."

"Well, then, why doesn't he ask you to marry him?"

"He's not ready yet," Tracy said. She stepped out of her skirt and tossed it over the back of the chair.

"I just think you—"

"Don't bother. I already know what you think."

That was the end of the discussion. Once Tracy decided not to talk about something, neither hell nor high water could get it out of her.

Lila was in the kitchen when Tracy came down the next morning. Her irritation with her daughter was obvious. Although she'd waved off Phoebe's comment, the truth was it had struck home. Since the funeral, Tracy had gone from being mischievous and carefree to downright irresponsible. Worse yet, she'd taken up with a group of friends that her daddy would most certainly have disapproved of.

Lila considered this her own fault. She was not a good disciplinarian, never had been. George was always the one to set rules and expect the girls to abide by them. If he said be home by eleven he meant eleven, not eleven fifteen. With Meghan it was never a problem. She was as precise as her daddy. If he said eleven, she was home by ten forty-five.

Not Tracy. She missed curfew on a regular basis, and more than once, Lila covered for her. She reasoned Tracy was just young and having fun; she herself had been the same way. Of course, back then it simply meant stretching the rules for an extra half hour or so. Now it seemed as if Tracy had tossed the rule book out the window. She came and went as she pleased and made no apologies for doing so.

"You missed dinner again last night," Lila said sharply, "and Aunt Phoebe wasn't too happy about it."

Tracy gave her no-answer shrug and plopped down at the table. "What's for breakfast?"

"Toast." Lila set a plate with two slices of burned toast on the table.

"That's it? No eggs? No pancakes?"

Lila handed Tracy a cup of coffee and sat across from her. "We have to talk."

Tracy rolled her eyes. "Meghan told you about the skirt, is that it?"

"Meghan didn't tell me anything. What about the skirt?"

21

"It's nothing." Tracy stood and opened the refrigerator door. "I didn't have dinner last night, and I'm starving. Isn't there something more than toast?"

"Oh, for heaven's sake." Lila sighed and stood. "Sit down, and I'll fry you some eggs."

She pulled a carton of eggs from the fridge and set a skillet on the stove. As she cracked an egg and dropped it into the pan, she said, "I thought you were out with Dominic last night. Why didn't you eat dinner?"

Tracy gave another shrug, but there was a faint smile playing at the corners of her mouth.

Lila noticed. Months earlier when George was the disciplinarian responsible for the girls, Lila might have seen that bit of a smile as simply mischievous. Now it seemed flat-out rebellious.

"This skipping dinners and staying out until all hours of the night has got to stop," she said. "From now on I expect you to be here every Tuesday night for dinner. No exceptions."

"You're kidding!"

Lila slid the eggs onto a plate and smacked it down on the table. "Do I look like I'm kidding?"

Tracy broke off a piece of toast and dunked it into the center of the egg. "What brought this on?"

Something about Tracy's casual attitude infuriated Lila. She wasn't a girlfriend or sister. Good grief, she was the girl's mother and should be treated as such.

"It's your total disregard for the rules," she snapped. "If your daddy were here, you wouldn't dare stay out until all hours of the night!"

"Mama, I'm not a child! Anyway, you said Daddy's rules were too strict, remember?"

Lila tried to maintain her composure, but inside she was seething. That was precisely what she'd said on graduation night when Tracy came home smelling of smoke and beer. Now her words were coming back to haunt her.

"That was an exception," she snapped. "It applied to that one instance, because it was a special night. It certainly wasn't permission for you to start living your life that way."

Tracy scooped up the last bit of egg and shoveled it into her mouth.

"Careful, Mama," she said with a grin. "You're starting to sound like Daddy."

Anger flushed Lila's cheeks.

"Good," she said, "because starting today, I'm also going to be enforcing the rules the same as he did!"

"Okay, whatever."

With that, Tracy scooted out the door.

For the remainder of that week, Tracy came home at a fairly decent hour. She seldom made the eleven o'clock curfew, but she did come in before midnight. Accepting that this was at least a show of effort, Lila let it go by without a row. When the weekend rolled around, she told Tracy Saturday night could be an exception to the rule.

"Good," Tracy replied. "Dominic and I have a party to go to."

Lila smiled. Parties were good—great, actually. She herself loved parties. It would be nice if Meghan would get out and . . .

Suddenly the thought hit her.

"Why don't you bring your sister along?" she suggested.

"Bring Meghan?" Tracy stood there looking as if such a thought were ludicrous. "She'd never go. Dominic's friends aren't her kind of people."

"How can they not be her kind of people?"

Tracy gave another of those no-answer shrugs. "They're just not."

Before Lila had time to pursue the subject, Meghan entered the room, and the discussion came to a screeching halt. Tracy started thumbing through the messages on her phone, and Lila busied herself with watering the ivy on the windowsill.

———— ⚬⌇⚬ ————

On Monday morning and again on Tuesday, Lila reminded Tracy of the dinner with Phoebe.

"I'm expecting you to be here," she said.

"You told me ten times already, and I said I would." Tracy gulped down the last of her coffee. "Okay if I bring Dominic?"

Believing this to be a turning over of the new leaf she was hoping for, Lila smiled.

"Well, of course it is. Phoebe has never met him, and it would be a good opportunity for her to—"

"Oh, crap. If Aunt Phoebe's going to start giving Dominic the third degree, I'm not inviting him."

"She won't," Lila replied. "I'll speak to her ahead of time." Still thinking about the weekend party issue, she added, "Meghan, why don't you invite someone, too? We could have a lovely dinner party. We haven't done that in ages."

"Okay. I'll ask if Amanda's available."

Amanda was Meghan's best friend, and it was easy to see why. They were both a bit reserved. Shy, you might say, but not painfully so. At the start of their freshman year at Magnolia Grove High, they sat beside one another in English Lit and formed a friendship that was almost unbreakable.

Almost, but not quite. Now that Amanda was dating Jeff Atkinson, she had little time for anything else. Couples got together with other couples, not single friends. She and Meghan still saw each other for an occasional lunch or trip to the mall, but now it was mostly text messages and phone calls.

Without missing a beat, Lila said, "I was thinking of perhaps a young man. Someone who'd make Dominic feel more at ease being with all of us women."

Meghan wrinkled her nose as if she'd suddenly caught the odor of dirty gym socks.

"Um, there's nobody I'd feel comfortable asking."

"What about Pete Mulligan?"

With her face still pinched into that look of skepticism, Meghan shook her head.

"Why don't you invite Wayne what's-his-name?" Tracy said. "The guy you went out with last week?"

Meghan pushed a piece of French toast around her plate. "I'd rather not."

"Why?" Lila asked.

"Because inviting a guy to a family dinner makes him think there's something more to the relationship. That's not a message I'm ready to give anyone right now."

"How about if Tracy asks Dominic to bring a friend?"

Meghan's face froze in horror. "That's as much as saying I can't get a date of my own, Mama! Are you trying to embarrass the life out of me?" She stood, scraped the remainder of her breakfast into the garbage can, and turned toward the *Snip 'N' Save* office. "I've got work to do."

Lila loved parties, and even if Dominic were the only male at the table, she was determined to turn the evening into a wonderful dinner. Instead of her usual chicken noodle casserole, she decided to do a crown roast of pork. This meant trips to the butcher shop and the supermarket, but it would be worth it.

Dinner parties were festive and made everyone feel good. Once Meghan saw what fun it could be, she'd be more willing to invite a date. And now that Tracy was introducing Dominic to Aunt Phoebe, they could conceivably make this a once-a-month event.

That afternoon, Lila chopped the celery and onions for the stuffing. She fried a skillet of sausage, melted three sticks of butter, and mixed it all by hand. Then she piled the stuffing into the center of the crown roast and slid her masterpiece into the oven.

By six o'clock, everything was ready. The table was set with the good china, crystal wineglasses, and the anniversary silverware George had bought to celebrate their twenty-fifth. She stepped back, looked at the table with its linen cloth and napkins tented in the center of each plate, then gave a wistful sigh.

If only George were here.

The table was set for five; the spot at the head of the table was left empty. Not just empty but painfully empty. Most nights Lila and the girls ate in the kitchen. With the hustle and bustle of moving around, fetching things like an extra helping of potatoes or the saltshaker, the emptiness seemed less pronounced. But here, in the dining room, a place where they'd all gathered for Sunday dinners, she saw the emptiness for what it really was—not just a vacant chair but a vast hole in her heart.

Lila stood for a moment, picturing the way George carved a roast with such flourish, then she brushed back a tear and returned to the kitchen.

Phoebe arrived at six fifteen. She eyed the fancy table setting and said, "You should have told me it was a dinner party. I would have invited a friend."

It struck Lila as strange that Phoebe, a woman in her early sixties, would have a readily available date, and Meghan, who was young, smart, and beautiful, wouldn't.

Shortly after six thirty, Tracy burst through the front door, hollering, "We're here!"

Lila called for Meghan to quit working, then hurried in to greet Dominic. She stopped short when she saw him. She thought by coming to dinner at their house he'd dress up a bit more, but it hadn't happened. He was wearing his customary T-shirt. This one read GRINDER'S SPECIAL and pictured a shapely dancer with her leg wrapped around a pole.

She forced a smile and shook his hand.

"It's nice to see you again, Dominic," she said. "You're looking well."

"Yeah, I work out a lot."

From the corner of her eye, Lila saw the smirk on Phoebe's face. Ignoring it, she said, "Tracy, will you pour a glass of wine for everyone while I get the food?"

The pork roast came out of the oven as perfect as any Lila had ever made. The whipped potatoes were without even the tiniest lump and the string beans just crisp enough. Once all the serving dishes were carried to the table, she called the group to dinner.

As they took their seats, Lila glanced over at Phoebe and asked, "Would you like to say grace?"

Phoebe nodded and folded her hands in front of her.

"Dear Lord," she said piously. "We thank you for this food and ask that you bless all young men by giving them a proper shirt." She might have said something more, but before she had the chance, Lila whacked her beneath the table.

As soon as the *amen*s were said, Dominic asked for someone to please pass the potatoes. Lila breathed a sigh of relief. Possibly he hadn't heard the comment, or, perhaps with not knowing Phoebe, he didn't understand the jibe she'd intended.

After that single incident, the dinner went amazingly well. Meghan chatted openly with Dominic, and when he told a few lame jokes, she laughed as though she found them funny. Watching the ease with which the conversation transitioned from one topic to another, Lila again wondered why Tracy had been so reluctant to invite Meghan to the party. True, sometimes Meghan came across as a serious-minded workaholic, but that was only because she had the responsibility of the *Snip 'N' Save* resting on her shoulders. Once she was away from it, she was quite pleasant to be with. Fun, you could even say.

The bombshell came after the main-course dishes were cleared away and Lila had begun to serve her homemade chocolate cake. She was in the process of lifting a slice onto Phoebe's plate when Tracy spoke.

"Dominic and I have an announcement to make." She glanced at him and grinned. "His cousin is getting him a great job working for the city, so we're moving to Philadelphia."

Lila stopped with the server midair, halfway between the cake stand and Phoebe's plate.

"You're doing what?" she exclaimed.

The slice of chocolate cake wobbled off the server and plopped onto the good linen tablecloth, but Lila barely took notice.

"Moving to Philadelphia," Tracy repeated. "Dom has an opportunity for this really great job, and we think—"

"I'm assuming there'll be a wedding before the move," Phoebe said sharply.

Dominic spoke up. "Well, yeah, we're planning to get married. Not right away, but maybe after I get settled in my job. You know, when I feel good about myself and comfortable with where I am."

Phoebe started sputtering like a Roman candle coming to its end.

"When *you* feel good about *yourself*? And what about my niece?"

"I forbid it!" Lila snapped. "I absolutely will not tolerate another word."

"Mama, I'm nineteen years old. You can't stop me."

"If your daddy were here, he'd sure as hell stop you!"

Dominic's eyes shifted to Phoebe, then Lila, then back to Phoebe.

"Maybe I'd better go," he said. "You might need to talk this over."

Before he could stand, Tracy clamped her hand down on his arm.

"You don't need to go anywhere, Dom. We're gonna settle this right here and now!"

With her face twisted into a knotted scowl, Tracy looked at Lila and said, "I'm going with Dom. You can either wish us well or lose me forever."

"Mama, maybe we're overreacting," Meghan said, trying to steady her voice as she spoke. "We need to respect Tracy's wishes. Let's wait and see how she and Dominic feel about this in a few days."

Tracy didn't change her expression one iota. "Don't count on me changing my mind, because I'm not going to!"

"Maybe not," Meghan said, "but it would give us all time to consider the situation and behave more rationally."

"I really think I should get going," Dominic repeated nervously.

"Yes, perhaps you should." Lila angrily grabbed the plate of chocolate cake she'd placed in front of him and carried it off to the kitchen even though he hadn't touched a bite.

When Dominic left, Tracy followed him out. For a few minutes, they stood there talking, then she leaned back and tilted her face to his. He pinned her against the car, pushed his body into hers, and covered her lips with his own. After a short while, they climbed into the car and left.

As Dominic and Tracy roared off, Meghan stood at the window and watched the red taillights fade away.

In the background, she heard her mama's and Phoebe's angry voices coming from the kitchen. Phoebe yelled that her brother would turn over in his grave if he knew such a thing was happening; her mama tearfully swore she was doing the best she could. A short while later, Phoebe stormed out.

In the kitchen, Meghan found Lila hunched over the kitchen table with her face buried in her hands.

"Why?" her mama said through her tears. "Why would your sister do a terrible thing like this to me?"

Dropping down into the chair beside her, Meghan wrapped a slender arm around her shoulders.

"Tracy's not doing this to you, Mama," she said softly. "She sees things differently, and she's just doing what feels right to her."

Lila

I am just about at my wits' end. If George were here, he'd know what to do, but I don't, and Phoebe sticking her nose into it isn't helping one bit.

I simply don't understand how the same parents can have two children who are so totally different. The girls were raised in the same household, and we didn't make a bean of difference in how we treated them, but look at how it turned out.

With George gone, Meghan is more dependable than ever. No matter what you ask her to do, you can trust she'll get it done without your ever having to mention it again. You don't have to ask, because you know she did exactly as she was told.

Tracy is just the opposite. Without George around to act as the disciplinarian, she's wilder than ever. She'll look you square in the eye, say okay, and then once you're out of sight, whatever you've asked her to do is gone from her mind. She wants to have fun today and let the devil take tomorrow.

I used to make excuses for her behavior. I'd laugh and say, "What can you expect? She's like her mama." I'm not laughing anymore. Now I'm worried sick and don't know which way to turn.

Tracy thinks I don't know what it feels like to be young and in love. I do, but I also know how it feels to look back and regret something you've done. When you're young and foolish, you can so easily make a mistake that will haunt you forever. It seems Tracy would understand I'm not looking to squash her spirit; I'm only trying to stop her from ruining her life.

I've seen men like Dominic before, and I know they're not to be trusted. If a young man doesn't look a girl's parent in the eye, then you know he's up to no good. The minute that conversation turned challenging, Dominic was ready to run out of here. If he'll do it now, just imagine what he'll do when real problems come along. It's one thing to have a fling with such a man, but following him off to another state is something else entirely.

The worst of it is that I know Tracy means what she says about us losing her forever. She's young and in love, and right now she thinks it's the only thing that matters. If I try to stop her, she'll stomp off in a huff, and that will be the end of our relationship. Once you cross a bridge like that, there are too many hurt feelings to ever turn back.

The sad thing is, regardless of what children do or say, they're still your children, and you don't stop loving them. Yes, there may be occasions when you scream and yell until you're blue in the face, but even then, you don't stop loving them.

There are times when I feel this challenge is way beyond me, but I'm not giving up. I'm determined to keep both my girls close and do my damnedest to see that they have a shot at happiness.

I pray Tracy comes to her senses and realizes this before it's too late.

Sad Goodbye

It was after two in the morning when Tracy came home and found Meghan waiting for her.

"Not now," she said wearily. "I can't deal with anymore arguments."

"I'm not here to argue," Meghan replied. "I just thought you might need someone to talk to."

"About my being a disgrace to the family?"

Meghan shook her head. "I think Mama and Aunt Phoebe have already beaten that horse to death. Anyway, I don't think you're a disgrace. You're simply a woman following her heart."

Meghan stretched out her arms, and Tracy fell into them. For a few moments they sat without a need for words, soaking in the bond of sisterhood.

Tracy was the one who spoke first. "I suppose Mama is pretty disappointed in me, huh?"

"I doubt that. She really loves you; it's just that she's worried Dominic won't give you the kind of life you deserve."

Tracy gave a cynical chuckle. "Maybe it *is* the kind of life I deserve."

"Why would you say that?"

Tracy shrugged and turned away, but Meghan took her by the shoulders.

"Tell me why you think you deserve a life that's less than wonderful," she demanded.

"I'm not you, Meghan," Tracy said. "I'm not smart like you. I can't set my mind to doing something and follow through the way you do. Look at us; we're as different as night and day."

Meghan shook her head emphatically. "We *are* different, but that doesn't mean one of us is less and the other is more. Yes, we're like night and day, but nobody wants to live a life that's all night or all day. Both have their place in the world."

"Maybe being with Dominic is my place."

"What about your job at the bank? What about the promotion to head teller?"

Tracy stretched her mouth into a tight line. "Ellen Bales got it."

"Is that why you're doing this? Because of a job?"

"No. I'm doing it because I love Dominic, and I believe he loves me."

"Then get married before you go. Do it here, where Mama and I can stand beside you and see the happiness on your face."

Tracy turned away and lowered her eyes. "Dominic's not ready yet. He said he wants to be sure of his job before we get married."

"Sure of his job?" Meghan's words were wrapped in irony. "That seems like a pretty lame reason. If you're married and he loses his job, you deal with it together like Mama and Daddy did. That's the 'for better or worse' part."

"Mama and Daddy didn't deal with it together. In case you've forgotten, when Daddy needed help with the *Snip 'N' Save*, you were the one who stepped in to help him." Tracy gave a weighted sigh. "I'm not you, Meghan, and I never will be."

"Why would you want to be? You're not the only one with problems. I wish I had some of the qualities you've got."

"Oh, come on, you've got to be kidding."

"No, I'm not. Everybody likes you. You're open and friendly. Even more important, you're not afraid to let yourself fall in love." Meghan's voice had a quality of sadness woven through it when she added, "That's something I envy."

That night she crawled into bed alongside Tracy. As they lay there in the dark talking of a shared past and an unknown future, Meghan realized what a huge hole would be left behind.

"Promise me one thing," she said. "Promise me that if you ever need help, any kind of help, you'll come to me."

"I promise," Tracy said, then she turned and kissed her sister's cheek.

That night they slept in the same bed, which was something they hadn't done since the year they were six and seven. Back then it had been exciting for each of them to have their own rooms. Now, being together as they were, Meghan wondered why they'd ever wanted to be apart.

The days that followed were like sitting on a time bomb, knowing it could go off at any minute. No matter how hard Meghan tried to keep peace in the Briggs household, the slightest thing erupted into a full-scale shouting match between Tracy and Lila. It generally started over something small, like a dish left sitting on the table or the last cup of coffee gone from the pot, but in a few minutes they'd circle around to the heart of the matter: Tracy's move to Philadelphia.

It didn't help that Phoebe called nearly every day with another suggestion on how to handle things. First she told Lila to lock Tracy in her room, then she suggested packing away her shoes, because the girl couldn't go running around town barefoot. When it got to the point where she railed about finding a reason to have Dominic arrested, Lila claimed she'd heard enough and said it would be better if Phoebe didn't call.

"Not call?" Phoebe said in a breathy voice. "When my brother's family is in need of—"

"You're not your brother!" Lila said, and slammed the receiver down.

She had come to the realization there were only two alternatives, like it or not. She could accept Tracy doing what she was going to do anyway, or she could watch her daughter disappear from her life. Perhaps there would come a time when Tracy would have a change of heart, a time when she needed a family to turn to, and Lila wanted to be there.

With the weight of this decision in her heart, Lila climbed the stairs, rapped on Tracy's bedroom door, and asked if she might come in.

"Not if you're going to yell at me again," Tracy replied through the door.

"I'm not going to argue. I just want to talk."

Given the bitterness of the past few days, Tracy found that hard to believe, but she opened the door anyway. For the first time, she noticed the lines of sadness in her mama's face as she stood there looking contrite.

"I'm sorry," Lila said. "I've been selfishly thinking of how much I'm going to miss you when I should have been thinking about you going off on your own and starting a new life. Please forgive me and let me continue to be a part of your life."

"Jeez, Mama, you're always gonna be a part of my life. You're my mama."

That afternoon, Lila sat on the bed and watched as Tracy pulled things from the closet and emptied out the dresser drawers, sorting what was going to Goodwill and what would be carried off to Philadelphia. Lila thought things like Tracy's pom-poms and the teddy bear she'd had for fifteen years would be left behind, but, no, they were tossed in the boxes marked PHILADELPHIA.

Two days later, when there was barely a glimmer of pink in the sky and the sun had not yet crested the horizon, Dominic pulled into the driveway and beeped the horn. Tracy gulped down one last mouthful of coffee and hurried to the door.

Meghan came behind her. "I'll help load the car."

Lila followed them out and handed Dominic the cooler she'd filled with sandwiches and soda.

"Be careful driving," she said. "And call when you get there."

"Don't worry, Mama," Tracy replied as she shoved a collection of boxes and bags into the trunk.

Meghan had spent the night dreading this moment; now it was here. She stood there feeling as useless as a single bookend. The bitter chill of the early November morning settled around her, and she tugged her robe tighter.

"I'm going to miss you," she said in a whispery thin voice.

"It's not like I'll be in Alaska," Tracy replied, laughing. "We can still talk on the phone and text each other."

"I know." Meghan swiped her palm across her right eye to brush back a tear. A text was a pitiful replacement for sharing a cup of coffee together, and a phone call could never be the same as having her sister in the next room.

They hugged each other one last time, then Tracy tossed her tote onto the floor of the front seat and climbed into the car. As Dominic backed out of the driveway, Tracy turned with a happy smile and gave one last wave.

Then they were gone.

Long after the old car with a blue fender that Dominic never got around to painting disappeared into the misty morning fog, Meghan and Lila stood looking down the road.

"Do you think there's a chance she'll be coming back?" Lila asked.

"Not anytime soon," Meghan answered solemnly.

Tracy

I know Mama thinks I'm making a mistake, but I'm not. Dominic really is crazy about me. It's just that he doesn't believe in doing things by the book. He said when two people really love each other, they shouldn't have to prove it by getting married.

Okay, I'll admit, I would have liked a nice wedding with a fancy gown and flowers. I would've asked Meghan to be my maid of honor, and she would have said yes in a heartbeat. I can just imagine how proud Mama would be sitting in the front row of the church watching us get married. But the truth is if I have to choose between a wedding and Dominic, I choose him.

That's how love is. Give and take. Sometimes you have to give up things you want, but in the long run you feel okay with it, because you know you're doing it for a good reason.

Anyway, Dom says that sooner or later we're probably gonna get married, and when we do, I'll know for sure it wasn't something he was pushed into doing. He believes knowing that is a lot more important than worrying about what everybody else thinks.

I understand what he's saying, but in my heart of hearts, I'm not sure I can see the merit of it.

A Remembered Love

During those first few weeks, there was a phone call or text from Tracy almost every day. She had so much to say about her new life. Dominic loved his job; they'd found an apartment; she was working as a waitress; they'd gone to the aquarium. None of it was especially exciting news, but it was a way of staying in touch. As weeks turned into months, the flow of daily updates slowed and then became little more than a trickle. E-mails that previously took a full five minutes to read were whittled down to a paragraph or two, and in time they shrunk to a single line. Texts were a few words followed by an emoji.

Nothing much happening here, Tracy would write, then ask how the family was doing.

Throughout that first year, Meghan buried herself in the day-to-day tasks of the *Snip 'N' Save*. After the work that needed to be done was done, she began to create new projects: a mailing to potential customers in the surrounding towns, a special edition to celebrate the coming of spring, coupon pages for advertisers who couldn't afford to run a quarter-page ad.

The town of Magnolia Grove was expanding—new homes springing up on streets that a few years earlier were vacant lots, businesses branching out from Main Street and the Chamber of Commerce adding new members, nineteen in a single year. To keep pace with the town's growth, Meghan began to include new features in the *Snip 'N' Save*. She started with listings of special events, then added spotlight features on local businesses. Before long, she found she could afford to take on an assistant and hired Sheldon Markowitz, a young man in his second year of studying design at the community college. Once he took over the layout and design of the magazine, she had enough time to call on customers and take them to lunch as her daddy had done.

It turned out to be the perfect arrangement. As ads came in, Meghan forwarded them to Sheldon, who worked remotely, and they communicated via e-mail. When the layout was complete, he sent everything to the print shop with a few keystrokes. Once or twice a month he and Meghan got together for lunch, and although it was supposed to be a business meeting, they generally ended up talking as two old friends.

She told him about her occasional dates with Pete Mulligan and the pharmacist who'd invited her to a dance at the Elks Club. He told her about his friend Sarah. At the moment, Sarah was just a friend, but Sheldon hoped one day to change that.

"We hang out a lot," he said, "but I'm afraid if I try to ramp it up a notch, she'll back away from our friendship."

"Don't be shy," Meghan advised. "Shyness will get you nowhere." She left off the part about knowing this from her own personal experience.

In early September, on a weekday evening at Walmart, Meghan was picking up a few items for Lila. She breezed through the grocery aisles and eventually meandered past the school supply section. Right there, smack in the middle of the aisle, were hundreds of black-and-white composition books.

Her heart skipped a beat. It had been more than a year since she'd written in a journal, more than a year since she'd made the fateful decision to delay going to Grady. For a moment she remembered the joy of scrawled words running across blank pages.

Suddenly a great longing filled her heart. It was the longing for thoughts that turned themselves into words and settled on pages to be forever preserved.

Moving closer to the display, she lifted a composition book and felt the familiar desire bristling inside her chest. Until now, she hadn't realized how very much she'd missed this old friend. She dropped the composition book into her basket and hurried along the aisle.

That evening, Meghan took the book to her room and began to write. She intended to simply make note of her trip to Walmart, but once she started, she couldn't stop. She wrote about all the things she'd kept bottled up inside her for more than a year: the heartache of Tracy leaving, the loneliness of an empty desk in the *Snip 'N' Save* office, the Thanksgiving that had come and gone without Tracy at the table, the late-night sobs she'd heard coming from her mama's room.

After she emptied her heart of those burdens, she wrote about Tracy's life in Philadelphia, giving page after page of details about things she knew only from phone conversations and text messages. She told of Dominic's new job and described the apartment as Tracy had described it to her.

One by one, she listed the *Snip 'N' Save*'s new customers and explained how in a little more than one year the business had nearly doubled. She also told of hiring Sheldon Markowitz and bragged on his quick wit and flair with design.

"I think of Sheldon not as an employee," she wrote, "but as a friend."

The grandfather clock in the hall struck three before Meghan closed the book. By then her eyes were rimmed with red and her fingers cramped from gripping the pen, but the weight of the words she'd carried in her heart for all those long months was gone.

The next day, Meghan returned to Walmart and bought another ten composition books.

One Sunday morning, a year after Tracy had left home, she sent a text saying she was expecting a baby.

Meghan read the message three times before the thought actually settled into her head. Something about the way the text was put together troubled her. The first two words were Good news! It was supposed to sound happy, but there was an undercurrent of sadness, a thread of melancholy that seemed unlike the sister she'd known.

She and Tracy were always so close. With news this important, it would seem as if she'd call. Meghan's first impulse was to call Tracy herself, but she hesitated, knowing there had to be a reason for the text instead of a call.

Maybe she's at work? Or hasn't told Dominic yet?

Meghan ran through a list of possible reasons, then hit on the one that was most likely. Tracy didn't want Mama to know.

She tapped out a reply.

Congratulations! I'm so excited for you and Dominic. BTW, call Mama. She'll love being a grandma.

Tracy's response came back seconds later.
Don't say anything to her yet, she wrote. Call you tomorrow.

The next day, Tracy called on the *Snip 'N' Save* line. That was the customer line, and it was a safe bet their mama wouldn't answer. The two sisters began talking at the same time.

"How wonderful—"

"I'm afraid—"

They both laughed.

"It's your news, so you go first," Meghan said.

"I've got a problem telling Mama and thought maybe you could tell her."

"That's crazy. Why would you not want to?"

"Because she's not going to be one bit happy. She tolerates my being with Dom but doesn't like it. Once she hears about the baby, I just know she'll go back to asking when we're getting married."

"No, she won't," Meghan said. "Mama just wants you to be happy."

"Yeah, happily married." Tracy gave a labored sigh. "It isn't like I don't want it, too, but Dom isn't ready yet."

"Have you discussed it?"

"Yeah. He said Angelina Jolie and Brad Pitt didn't get married before having a baby, and if it's good enough for them it's good enough for him."

They spoke for a long time, and in the end, Meghan agreed to smooth the way with their mama if Tracy would call that evening and talk with her.

"You'll see. Mama will love being a grandma," Meghan assured her.

"Maybe," Tracy replied doubtfully.

That evening, when Tracy called, Lila put the call on speaker. By then she had come to grips with the fact that the baby would be born out of wedlock. It wasn't what she would have wished, but Tracy was her daughter, and that outweighed both her dislike of Dominic and the impropriety of the situation. Keeping these opinions to herself, Lila stuck with expressions of happiness as the three women chatted.

"Perhaps you could come home for a visit," she suggested.

"We've got too much going on right now," Tracy said, but promised to think about it after the baby was born.

"You just know I'll be itching to see my grandbaby," Lila replied.

The conversation lasted a full twenty minutes, and during all that time there was not a single mention of Dominic. By anybody.

In April, Tracy gave birth to a baby boy. She named him Lucas, and he did indeed have her dark hair and eyes. When Meghan received the first picture, it was one of Tracy sitting in the hospital holding the baby in her arms, with Dominic standing beside her, leaning in. They appeared to be a family, married or not.

"You see, Mama," Meghan said. "They're happy together. Isn't that the most important thing?"

Lila nodded reluctantly. "It should be, but I doubt Aunt Phoebe will see it that way."

Surprise Visit

In the year that followed, Tracy sent countless pictures of Lucas. She marked each milestone with another photo. There was his first smile, his first bath, the day he rolled over, the day he began to crawl, and dozens of selfies showing her with the baby. They'd be squeezed into the picture nose to nose or his cheek squished next to hers. In one, his tiny hand was covering her mouth, and in another his foot was in front of her nose. In all that time there was just one of Dominic holding the baby, and in it, he stood ramrod straight as he flashed a chagrined smile. Lucas looked as if he'd been photoshopped into his daddy's arms.

On Lucas's first birthday, Meghan and Lila telephoned Tracy, and the three women talked for nearly an hour.

"We'd love it if you could come home for a visit," Meghan suggested.

"I'd love it, too," Tracy replied solemnly, but then she went on to explain that they had too much going on right now, and it wasn't a good time for her to leave Dominic alone.

Lila's arms ached to hold the baby, but she was determined not to nag Tracy. "Maybe you could all come for Thanksgiving," she said wistfully.

"Yeah, maybe." Tracy's words were weighted with the sound of doubt.

A few months later, on an ordinary Monday morning when nothing of importance should have been happening, Meghan logged on to the *Snip 'N' Save* e-mail and found a message from Tracy. She clicked on it and read the first line, which said in all caps,

DON'T SHOW THIS TO MAMA!

The next paragraph went on to say Dominic got fired from his job and let their health insurance lapse. Tracy wrote:

> I'm having it reinstated with that COBRA plan, but in the meantime I'm really worried about Lucas. He's fourteen months old and hasn't said a single word. I call to him, and he doesn't pay one bit of attention.
>
> Margaret, the woman who works with me at Wawa, said she has a friend with a three-year-old son who is autistic, and that's exactly how he acts. She said boy babies are more prone to autism. Dear God, I hope it's not that!!!!
>
> I want to have Lucas tested, but I'm afraid of what they might find. Dominic claims nothing's wrong, but I'm not so sure.

Without a moment's hesitation, Meghan fired off a response suggesting Tracy bring Lucas to Georgia, and she'd make certain he was tested.

"Don't worry about the money," she wrote. "Mama and I will cover it."

Tracy's response came minutes later.

I can't leave Dom right now. Whatever is or isn't wrong, we'll have to work through it together. Please don't worry. I'm okay. Just needed a sisterly shoulder to cry on.

It was fine to say *don't worry*, but there was no way Meghan could hold back. In the hours that followed, she reread Tracy's e-mails a dozen times, and before the day ended, she'd made her decision. She'd finish up the current issue of the *Snip 'N' Save* and fly up to Philadelphia on Saturday. No matter how much it cost or what she had to do to make it happen, she was determined to have Lucas checked out by a doctor.

For the next two days, Meghan put in long hours at work. It was possible she'd be away for a week, maybe longer. Before leaving, she had to get the ads scheduled and roughs out to Sheldon. He could take it from there.

Late Wednesday night, she was in the *Snip 'N' Save* office when she heard the doorbell chime. She glanced at the computer screen and saw it was 10:47. Baker Street was a family neighborhood, a place where people went to bed early, and no one went about ringing their neighbor's doorbell at this time of night.

She moved cautiously through the hall. Then, before opening the door, she asked, "Who is it?"

"Me," Tracy replied. "Open the door."

Meghan yanked the door back and saw her sister standing there with Lucas in one arm and a diaper bag in the other.

"Good grief!" she gasped. "What happened?" Too anxious to wait for an answer, she continued asking if Tracy and Lucas were okay.

"We're fine. Give me a minute, then I'll tell you everything." Tracy stuck her head through the doorway and looked around. "Is Mama still up?" she whispered.

"No, she's in bed." Meghan lifted Lucas into her arms and cuddled him to her chest. "So this is my adorable little nephew," she cooed. "Why, you're ten times cuter than those pictures your mama sent."

Half-asleep, Lucas looked at her for a moment, then dropped his head onto her shoulder.

Tracy gave a sigh of relief. "I'm glad I won't have to deal with Mama until tomorrow."

Meghan was about to ask why, but as she pushed the door shut, she noticed Dominic's car with its one blue fender parked in the driveway.

"You drove down from Philadelphia?"

Tracy nodded. "Yeah. I left Dom."

At first she couldn't believe what she'd heard. Two days earlier, Tracy had said she was trying to work things out. Now here she was, saying she'd left Dominic. Meghan could understand why her sister wasn't ready to face Lila, but she couldn't help but wonder what unforgivable thing had brought about such a change.

With a look of surprise still stuck to her face, she said, "You left him? And he let you take his car?"

"He didn't know where I was going. He probably figured I'd go somewhere, get over being mad, and then come home."

"What happened?"

"I don't want to talk about it right now," Tracy said wearily. "Let me grab Lucas's crib out of the car. He's tired, and I need to get him into bed."

Moving as quietly as they had when they were youngsters making a midnight run on the cookie jar, they set up the crib in the room next to Meghan's, the room that was now their mama's sewing room. Tracy got Lucas settled, stashed her bag in the guest room, then tiptoed back downstairs to the kitchen.

"Is it too late for a cup of coffee?"

"Of course not." Meghan filled the pot and turned it to brew. "It's so good to have you back home."

Tracy gave a half-hearted smile. "It's good to be home."

In an odd way, it seemed as if nothing had changed in the two and a half years she'd been gone. Meghan reached into the cupboard, pulled down two of the same yellow mugs they'd always used, and set them on the table.

"Got any cookies or cake?"

"With Mama, there's always cake. She's not happy unless she's baking up a storm."

Meghan pulled a chocolate Bundt cake from the refrigerator, carved off two pieces, and set the plates on the table. She poured the coffee, then slid onto the chair on the opposite side of the table.

"I guess you're wondering what happened," Tracy said.

"You told me you didn't want to talk about it."

"Yeah, I know." Tracy sat looking pensive for a few moments, then said, "You won't believe what he did."

Once she got started, the words came pouring out like a festered wound popped open. She told about how she'd come home from work unexpectedly and found Dominic in bed with Kristen, the girl who was supposed to be babysitting.

"Lucas was crawling around the living room floor, and they were in the bedroom with the door closed. Lucas could have fallen or pulled something over on himself, and they wouldn't have heard a thing."

Once the truth was laid bare on the table, Tracy continued.

"I'm a fool," she said. "I could feel in my bones that he's been cheating all along, but I kept trying to please him. I thought it was a fling and sooner or later he'd settle down so we could be a real family."

She pulled a tissue from her pocket, wiped the tears back, then blew her nose.

"I figured I owed it to Lucas. A child needs both parents."

Tracy blew her nose again, and by then, the tissue was in shreds. She stood, opened the cupboard door beneath the sink, and tossed the tissue in the garbage can, then reached over to the far end of the counter and grabbed a few more. It felt good to be home in a place where you could count on things staying the same.

She returned to her seat. "After Dom left Lucas alone in the living room, I knew he was never going to be a real parent. That's when I realized I was just fooling myself in hoping he'd change."

"I know it's hard," Meghan said, "but you did the right thing. Someone like Dominic is so self-centered, I doubt he's capable of changing."

They talked for a while longer. Then Meghan went back to the *Snip 'N' Save* office and turned off her computer. Afterward she returned to the kitchen, and the two sisters sat at the table drinking coffee and talking until the first light of dawn glimmered on the horizon.

When they finally trudged up the stairs together, Meghan asked, "Are you back to stay?"

"I'm not sure. Right now I'm just trying to sort out my feelings."

"Tomorrow we can start trying to find a doctor for Lucas."

"Let's wait a few days. Let me get settled and back on my feet."

When they got to Meghan's room, instead of moving on down the hallway to the guest room, Tracy just stood there. Meghan wrapped her arm around her sister, and it seemed as if they were six and seven years old again.

"Do you want to crawl in bed with me for a few hours?"

Tracy nodded and gave a sheepish grin.

Tracy

On the drive down here, I kept thinking of how Mama had tried every which way to keep me from going to Philadelphia with Dominic. At the time, I thought she was too blind to see how in love we were. Now I realize I was the blind one.

I can't help wondering if someday I'll find myself standing in Mama's shoes and trying to keep Lucas from making the same kind of dumb mistakes I've made. Lord God, I hope not.

I used to think being a mama was the easiest job imaginable. Now I know it's the hardest. You start worrying about your baby before he or she is even born, and you don't stop until the day you die.

Knowing what I know now, I'm truly sorry for all the grief I caused Mama, and someday soon I'm gonna tell her so. Of course, my admitting such a thing might cause her to keel over from the shock, but I'm hoping all she feels is happy. If it were anybody other than Mama, they'd probably jump at the chance to say I told you so, *but she won't.*

You know how I know that? Because now I'm a mama myself. Once you've got another life that you're responsible for, you don't care about being right. You just care about making things right for your baby.

It's sad that it took almost twenty-two years for me to understand Mama's motives. All the while I thought she was just trying to make me miserable, but I know she was doing exactly what a mama is supposed to do—take care of her child. Now that I've finally come to realize this, I'll always be thankful to Mama for never giving up on me. I'm not ever going to forget it.

The Threat

Dominic didn't worry the first night Tracy failed to come home. He'd apologized and said the thing with Kristen was a meaningless fling. A diversion to ease the stress of trying to find a job. He'd promised it wouldn't happen again, but still she'd slept on the sofa, and then the next morning she and Lucas were both gone. Other than Wawa, Tracy had no place to go, so it was a safe bet she'd be back once she had time to cool down.

But after a second night passed without a phone call, he felt a twist of panic working its way into his chest. He tried calling her cell a number of times, and each time he got her voice mail. On three different occasions, he left a request for her to call back. The fourth time he said it was urgent, but still there was no response.

At six o'clock Thursday morning, Dominic walked the fourteen blocks to Wawa and pushed through the door. Tracy was extremely conscientious about her job. She wouldn't blow that off no matter how mad she was.

The man at the register wore a name tag indicating he was Nico Parks, Assistant Manager.

"Need help?" he asked.

For a moment Dominic stood there, stretching his neck in one direction and then the other as he searched for Tracy.

"I'm looking for my wife—"

Not knowing if she'd used her last name or his, he hesitated a moment. She liked pretending they were married, so it seemed more likely she'd use his name.

He finally said, "Tracy DeLuca."

"No DeLuca here."

"What about Briggs? Tracy Briggs?"

"Not anymore," Nico said. "She quit Tuesday morning."

Dominic's chest got tight, and he struggled to draw a breath. "Quit? Permanently?"

"I imagine so. She took her pay in cash and left."

"Did she say where she was going?"

Nico shook his head. "Afraid not."

On the walk back to the apartment, Dominic tried to think of where Tracy would go. She had few friends in Philadelphia. She was friendly with some neighbors, but they weren't the kind of people he'd consider close. Anyway, if she were in the building, the car would be parked on the street or in the courtyard, and it wasn't. As he walked he made a mental list of places she might go, then crossed the names off one by one.

In the end he was left with a single feasibility: as she so often threatened, she'd taken Lucas and gone back to Georgia. By the time he reached the apartment, he decided that was precisely what had happened. He picked up the phone and dialed Lila Briggs's number.

———— ✄⁓✄ ————

Lila hadn't yet opened her eyes when the sharp sound of the phone pierced her ears. Fearful that calls at this early hour brought only bad news, she grabbed the receiver and said, "What's wrong?"

"Put Tracy on the phone," Dominic replied.

"Who is this?" Lila asked.

"Dominic. I know she's there, so just put her on the phone."

Relieved to find the call was not news of a tragedy, Lila asked, "What on earth are you talking about? Tracy's not here; she's in Philadelphia."

"Don't give me that shit!" Dominic shouted.

"How dare you speak to me like that! Either you keep a civil tongue in your head, or I'll—"

"PUT TRACY ON THE PHONE!" Dominic screamed.

Lila slammed down the receiver without bothering to say good-bye. She climbed out of bed, walked to the window, and peered down. Dominic's car was parked in the driveway. There was no mistaking it.

"Well, I'll be . . ."

Sliding her feet into a pair of slippers, she padded down the hallway and opened the door to the sewing room. Standing up in his travel crib, Lucas smiled when he saw her.

"Well, bless your darling little heart . . ." Lila cooed as she lifted him into her arms for the first time. "Meghan! Come see who's here to visit Grandma."

Moments later the two sleepy-eyed sisters ambled into the room. First there was an affectionate hug. Then Tracy asked, "How'd you know I was here?"

"Dominic called, and he was in an extremely foul mood."

"What'd you tell him?"

"Nothing. He started yelling in my ear, so I hung up."

Overjoyed to have everyone together again, the group moved down-stairs, and Lila pulled a collection of pots and pans from the cupboard to begin fixing a huge breakfast: scrambled eggs, pancakes, bacon, and sausage, more than they could possibly eat. It was the same breakfast she had made every Sunday morning when George was alive.

Some people saw cooking as a chore, but not Lila. For her it was a way to express her love. It made her feel motherly and full of life.

Although the table was laden with food, Lila added a second basket of Tracy's favorite blueberry muffins still warm from the oven. Then she sat and took Lucas onto her lap.

The phone rang, but the caller ID read "Unknown," so no one felt compelled to answer. When the call ended, there was the space of a minute, perhaps less, then it rang again. Before the table was cleared, there had been a total of five calls, all "Unknown," all unanswered.

When the calls finally stopped, Tracy thought that was the end of it, but it turned out to be just the beginning.

A few minutes after eleven, the doorbell chimed. Confident there was no way Dominic could get from Pennsylvania to Georgia in that amount of time, Meghan opened the door. The guy standing there was thin as a broomstick and had attitude written all over his face.

"You Tracy?" he asked.

Meghan felt her back stiffen. She knew by the antagonistic tone of his voice that this was not good.

"Who wants to know?" she said, sounding braver than she felt.

Instead of answering, he eyed her with a contemptuous smile.

"I got a message from Dominic. He said for you to get your ass on the road and bring his car back, or he's gonna report it stolen."

Broomstick turned and started for the porch steps, then he looked back and added, "Oh, yeah, Dominic also said to make sure you bring the kid; otherwise he's gonna charge you with kidnapping."

He gave an evil-sounding snigger and disappeared down the walkway.

Meghan hesitated a moment, her heart thumping against her chest, then she closed the door and returned to the kitchen. Tugging Tracy into the *Snip 'N' Save* office, she closed the door and repeated her conversation with Broomstick.

"You know who this guy is?" she asked.

Tracy shook her head. "Probably one of the guys Dominic knew from before."

"Well, we've got to do something," Meghan said, "or else he's going to report his car stolen."

"Crap," Tracy said with a groan. "What do I do now?"

Meghan thought for several minutes, then offered up a plan. "It sounds like he's more upset about you taking the car than kidnapping the baby, so let's just ship it back to him."

They spent the next two hours making calls and finally found a transport company with a truck leaving Jacksonville the next morning, headed for New Jersey.

"We've got room for one more vehicle and can do a pickup in Georgia," the salesman said, "but it'll be an extra seventy-five, plus the two forty for transport."

"Three hundred and fifteen dollars?" Tracy sputtered. "To deliver a car that's barely worth fifty?"

"Not my problem," he replied. "That's our rate. Take it or leave it."

The thing was, Tracy couldn't just take it or leave it. She had to get the car back to Philadelphia one way or another. The only alternative would be for her to drive it back, and she wasn't about to do that.

"I'll take it," she said begrudgingly.

Once that was done, Meghan backed her car out of the garage, and Tracy pulled Dominic's inside. If Broomstick came by again, he'd hopefully think she was on the road headed home. There was still the problem of Dominic's claim to Lucas, but they'd take it one step at a time.

On Friday morning, Meghan woke with a raging headache. She'd spent a sleepless night worrying that any minute she'd find Dominic pounding on the door or Broomstick tossing a rock through the window. Several hours had passed before she decided that if such a thing happened, she'd simply call the police.

Once that worry was put to rest, she moved on to thinking about Lucas. At times he appeared to be a perfectly normal fourteen-month-old baby; other times he seemed detached, off in a world of his own. There but not there.

Meghan couldn't help but wonder if that were normal. She thought about other babies she'd known and tried to remember when they began talking. Marjorie Campbell's boy came to mind; that baby was saying *mama* before he was a year old. And then there were the Cooper twins, both of them already chattering like magpies.

It seemed odd that Lucas wasn't trying to form words. He grunted, reached for what he wanted, and bucked like a bull when he didn't get it, but there was no attempt to mimic sounds like *ba-bee* or *ma-ma*. Now this morning, he'd decided to throw a tantrum. Over what, no one could say.

One thing at a time, Meghan told herself, but it did little to relieve the pounding in her head.

When the transport trailer arrived before she finished her morning coffee, Meghan's headache worsened. The sight of Dominic's junky old car being rolled onto a trailer carrying Lincolns and Cadillacs would have been laughable were it not for the pounding in her head. After nearly twenty minutes of clanging, banging, and moving cars around, the transport was gone. By then, Lila had quieted Lucas down, and he was ready for a nap.

Tracy looked into the *Snip 'N' Save* office and asked, "Am I interrupting anything?"

Meghan shook her head. "Come on in."

Tracy plopped down in what once was Meghan's chair. "Thank God that car's gone."

Meghan gave a half-hearted chuckle. "I heard Lucas screaming. Is he okay?"

"He's fine. Mama's putting him down for a nap. He was obviously frustrated with something, but God knows what it was."

"I was thinking if you want to take him to the doctor—"

"Tomorrow, okay? First I want to make sure Dom can't send a sheriff after us."

"How are you going to do that?"

"If you don't mind my using your computer, I can google parenting laws and figure out what rights Dom has or doesn't have."

"Sure, go ahead." Meghan pushed back from the desk and stood. "Take your time. I'm going down to the lake for a breather."

She grabbed the black-and-white composition book from her top drawer and pocketed a ballpoint pen.

"I'll be back in an hour or two," she said, and disappeared out the door.

The sky was thick with clouds pushed up against one another, and as Meghan walked to the lake she could feel the heaviness of it overhead. The smell of last night's rain was still in the air, but now that the wind had picked up, it seemed the storm was gone.

The lake was a twenty-minute walk from the house. She could have driven it in five, but it felt good to be walking in the fresh air. Already her head felt better. She quickened her steps and began wondering what she would write about today. The words in her journals were seldom planned. They were always ideas that popped into her head when she opened the composition book to a fresh new page and began to write.

Today there were a thousand thoughts rolling through Meghan's head. Perhaps she would write about Lucas and the strange way his behavior swung back and forth: happy one moment, screaming for something he couldn't name the next.

Or the topic could be Tracy; she'd become a different person in the years she was gone. Tracy was always the fun sister, the one who could find humor in even the direst circumstances. Now her cheeks were thin and her mouth set in a rigid line. Instead of slathering on sunscreen and lying out in the yard, she was at the computer searching for a way to hold on to her child. She had the stooped look of a woman carrying the weight of the world in her pocket.

And then there was Mama, snatching up Lucas every time he screamed and cooing that there was nothing to worry about, when a look of concern was already etched onto her face.

Meghan dropped down onto the grass in front of the lake, close enough to hear the bass splashing but beyond the reach of the water. The earth was still moist from last night's rain, and the dampness soaked into the seat of her shorts. It was good, cooling almost. She stretched her legs out in front of her, kicked off her sandals, and opened the composition book to a fresh page.

Although she'd thought through a number of things she wanted to write about, her first words were about Broomstick and the noise of loading Dominic's car onto the transport trailer. From there, she continued documenting her thoughts of Lucas, Tracy, her mama, and even Aunt Phoebe.

At the bottom of the fourth page, she wrote, "They say that every cloud has a silver lining, but right now I can't see . . ."

Before she could finish the sentence, a dark shadow fell across the page. Meghan looked up and saw angry gray clouds rolling across the water. The storm had turned and was coming her way. She closed the book, stood, and reached for her sandals.

That's when she spotted the dog splashing around in the middle of the lake. From where she stood, it appeared to be a brown-and-white pup about the size of Clancy.

At first she thought he was playing—swimming out to fetch a stick or some other game—but there was no one on the opposite bank. She watched for a second or two, then realized the dog wasn't playing. He was floundering, trying to keep from going under. Although it had been almost six years since Clancy disappeared from the backyard, the thought of him came into Meghan's mind.

With her heart pounding like a trip-hammer, she ran into the water and started swimming toward the dog.

Meghan was a strong swimmer, and the lake wasn't all that large, but before she got to the dog, the rain started. It came in droplets so heavy they had the feel of hail.

She saw the dog, and seconds later he was gone. She pushed forward frantically, her arms reaching out in long strokes, her legs kicking harder and faster. Seeing nothing but the splash of rain around her, Meghan bobbed in the water and gasped for air.

"Here, boy!" she called, but the sound of her voice was lost beneath the roar of the wind and rain.

Treading water, she squinted and searched the surface. Suddenly she caught sight of him again. A tiny speck in the water that had begun to churn and swell. Keeping him in her line of vision, she lunged forward.

In that instant before she reached out and grabbed hold of him, she saw the pup's face, his eyes big and round with fear. Meghan circled her arm around his middle and pulled him close.

"Hang on, buddy," she said, and turned back in the direction she'd come from.

The sky had grown black as night, and the storm was all around them. With the rain pinging against her face, Meghan could no longer tell where the shore was. The lake wasn't wide, but it was long, and if she were headed in the wrong direction they'd never make it.

The water was rougher now, and with one arm wrapped around the dog, she moved slower. Using mostly her legs and torso, she propelled herself forward, hoping—praying—that she was headed in the right direction. Her breath came in ragged gasps, but there could be no rest. The sound of thunder was directly overhead.

Stroke after stroke, she moved through the churning water, and then her legs began to slow. Each kick felt like lifting a heavy weight, and each stroke brought with it a stab of pain to her side. In her mind, there was only the thought of saving Clancy. But this pup wasn't Clancy . . .

Realizing she was most likely swimming the length of the lake, Meghan was as close to giving up as she had ever been. Her legs stopped pumping and dropped deeper into the water. A storm swell pushed against her back, and she rushed forward. That's when she felt her foot touch the ground beneath her. Propelled by a sense of desperation, she reached the edge of the lake and stumbled. She fell to her knees, released her grip on the dog, and crawled onto the shore.

After coughing up a mouthful of black water, Meghan passed out.

The Dog

When Meghan came to, she was lying on the grass with the dog's tongue lapping at her arm. In those foggy first few seconds, she believed it was Clancy beside her. She opened her eyes slowly and saw the dog. It wasn't Clancy. It was a medium-size brown-and-white pup with his body low to the ground and those huge pleading eyes looking up at her.

For a few moments, everything remained fuzzy and out of focus. She felt uncertain about where she was and how she'd gotten there. She rolled to her side, leaned on her right elbow, and tried to push herself to a sitting position. A sharp pain shot through her hip, and she dropped back to the ground. She closed her eyes again.

The day was warm, hot almost, yet she shivered as she began to remember those last few moments of desperation when she'd held on to the dog, fearing the next breath would be her last and she would take him down with her. In a voice that was no more than a whisper, she said through a groan, "Thank God." A well of tears overflowed her eyes and rolled down her cheeks.

The dog moved closer. Keeping his body low, he stretched his paws and placed them on her shoulder, then cautiously eased his snout forward and began to lick the tears from her face. Instinctively Meghan wrapped her arm around him and held him close. She found a measure of comfort in having the thump of his small heart next to her own.

As several minutes ticked by, she remembered the blinding rain and the rush of water at her back, but she couldn't remember the actual moment of climbing out of the lake. It was something she'd most likely never remember, and perhaps it was better that way.

The last drizzle of rain finally disappeared and left behind a gray sky with a few dark clouds hanging low. Meghan remained there until the throbbing in her hip was bearable, then she pushed herself to a sitting position. The dog scrambled into her lap and went back to licking her arm.

Gradually a sense of steadiness came back to her. Her hip ached, and her legs felt as if she'd run a 10K race, but she was alive, and the dog was alive. It was a lot to be thankful for. She affectionately rubbed his ears, and he leaned into her touch.

"Poor baby," she said softly. Again she wondered how it came to be that he was out there in the middle of the lake.

Now with the rain gone, she could see across to the other side of the lake. She looked up and down the shoreline, but no one was standing there. No owner calling for a lost puppy or looking to pull him from the water.

The dog was affectionate and sweet; surely he belonged to somebody. She ran her hand around his neck looking for a collar or tag, but there was none.

"You must belong to somebody," she said, "but whom?"

The more Meghan looked at the pup, the more he reminded her of Clancy. He wasn't Clancy, she knew, but his mannerisms and the way he curled himself into her lap were exactly like Clancy. The two dogs were about the same size, but this pup had paws too big for his body. He was still young and would most likely grow to be the size of a shepherd or golden retriever.

They sat there for a long while, her stroking the dog and lovingly plucking bits of leaf and twig from his fur, him licking at her hand, arm, leg—anything he could reach. When Meghan stood and began looking around for her sandals, he was right behind her.

She had climbed out of the lake in a different spot than where she'd gone in, and it took a good fifteen minutes before she found her shoes. The journal she'd been writing in was nowhere to be seen. As she sat to pull on her sandals, the dog cozied up beside her and licked her leg.

Meghan smiled. "Since you don't seem to have an owner anywhere around, do you want to come home with me?"

The dog wiggled his rear end, looked up at her with those heart-rending eyes, and gave a soft whimper. To her ear it had the sound of "Please."

She bent down and ruffled the soft fur on the underside of his snout. "I was hoping you'd say that."

He cocked his head and barked, his tail swishing back and forth happily. There was something about the way he looked at her with such direct eye contact; she could almost swear he understood what she was saying.

"You are so stinkin' cute," she said, laughing. "I just know a sweetie like you belongs to somebody, so we've got to at least try and find your owner."

Keeping his eyes fixed on her face, he gave another pitiful whine.

When Meghan called him Sox, it was nothing more than a description of his looks. Despite the dirty lake water clinging to his fur, she saw three completely white paws and a fourth fringed with white. He looked as if he were wearing sweat socks, the kind she wore for a run or a workout at the gym. That fourth paw had the look of a sock without much elasticity, like it had slipped down.

When she said, "Let's go, Sox," he followed along.

Apparently he was okay with the temporary name.

Calling him Sox meant she hadn't given him a real name. If she gave him a real name, it would signify she was going to keep him. As much as she wanted to, he wasn't hers to keep. She reminded herself this was short-term. He was hers for today, but after that . . .

As they started toward the road, she looked down at the dog and laughed.

"We look like a couple of drowned rats, don't we, Sox?"

The dog responded by vigorously shaking his body. A spray of water went flying and doused her again.

Her hair was dripping down her back, her clothes were soaked, and with every step, she could feel the wetness of her sandals squishing between her toes. Yet none of those things seemed to matter. At the moment Meghan had a feeling of contentment that had been missing for a long time. It was a warmth that settled into her chest and gave a jauntiness to her step, even though her legs still ached.

On the walk home, she again reminded herself that this dog wasn't Clancy and in truth she had no right to him. But in the back of her mind, there was a small voice arguing *You saved his life, so now he's yours.*

By the time they arrived back at the house, Meghan and the dog were both still trailing muddy lake water, so she circled around to the back and came in through the kitchen. Tracy heard the door open and came from the *Snip 'N' Save* office.

"Hey, Meghan, wait until you hear what I've found out!" She stopped, eyed Meghan, and asked, "What happened? You're soaked!"

"A storm came up and—"

"Storm?" Tracy spotted the dog and bent to pet him. "Aw, isn't he a cute little rascal. Where'd you get him?"

"Rescued him from the lake," Meghan said. "I was getting ready to leave, and this huge storm rolled in."

"Strange. We didn't have a drop of rain here."

"Good grief, it was like a hurricane blowing through. I don't know how you could have missed it."

The dog shook his body again, and a spray of muddy water splattered across the kitchen floor.

"Uh-oh. Mama just cleaned up in here. She's gonna have a fit about this mess."

The dog went down on his belly and lowered his head as if he were ashamed.

"If she has a fit, then she has a fit," Meghan said. "Too bad."

Tracy laughed. "After all these years, don't tell me you've decided to take a turn at being the rebellious daughter!"

Meghan gave a sheepish grin. "Afraid not. It's just that I feel very protective of this dog. He reminds me of Clancy."

Tracy scrunched her nose and frowned. "He doesn't look at all like Clancy."

"It's not the way he looks," Meghan replied. "It's something more. I think what happened back at the lake created a bond between us and—"

"What actually happened at the lake?"

Meghan recounted how she'd seen the dog and gone in after it. When she told of the blinding raindrops and the desperation she'd felt, fearing she wasn't going to make it back to the shore, Tracy's face went white.

"Good Lord, Meghan, you could have been killed!"

"But I wasn't, which leads me to believe I was there because fate wanted me there to rescue Sox."

"Are you serious?" Tracy rolled her eyes and gave an exasperated huff. "You've spent too much time writing stories. Now you're starting to believe them."

"That's not true. Those things have nothing to do with each other. Fate isn't controlled by wishes. It just is what it is, and it happens whether you want it to or not."

Tracy twitched her mouth to the side with a look of skepticism. "What if the dog was fated to drown, and you interfered by saving him? Isn't that the same as controlling fate?"

Meghan hesitated a moment. She didn't have a comeback. The only thing she could do was tell what was in her heart.

"Think whatever you want," she said, "but I know I was meant to save this dog. I know it, and I believe he knows it, too. We were as good as dead, and then when I opened my eyes we were on the shore. He was right there beside me, just as Clancy would have been, and I could see the gratitude on his face."

"Gratitude on his face?" Tracy repeated laughingly.

She didn't necessarily believe such a thing possible, yet she had to admit there was a certain something about the way the dog stayed alongside Meghan. He didn't wander or go sniffing around the kitchen the way she'd expect a stray to do.

"So I guess you're planning to keep him," she said.

"I'd like to, but . . ." Meghan gave a soulful sigh.

The thought of giving up the dog felt like a sharp-edged rock dropped into her chest, but remembering the heartbreak she'd felt when Clancy disappeared, she knew it was something she had to do. She squatted and affectionately rubbed the spot behind his ears.

"You understand, don't you, Sox? I have to try to find your owner, because they probably love you the way I loved Clancy."

Looking up at Tracy, Meghan said, "Tomorrow I'll take a picture of him and run a found-dog ad in the *Snip 'N' Save*. Everybody in town reads it."

"And if no one claims him?" Tracy replied.

A smile slid across Meghan's face. "Then he was meant to be mine."

The dog shimmied up against her leg, and she continued to rub his ears.

Tracy laughed again. "I think he's already yours."

Something New

By the time Lila came downstairs with Lucas, Tracy had disappeared back into the *Snip 'N' Save* office to print out the information she'd found on the computer. The kitchen floor was wiped clean, and Meghan had changed into dry clothes. She'd also rinsed Sox's paws, so they looked whiter than ever.

Lucas toddled in and saw her on the floor combing tangles from Sox's fur. He stopped, stood looking wide-eyed at the dog, and raised an arm almost as if he were going to reach out. Then, for some unknown reason, he turned back to Lila, grabbed her leg, and buried his face in the fabric of her slacks.

With a nod toward Sox, Lila asked, "Where did that dog come from?"

"I rescued him."

"Rescued?"

Meghan nodded. "I was down at the lake and spotted him out in the middle of the water. He was just about to go under when I swam out and pulled him in."

She didn't mention the danger of the storm. Her mama had a dozen different superstitions, and the thought of such a storm being in one place and not the other would surely incite a prediction of misfortune.

Lucas again glanced at the dog, then shrieked and turned back to Lila.

"Aw, don't be afraid, sweetie. Grandma won't let that doggy bother you." Lila squatted, scooped Lucas into her arms, then glared at Meghan. "I hope you're not planning to keep him."

Meghan shrugged. "Well . . ."

"What about Beulah?" Lila's cat was fourteen years old and moved through the house like a shadow, but still it seemed unlikely she'd welcome a newcomer.

"Mama, I doubt this one little dog is going to upset Beulah. Besides, Sox may already have an owner. If not, then I'd like to at least consider—"

"Absolutely not," Lila cut in, using a rather brusque tone.

"Why?"

"Well, for one thing, Lucas is frightened of him."

"He's not really frightened. It's just that the dog is something new. Put him down, and let's see what he does."

An apprehensive expression settled on Lila's face, and she stood for a few moments before lowering Lucas to the floor. Meghan cradled Sox in her lap and told him to lie down. When he lowered his head onto her thigh, she called to Lucas.

"Do you want to play with the puppy?" she asked in a soft voice. "Sox is a good doggy. See how sweet he is? He likes babies. See? Gentle, gentle."

Meghan stroked the underside of the dog's neck with a tender touch, and he lolled his head to one side to make room for more. Still using that same singsong voice, she held out her other hand, motioning for Lucas to come closer.

"Come play with the puppy," she said.

Lucas didn't budge. He remained in the same spot, looking as bewildered as an old man who'd come to fetch something and then forgotten what. After a few minutes, he turned back to Lila with his arms upstretched, signaling he wanted to be picked up again.

"Well, I guess that proves my point."

"That's not fair, Mama. Lucas is probably still a little sleepy from his nap. In a day or two I'm sure—"

"Never mind a day or two. Take the dog to a shelter, and let them find a home for him."

"But Mama—"

"This is not a subject open for discussion! I will not have my grandchild scared out of his wits because of some stray you've brought home."

Moments later, Tracy came from the office. Lila handed Lucas to his mama and turned toward the door. She looked back, gave an ominous nod toward Meghan, and said, "Do it today."

Lucas's eyes followed Lila as she left the room, then he gave a quick glance down at the dog and turned back to Tracy. It was a glance, nothing more; no look of either fear or fondness. He stuck his thumb in his mouth and started picking at the button on his shirt.

Sensing something was askew, Tracy asked, "What's wrong with Mama?"

Instead of answering, Meghan shrugged. It was a movement that was barely discernible. She hiked her shoulders a fraction of an inch, then lowered them. Someone else might not have noticed the despondency in Meghan's action, but Tracy did. She understood the feeling of helplessness.

"Something's wrong," she said. "Tell me, or I'll keep nagging you."

"It's nothing. Really. Nothing."

With Lucas still in her arms, Tracy crossed over and squatted beside Meghan. "I don't believe you. I know how Mama can be, and I bet she said something."

There was no way Meghan could add guilt to Tracy's worries. "It was just stuff about the *Snip 'N' Save*. Nothing important. Really."

Tracy lowered herself into a sitting position and lifted Lucas into her lap. "Well, now that I'm back, maybe I could help with some of the work. I know it's been a lot for you, and it's unfair—"

"Don't give it a second thought," Meghan said. "Mama was just making a mountain out of a molehill. By tomorrow the whole thing will have blown over, and she'll move on to fussing about something else."

Both girls laughed, and the conversation segued to what Tracy had found on the computer. Once she began talking about what rights Dominic might or might not have, Tracy ignored the way Lucas was listing to the right and reaching out for the dog.

Lucas didn't say words. He didn't even make definitive sounds, not one thing for yes and another for no. His only sounds were just that: sounds. Grunts and squeals with no meaning or consistency.

It wasn't because there had been a lack of effort on Tracy's part. She tried to teach him to talk, to say *mama*, *dada*, or even the dreaded *no*. In the evenings when Dominic was tending bar, she had sat with Lucas, repeating *ma-ma* and emphasizing each syllable until it echoed in her ears like the bleat of a lost lamb. She stuck to the easy words, hoping he would show a tiny bit of progress. Still there was no attempt to mimic her sounds.

For a while Lucas would be relatively content with the attention. Then his eyes would wander, and he'd gaze off into space. When that happened, she gently turned his face back to her and continued repeating the word over and over again. Now she'd grown accustomed to hearing the strange sounds and paid them little attention.

With no one pulling him back, Lucas wriggled forward until he finally plopped facedown on the dog's back. He laughed, then stretched his tiny arms around the furry body. Sox wagged his tail, and it thumped against the floor.

"Good grief, will you look at that!" Meghan said.

Tracy glanced around the room. "Look at what?"

"Lucas. I think he likes Sox."

Tracy chuckled. "Most kids like dogs. Hardly a groundbreaking observation."

"No, you don't understand. Mama said I couldn't keep Sox because Lucas was afraid of him, but now it seems he's not."

"Why didn't you tell me that to start with?"

Meghan gave another shrug. "Maybe I should have, but I didn't want to—"

Tracy cut in. "Let's make a pact to always tell each other the truth, no matter how painful it may be."

Meghan raised an eyebrow. "Always?"

"Always."

They offered one another their pinkie fingers, then linked them in a pinkie swear. Knowing Lila had retreated to the upstairs sewing room, Tracy got up and sprinted into the hallway.

"Hey, Mama!" she hollered up the stairwell. "Poor little Lucas loves this dog so much we've got to keep him."

Meghan laughed. "I'd like to believe that's true, but don't forget— Sox may already have an owner."

Hearing his name, Sox stood, put his front paws on Meghan's chest, and lapped a wet tongue across her cheek.

"You're not making this easy," Meghan said as she held him close and nuzzled her face to his.

Meghan

When Mama gets that stern no-nonsense attitude, you know she's worried about something. Right now, I believe it's the memory of Clancy. That memory is almost as painful for her as it is for me. She felt guilty about what happened back then, and I think she still does. Daddy tried to tell her it wasn't her fault, the lock on the gate was broken, but Mama never quite believed him.

After Clancy disappeared, she quit making her oatmeal raisin cookies just because they were a reminder of what she was baking that day. I think when Mama looks at this dog, he's another reminder. She's afraid I'll become attached to Sox, then someone will claim him, and I'll end up as brokenhearted as I was when I lost Clancy. Once you understand Mama's reasoning, you can't fault her.

Loving your children so much that you can't stand to see them hurt is not a fault.

Daddy always said we've got to be forgiving of Mama, because she means well, but she's a talker not a listener. He claimed that's how she got rid of anxieties. When she and Daddy had conversations, she'd sometimes go on and on telling about some inconsequential thing that was troubling her mind. Then when she finished, she'd ask Daddy's opinion, and he'd say one of his two favorite words: possibly or probably.

One day, Mama told him he wasn't giving enough thought to her question, because those two answers were almost the same thing. Daddy said they *were totally different.* Possibly, *he said, meant there was more likelihood of something not happening than happening, but* probably *meant there was a greater chance of something happening.*

Mama stood there looking at him for a minute or two, then said she really didn't see all that much of a difference.

"Possibly not," he said, and that was the end of the conversation.

Daddy had plenty of worthwhile thoughts and ideas, but he kept most of them inside his head, the way I keep my thoughts in a journal.

He understood me in a way no one else did. After Clancy went missing, Mama did everything imaginable to cheer me up: she baked cookies, bought me new sweaters, even painted my room the shade of pink I liked at the time. But the thing she didn't understand was that nothing could take the place of Clancy.

Daddy understood; he never tried to do all those special things. Instead he walked alongside me every night as we went up and down the streets calling out for Clancy. I knew some nights Daddy was tired and just wanted to go home, sit in the chair, and read his paper, but he never let on. All those months I was looking for Clancy, he kept looking right alongside me. Daddy doing that made me love him more than you'd imagine possible.

They say that after a person goes to meet their maker, a part of them stays behind with those they've loved. According to legend, the person can be found in things like a flower pressed between the pages of a book, a locket, or even the melody of a song. Finding Sox in the middle of the lake with no one else around makes me wonder if somehow Daddy could have put him there, knowing full well I'd swim out to save him.

True or not true, it's what I'd like to believe.

Remembering Clancy

Once Lila saw how Lucas took to Sox, she softened her stance on keeping the dog, but only marginally. She still insisted Meghan search for a possible owner before becoming attached to it.

Still wary of what this could lead to, Lila wanted to keep some distance between her family and the interloper. It wasn't that she disliked dogs; in fact, when she saw the way Lucas followed the pup around, it gave her a warm fuzzy feeling. That feeling was what she disliked. She knew from experience the heartache having a dog could bring. She still remembered Clancy.

He had been Meghan's dog, and there was no doubt about it. Wherever you saw one, you'd see the other. Clancy followed her everywhere. On school days, he'd be sitting on the front porch waiting when she rounded the corner. When she read, he'd be sitting in her lap, and when she studied at the desk, he'd be right there at her feet. Meghan loved that dog the same way she loved her daddy—wholeheartedly and without reservation.

Lila knew if Meghan became attached to this dog and then someone came to claim him, it would be the Clancy thing all over again. She was determined not to let that happen.

"How do you plan to go about finding the owner?" she asked.

"I'm going to place a found-dog ad in the *Snip 'N' Save*." Meghan's words were flat and without enthusiasm. "Everyone in town reads it, so I'm sure . . ."

"I suppose that's as good a way as any."

Lila hesitated for a moment, then remembered how week after week George had called the police station and the ASPCA to see if anyone had found the dog.

"His name is Clancy," George would say hopefully. "He's wearing a blue collar with a tag . . ."

"Try the police station and the ASPCA," Lila suggested. "Ask if anyone has reported a lost or stolen dog."

"Okay," Meghan answered reluctantly.

The remaining hours of the day passed, and it seemed there was no good time for making those calls. Meghan managed to find things to keep her busy. First she discovered a number of ads that needed to be redesigned, and after that, there were several e-mails to answer. Not surprisingly, she didn't have a free moment until it was nearly supper-time, and then she reasoned it was too late for calling.

When they sat down at the table, Lila asked if she'd made the calls.

"Not yet," Meghan answered. "It's too late for the ASPCA. They're probably already closed."

"Probably?" Lila repeated, noting how Meghan used her daddy's noncommittal word. "Well, the police station is open twenty-four hours a day. I'm certain you could call them."

"Yes, I suppose I could."

Meghan promised to do it after supper, but when they finished eating, she jumped up and began clearing the table. When that was done, she polished the counter, watered the ivy on the windowsill, and straightened the mess in the pot-holder drawer. With one thing after another, it was almost ten o'clock before she finally got around to calling the police station.

Trying to make the question sound as insignificant as possible, she asked, "Did anyone happen to report a missing dog?"

Officer Brogan said to the best of his knowledge there'd been no such report.

"Want me to take your number and let you know if one comes in?" he asked.

"No, thanks," Meghan replied. "I can call back some other time."

She breathed a sigh of relief and hung up the receiver. A few minutes later, she headed for her room, and Sox was right at her heels.

That night Meghan sat at the desk and wrote in her journal. She wrote about the memories of her daddy and her hopes that Clancy had somehow found a good home. In words that were crowded together like the whispers of a secret, she prayed Sox had no owner and would be hers to keep. She reasoned it was good for Lucas and told how he happily trailed the dog from room to room, and she went on to explain how patient Sox was with the baby.

"I think he understands Lucas is fragile," she wrote.

Hours passed, and Meghan continued to write. She penned page after page saying how she'd missed Tracy and how in the future they needed to spend more time together to do the things sisters often did.

She started to list the things she had in mind, but when it came right down to it, she couldn't put her finger on one specific activity. She tried imagining the two of them doing the things she enjoyed—sitting by the lake, strolling through the stacks at the library, walking a wooded trail—but remembered that Tracy found those things boring. She tried to imagine them going to a rock concert or racing along the highway in a top-down convertible, and while that would be fine with Tracy, it didn't work for her.

In the end she simply wrote that she could walk Sox on a leash while Tracy pushed Lucas in his stroller. That picture was easy enough to see, but it still hinged on the looming question of whether or not she would be able to keep the dog.

It was nearly midnight when Meghan closed the notebook and pushed her chair back. Sox was sleeping alongside the desk, but when she stood, he stood, and when she climbed into bed, he jumped in after her.

She playfully ruffled his fur. "Oh, so you want to sleep with me, is that it?"

The dog whimpered, lowered his head, inched forward, and started licking her hand. He made it clear he knew she was the boss, and he was asking, "Please."

Meghan couldn't help but laugh. "You know I'm a sucker for you, don't you?"

She slid beneath the blanket and patted the spot next to her. It was the okay signal he was waiting for. He scooted up, rumpled the blanket until it was just so, then curled his back into her chest. A few minutes later, his head dropped down onto her arm.

As she drifted off to sleep, Meghan could almost swear she caught the aroma of the pipe tobacco her daddy had smoked.

Making Plans

When everyone gathered for breakfast the next morning, Lila reminded Meghan about calling the ASPCA.

"And be sure to put that notice in the *Snip 'N' Save*," she added.

"I will," Meghan promised. "But first I have to finish up a few other things."

As soon as Lila began clearing the dishes, Meghan tugged Tracy into her office and whispered that their first priority should be to find a pediatrician for Lucas.

"I'm not so sure," Tracy replied hesitantly. "Mama said some babies are just late talkers. It may be that Lucas is—"

"Wouldn't it be better to know for sure?"

"I suppose so, but . . ."

Although fear of the truth was what held Tracy back, she claimed there were a number of other considerations. She first needed to get settled and make sure the COBRA insurance had gone through. Then there was the problem of Lila. Given her tendency to worry, she'd be frantic if she suspected something was actually wrong with Lucas. Right now, Lila believed he was simply a late talker.

"Boys are almost always slower than girls when it comes to talking," she'd said. "Why, you were talking a blue streak before Cindy Hendricks's boy said his first word."

Tracy hadn't argued the point. Instead she'd taken hold of it and swallowed the belief, because it was what she'd wanted.

"Without Dominic and me yelling at one another, Lucas will probably have more of an interest in talking," she suggested hopefully.

"Possibly, not probably," Meghan replied. "You should at least have him checked. I can make the appointment. You don't even have to tell Mama."

"And what if there's a problem with the insurance?"

"COBRA has to let you keep the plan. It's the law," Meghan said. "And if the paperwork doesn't come through in time, I'll pay for the visit."

Tracy heaved a disheartened sigh and lowered her eyes. "Suppose something really is wrong with Lucas? I don't know how I'd manage—"

"Don't even go there." Meghan's voice was strong and definitive, with no extra words thrown in to cloud the issue. "We'll cross that bridge if we come to it."

Tracy noticed her sister didn't say *you'll* cross that bridge. She said *we'll* cross that bridge. She'd also said *if* not *when*.

Tracy looked up with a smile, then flung her arms around Meghan's neck.

"I don't deserve a sister like you!" she said.

Meghan laughed. "I know, but you're still stuck with me."

Together they spent most of the morning calling around asking for pediatrician recommendations. After three strikeouts with friends, Meghan suggested they call Tracy's old pal Kelly MacPharland. Kelly had married her high school sweetheart two weeks after graduation and had a baby six months later. She now had three little ones, so she was certain to know a pediatrician.

Once Kelly heard Tracy was back in town, she wanted to know the whole story. After nearly twenty minutes of chitchat, she finally gave them Dr. Driscoll's name and number.

"Make sure you see him," she said. "Not Manners, his partner." She then went on to say Manners had misdiagnosed Kristie's runny nose, claiming it was just sniffles rather than a pollen allergy.

Once Meghan got Kelly off the line, she called Dr. Driscoll and learned the earliest appointment they could get was six weeks out.

"That's crazy," she said. "What if this were an emergency?"

"Then you'd take the child to the ER at Magnolia Grace," the nurse replied.

The only other alternative the nurse could offer was an appointment three weeks out with the new associate, Dr. Manners.

Having been forewarned about Manners, Meghan said no, they'd wait.

The morning flew by, and although she had every intention of making the call she'd promised, Meghan never got around to it. When she eventually did phone the ASPCA, an answering machine said they were out to lunch. Without leaving a message, she hung up, figuring she'd call back later.

Then there was the found-dog ad that was supposed to go in the *Snip 'N' Save*. But to create the ad, she needed a picture of Sox. With Lucas hanging onto the dog, it would be impossible to get a decent shot until after he went to bed. She quickly tabled the idea and moved on to some overdue billing.

Although it was nothing more than wishful thinking, it somehow seemed the longer she held on to the dog, the less likely it would be for another owner to come forth claiming him.

The following afternoon, Meghan finally called the ASPCA. The only missing-dog report they'd received was for a female Chihuahua that answered to the name of Princess. Feeling she'd crossed two major hurdles, she breathed a sigh of relief and allowed yet another day to roll by before she took the photograph of Sox.

After Lucas was in bed, she snapped a single shot of the dog sitting between the brown sofa and matching chair. The picture came out grainy and dark. The only thing clearly visible was the white of Sox's two front paws, so it seemed a waste of time to upload it to the computer.

Two days later, Dominic's car arrived back in Philadelphia, and he called screaming like a banshee. His voice was so loud, Tracy held the phone at arm's length.

"What the hell do you call this?" he yelled. "I tell you to get your ass back here, and you send some bozo home with my car?"

Tracy half expected something like this to happen, and she was ready.

"You said you wanted your car back," she replied, "so I sent it back. The delivery service was bonded and insured."

"Don't give me that crap!" Dominic screamed. "You knew what I meant. I want you and Lucas back here by tomorrow!"

"You *want*?" Tracy repeated angrily. "I'm sick of doing what you want! You can forget it, Dom. We're not coming back."

"Like hell you're not! He's my kid, and you've got no right—"

"Actually, I do. I'm his mama, and you're nothing."

"Your smart-ass sister tell you that? Well, it's not true! I'm his daddy and—"

"You're not his daddy. At least not legally."

There was a moment of hesitation before Dominic spoke again. "Not legally? What's that supposed to mean?"

"You're not listed on the birth certificate. I left it blank, remember?"

"Oh, so that's what this is all about! You're thinking you can hold this over my head and force me into marrying you?"

Their getting married had been a bone of contention for more than two years. His single statement wiped away any illusions Tracy might have had about Dominic trying to win her back.

"I wouldn't marry you if you were the last man on earth!" she snapped. "And forget about ever seeing Lucas again! He's a good kid and deserves a better father than you!"

Without giving him time for a response, she slammed the receiver down.

The conversation had been angry and loud. Even after ending the call, Tracy stood rooted to the spot with a swell of heartache and anger rising up inside her. Fearful such a scene would upset Lucas, Lila scooped him up and rushed him out to the backyard.

"What you need is some fresh air," she cooed as she carried him from the room.

Tracy didn't object. She blinked back the tears and bit down on her lip. Meghan crossed the kitchen and wrapped an arm around her sister's shoulders.

"I know this is painful, but you're doing the right thing."

It had taken every last ounce of Tracy's resolve to remain strong against Dominic's tirade, but given this gesture of kindness, she let go. With her face buried in the hollow of Meghan's shoulder, she began to sob.

"It doesn't feel right," she said tearfully. "Nothing feels right. It seems as though all I've done is make a mess of my life and Lucas's."

"Nonsense. What you're doing will make a better life for him. And you're right—he does deserve it."

The phone rang again. Unknown caller. Neither sister answered it. After a while the ringing stopped. Less than ten minutes later, the ringing started again. Still they ignored it.

Tracy followed Meghan into the living room, and they sat side by side on the sofa. This room was nothing like the living room in the apartment Tracy had left behind. That living room was a mishmash of colors and thrift-shop finds. The sofa had a wobbly leg and a burn hole in the armrest. The table was too small for even a lamp.

The sofa they sat on now was a warm brown. It was plump and cushiony with colorful throw pillows. Tracy sank into it and felt the comfort of a place to call home, but even this didn't soothe the ache in her heart.

She gave a gloomy-sounding sigh. "What's wrong with me?"

Although her sister was sitting beside her, the question wasn't aimed at Meghan. It was a question Tracy asked of herself.

"I know Dominic is bad for me," she said. "I know he lies and cheats, but I keep thinking about the times when it wasn't this way. I think about the early days when we made love every night. It was good back then. We found a thousand things to laugh about and never worried about the future. Dominic used to say, 'We live life in the present; the future will take care of itself.'"

"But wasn't that before you had Lucas?"

Tracy nodded. "I thought Dominic would be thrilled to pieces knowing we were going to have a baby, but he wasn't."

She lowered her eyes and studied her hands in her lap. She'd hoped to see a wedding band on her finger one day. Now that dream was gone. There was nothing except anger and bitterness.

"Once I was certain about the pregnancy, I told Dom it would be a good time for us to get married. He looked at me like I was crazy and said absolutely not. That was it, a flat-out no. He wasn't even willing to discuss it." Tracy's eyes grew teary. "He claimed we weren't ready for marriage or a baby and suggested I get an abortion."

Meghan's surprise was obvious. "An abortion?"

Tracy nodded, and her eyes narrowed as she settled into remembering. "He said a baby would be the end of everything. We argued the whole nine months. Every day. Every night. It was nonstop."

"I'm so sorry." Meghan stretched out her arm and placed a sympathetic hand on her sister's knee.

"The morning my labor started, Dominic and I had another huge argument. He stormed out and didn't say where he was going. I figured with knowing the baby was on the way he'd be back in an hour or two to take me to the hospital, but he wasn't. I waited all day, and then that night when I felt the baby coming, I called for an ambulance. Lucas was born minutes after the medics got there."

"You didn't make it to the hospital?"

Tracy shook her head. "There was no time. The EMTs delivered him."

"But what about the picture you sent?"

Tracy looked down again; it was obvious she was embarrassed.

"The EMTs took us to the hospital so they could make sure everything was all right, but when Dom got there the next morning, we checked out."

"Why?"

"Because I knew we couldn't afford even one extra day."

"You had health insurance, didn't you?"

"Not then. Dominic joined the group plan after he went to work for the city. When Lucas was born, all he had was that temp job at the bar."

Tears welled in Meghan's eyes. "You should have called. Mama or I could have come to help out."

Tracy pinched her brows, and her expression tightened into a grimace. "I was too ashamed to say anything. You and Mama both warned me about Dominic, and when all this happened, I felt it was payback for my not listening."

"That's nonsense. Mama and I only want the best for you."

"I can see that now, but it was different back then. My feelings were all mixed up. I cried and cried about how thoughtless Dom was with me and how he didn't care about our baby. I wanted to hurt him the same way he hurt me, so I deliberately didn't put his name on Lucas's birth certificate. I wanted to punish him for the way he'd acted . . ."

She hesitated a moment, then let loose an embittered sigh. "But the irony of it was he didn't care. I'd planned to add his name when I got over being mad, but I never did."

They sat and talked for a long while, not finding a solution to any of the problems, simply letting out the anger and hurt of the past. Tracy told of the small slights and big disappointments that consumed the last two years of being with Dominic: day after day of not speaking, evenings of loneliness wondering where he went when he left the bar, and endless nights of climbing into bed with his back turned to her.

"Given the way he felt about having a baby, I would have thought he'd be glad to get rid of Lucas and me."

"Obviously not," Meghan said. "But now that he understands you're not coming back, maybe you won't hear from him again."

"Yeah, maybe." Tracy's words suddenly had the hollow sound of sadness in them.

Meghan heard it. "You're not thinking of going back to him, are you?"

"I guess not," Tracy replied, but her words were weak and wobbly.

Book of Wishes

Long after everyone was asleep and the house was so quiet Meghan could hear the *thump-thump-thump* of the dog's heart, she lay in bed looking at walls lit only by the glimmer of a pale moon. The events of the day kept cycling through her mind. She remembered how Tracy's eyes blinked nervously and how her hands trembled after she'd slammed the receiver down. It wasn't just anger; it was fear. Was Tracy fearful for herself, Meghan wondered, or was she concerned about Lucas?

She reached out and absently ran her hand along the smooth fur of Sox's side. He rolled onto his back and offered up the underside of his belly. She stroked it, and he squirmed closer.

Although she was still troubled about the events of the day, a smile softened the corners of her mouth as she tightened her arm around his warm body. Pushing himself deeper into the hug, Sox stretched his neck and nuzzled his snout in the curve of her neck. He settled himself, then sighed with satisfaction.

"Oh, Sox," she whispered softly, "you understand everything, don't you?"

There was a muffled chuff. It was the dog's way of answering.

"Please don't let me fall in love with you if you belong to someone else."

The dog snuggled closer, his fur soft and warm against her skin.

"If only you could talk," she said. "Then you could assure me no one will ever show up and take you away."

Her words were still hanging in the air when she could have sworn she heard a chortle that sounded like her daddy.

For a long while they stayed side by side, Sox nuzzled close and Meghan gently scratching the feel-good spot behind his ear. She spoke to Sox the way she'd once talked with her daddy, confiding in him the troubling thoughts that picked at her brain.

"I'm worried about Tracy," she said, "but more worried about Lucas. I know Tracy needs time to work through this, but I can't help feeling I need to do something. How do I help a person who's not ready to be helped?"

She rambled on for several minutes. Then Sox wriggled free and jumped down from the bed. He trotted across the room and sat beside the desk, looking back at her.

"Do you need to go out?"

The dog didn't respond as he usually did. He sat there eyeing her as if to say, "Nope, guess again."

"I know you want something, but I have no idea what," she said, smiling.

He stood, put his paws on the chair, and eyed her again.

In an odd and almost indescribable way, she felt he was telling her to write in her journal. She laughed. Such a thought made sense.

"Sox, you know me as well as Daddy did."

It was always easier for Meghan to sort through problems when she saw them written out. Things that were gray and fuzzy in her head became crystal clear once they were penned in her journal. She swung her legs from the bed and started across the room. As she dropped into the chair, Sox gave a sigh of contentment and curled up alongside the desk.

Taking a new composition book from the drawer, Meghan began to write. She wrote page after page of words describing all that had happened. When she wrote of Lucas, the letters were scripted with a flourish and flowed easily into one another. When she wrote of Dominic, the words were scrawled in bold heavy-handed strokes of anger.

As she told of Tracy's fear, her hand trembled, and the words fell into a slant as if they were leaning against one another—the same way Meghan hoped her sister would lean against her. Although she felt neither fearless nor bold, she wrote of these attributes as her wish for Tracy.

Pages flew by. Some words released the anger in her heart, and others asked for a stroke of luck to turn possibility into probability. When the pages of the composition book were full to the center, she turned another page and continued to write.

She told of the doctor Lucas would see and counted the days until it would happen. After numbering the days, she gave each day a specific wish: that Lucas might speak a word or mimic a sound. She asked that Tracy's fear be lifted from her shoulders and that their mama's wisdom of boys who are late to talk be changed from speculation to fact.

After Meghan had emptied her heart of all those things, she wrote of Sox. Those words were penned with a gentle touch. The ink seemed to grow paler as she acknowledged a responsibility to at least try to find his owner.

"I'm certain someone loves him," she wrote. "It's impossible not to."

When there was only a single page left in the book, she penned a prayer for herself.

"Please, God," she asked. "Let Sox be mine."

She closed the book, then stood and pulled a box from her closet. Beneath the lid was a nest of ribbons in a perfusion of colors: white, blue, pink, yellow, green, silver, gold, black. All of them were exactly one yard long and one-quarter-inch wide.

Tonight she would do as she had done with all the other composition books. Once the pages were filled, she tied a ribbon around the book and sealed the thoughts inside. Knowing the book would forever remain closed enabled Meghan to write the deepest secrets of her heart, no matter how foolish or hopelessly sentimental. She was free to wish for the moon or entertain thoughts of romance that would turn her cheeks crimson if they were spoken aloud.

Each time, the color of the ribbon was chosen according to the mood of the book. After Clancy's disappearance she'd filled five notebooks with hopeless prayers for his return; all five of those books had been tied with a black ribbon. These pages were more hopeful, so Meghan chose a sash of rose-colored satin, looped it into a bow, and then slid the book into the box beneath her bed.

When she snapped off the light, Sox padded across the floor and jumped into bed. As she climbed in beside him, Meghan noticed a thin band of rose-colored dawn feathering the horizon. A whispered sigh escaped her lips as she closed her eyes. This was indeed a good omen.

It was almost nine when Meghan awoke. By then Lucas had already eaten breakfast and was toddling from room to room in search of Sox. The minute the dog thumped down the stairs, Lucas squealed and ran toward him.

Meghan hoped to get a picture of Sox for the *Snip 'N' Save* ad, but instead she ended up with more than a dozen photos of Lucas and the dog. In one, he was lying on the floor beside the dog, so squished together there was not a sliver of space between them. In another, he squatted nose to nose with Sox. Each picture was cuter than the previous one, and Meghan kept clicking the camera.

When she loaded the photos onto the computer and scanned through them, it crossed her mind to use one of these wonderful photos for the *Snip 'N' Save* ad, but it seemed unfair. If Sox did have an owner who wanted him back, it would appear heartless to snatch the dog from a baby who so obviously loved him. As much as Meghan wanted to keep Sox, she wasn't going to resort to underhanded tricks.

Hopefully she didn't have to. Hopefully her prayer would be answered, and Sox would end up being her dog. If not . . .

In her mind, there was no "if not." Sox was simply meant to be her dog. She'd already fallen in love with him.

At eleven o'clock, when Lucas went down for his nap, Meghan took Sox into the backyard to snap a picture of him alone, but for some odd reason the dog wasn't cooperating. He'd sit in the right position for a second or two, but the moment she began to focus the camera, he turned away.

The first shot was of the back of his head. The second shot caught his tail as he walked off. The third shot showed him lying down with his face buried in his paws. After each ruined shot, Meghan moved him back into position and started over. The ninth shot, although not head-on, at least caught his profile and was a reasonable likeness. She decided to use that one.

She loaded the picture into the computer and began assembling an ad; that's where she got stuck.

Meghan had written hundreds, maybe even thousands, of words about Sox, but now she couldn't find the right ones for an ad that could conceivably take him away from her. If she were to tell the absolute truth as she saw it, the ad would read "Awesome, wonderful dog who understands every thought." But, of course, that was only her perception of Sox, and if she wrote something like that, it was possible every person in Magnolia Grove would want to claim him.

One by one she ran through the words she'd written in her journal: *gentle, loving, smart, loyal, funny, good with children.* There were so many words and not one of them right.

After nearly an hour of deliberation, she wrote, "Found: What appears to be a mixed-breed puppy with white paws. For more information, contact the *Snip 'N' Save.*"

Meghan leaned back in her chair and eyed the finished product.

Even turned away, Sox looked far too cute. Dozens of people would want an adorable pup like this, and it would be heartbreaking enough to let him go if someone else were the rightful owner. No way could she risk having a stranger show up and lay claim to Sox. In these few days, he had gone from being a stray to one very tiny step away from being her dog.

She clicked on the picture, dragged it out of the layout, then reduced the size of the ad from a half-page feature to a one-eighth insert that would go back by the classified listings.

Perfect, she thought, and slid the ad into the FILLERS folder. If there was space, she'd run it in the next issue. If not, she could do it the week after or even two weeks out.

A Spiteful Deed

After a full day passed without any more calls from Dominic, Meghan thought for sure the wish she'd written in the black-and-white composition book had been granted, but the following night at nearly 3:00 a.m. the phone rang and woke everybody in the house.

Lila, fearful that something catastrophic had occurred, was first to grab the receiver.

"What happened?" she asked in a rush.

"Nothing," Dominic replied. "Just let me talk to Tracy."

Suspecting something like this, Tracy had already picked up the receiver in the guest room. The moment she heard the thickness of his voice and slurred words, she knew Dominic was drunk. Chances were he was still at the bar.

"Good grief," she grumbled. "It's three o'clock in the morning! Go home, Dominic, and get some sleep."

Tracy plunked down the receiver, but it was too late. Everyone in the house was already awake. Lila pulled a bathrobe over her gown and headed for the guest room. Meghan came right behind her, and Sox followed along.

Seconds after they walked into the room, the phone started ringing again.

Tracy knew from past experience when Dominic was drinking he became more obnoxious and more persistent. If no one answered, he'd sit there and let the phone ring all night.

"Let me answer it," she said. "I'll tell him to stop calling this late."

She lifted the receiver and in a fairly calm voice said, "You can't keep calling this late at night, Dom. Everybody's trying to sleep."

"I've got something to say—"

"Well, call tomorrow and I'll—"

"No, I'm not gonna call tomorrow. I got every right—"

"You don't have a right to keep waking everybody up. If you call here again, Mama's going to telephone the police and say you're harassing us."

"I got something important to say—"

"Whatever it is can wait until tomorrow. Call back in the morning, and I'll talk to you then."

He gave an evil-sounding chuckle. "I think you maybe need to hear this right now. I canceled your and the kid's health insurance. I told 'em you're not really my wife, and my name's not even on the kid's birth certificate."

Tracy gasped. "You what? Are you crazy? You know Lucas needs—"

"Yeah, well, you should've thought about that when you decided not to put my name on his birth certificate. Now, if you'd get your ass back here—"

"Dominic! This isn't about us and our problems. It's about Lucas. He—"

"Unless you're ready to come home and apologize for aggravating the crap out of me, I'm not interested in hearing it."

Tracy stood there for a few minutes saying nothing as tears welled in her eyes, then rolled slowly down her cheeks. She knew Dominic had a mean streak, but she never thought he'd do something to Lucas just to spite her.

"I am home," she finally said, and hung up the receiver.

Through the thin cotton of Tracy's sleep shirt, Meghan could see her sister's heart pounding against her chest.

"Calm down," Meghan said. "I told you, whatever the problem is we'll work through it together."

Feeling somewhat in the dark, Lila eyed one daughter and then the other.

"Would someone mind telling me what is going on?"

Tracy sat on the bed next to her mama and tried to explain.

"The only way we could afford health insurance for Lucas was through Dom's Municipal Workers Union group policy, so he listed us as his wife and baby."

"Well, isn't Lucas his baby?"

"Yes, but . . ." Word by painful word, Tracy told of how she'd had the baby at home and, because of her anger, refused to put Dominic's name on the birth certificate. She went on to say he'd now told the insurance company they weren't married and Lucas wasn't his baby.

A washboard of ridges settled on Lila's forehead. "Health insurance isn't something you should have to worry about. I'm certain we can get you and Lucas an individual policy."

"It isn't that easy. It's expensive, and there's a chance they'll consider Lucas's problem a preexisting condition."

The look of concern on Lila's face deepened. "What problem?"

This wasn't a discussion Tracy wanted to have, but now it seemed she had no choice.

"We've got to face facts, Mama. Lucas still isn't talking, and by now he should be saying several words. I think there's a possibility he might—"

Lila eyed Tracy with an angry glare. "I told you, boy babies are late talkers!"

"It's not just his talking, Mama." Tracy seemed to fold in on herself as she spoke. "Haven't you noticed when you're talking to Lucas he pays no attention? It's like his mind is a million miles away."

"Well, shoot, that's a baby thing. He'll outgrow it."

"Maybe, maybe not. We've got an appointment with the pediatrician . . ."

As Tracy spoke, Meghan was running a dozen different scenarios through her head, thinking, *What if . . .*

"I've got an idea," she finally said, and outlined the plan.

The next morning, Meghan sat at the computer and redid the "About Us" page of the *Snip 'N' Save* website. Before noon, Lila was listed as the bookkeeper, Sheldon the production manager, and Tracy the graphic designer. That afternoon, Meghan applied for a group insurance policy. By pooling what she, her mama, and Sheldon all paid for individual policies, they could almost cover the cost of Tracy and Lucas. Plus, there was no preexisting exemption.

Tracy

I know you'll find this hard to believe, but there was a time when I had a bug up my nose about Meghan. Not that I didn't love her; she's my sister, so of course I love her. I always have. She's the kind of person it's impossible not to love.

That was what irked me. She was too damn perfect.

For a long while, I actually believed she was being good just to make me look bad. Thinking back, I realize I didn't need anyone to make me look bad; I did it all by myself. If there was a speck of trouble to get into, I was there. It was kind of like if Meghan cornered the market on good grades and obedience, I was determined to do so with being the popular party girl. I was the fun sister, the one who was reckless and carefree.

I was also the sister who was always in trouble.

Mama once said she was a lot like me when she was younger. But now I've got to wonder how she got lucky enough to marry a settled-down man like Daddy. My bet is that she wasn't anywhere near as wild as I was.

In my junior year, Daddy grounded me for a month. I'd tell you about it, but it's another one of those stories I'd sooner forget. Anyway, Meghan stayed home with me almost that whole month. We rented movies and watched them together. We gave ourselves manicures and pedicures, and some nights we'd stay up until after midnight playing Monopoly. I actually had a better time that month than I did with some of my "cool" friends, but of course I didn't tell Meghan that.

I'm lucky to have a sister like her, and this time I'm going to let her know how I feel. Regardless of how hard it is, I'm gonna stay here and help her with the Snip 'N' Save.

Dominic is not the last man on Earth, and it's high time I stopped thinking he is. Sure, I miss him something fierce, but what Meghan says is also true. We're better off without him. I've got to stop remembering how it used to be and start thinking of how I can build a future for Lucas.

I know Meghan really wanted to go to college after Daddy died, but she gave it up because she cared more about our family than pursuing her own dreams. Now it's time for me to do the same.

When I start missing Dominic again, I'm going to remind myself of how stupid it is to love a man who doesn't give a fig about his own child.

Sister Love

Once she was listed on the *Snip 'N' Save* website, Tracy began helping out. She spent most of the week sitting beside Meghan at the computer learning how to use templates to create an ad.

"It's not all that hard," Meghan said, sliding a photograph of work boots into place. "Upload the image, then click on it and drag it into position."

Tracy watched, and it looked easy enough, but when she moved into Meghan's seat and tried to do it herself, the ad looked overcrowded in some places and bare in others. The block of copy was squashed together with a ragged edge on the right, and the headline floated several spaces above the spot where it was intended to be.

It didn't take an expert to see the layout needed help.

Her hand poised atop the mouse as if she were still working, Tracy eyed the layout on the screen and frowned.

"I'm not exactly sure what I did wrong, but this looks—"

"It's fine," Meghan said. "You just have to tweak the copy."

She reached across, covered Tracy's hand with her own, and slid the cursor to the navigation bar. "Let's left-click on the text box here . . ."

Both sisters moved their index finger up and down at precisely the same moment and then laughed. Their laughter had a girlish sound. It was light and flowery like it had been all those years ago. Before the *Snip 'N' Save*, before high school.

Before Dominic.

Tracy turned and glanced at Meghan. "This is nice. I mean, us working together. It feels . . . I don't know. Sort of comfortable."

Meghan smiled. "Yeah, it does."

She looked at Tracy with her dark hair in loose curls, one strand dropping lazily onto her forehead. Despite the hardship of the past three years, Tracy hadn't changed a lot. Her skin was still dewy and glowing. The only thing that appeared to be different was the look in her eyes. Meghan thought back to the time when they sparkled with the fire of mischief. Now they were softer, a more sensible shade of brown.

Tracy clicked "Justify," and the ragged right edge of the text disappeared. It was replaced with a square of copy evened out on both sides. She laughed.

"You're right, this isn't as hard as I thought it would be." She again turned to Meghan. "I wish I'd done this sooner."

"Me too," Meghan said.

She thought back to the early years when they'd walked to school together every morning. Although Tracy was only a year older, Meghan felt grown up walking beside her. Back then they'd been more than sisters; they'd been best friends. Friends no one could separate. Not Elise Conklin with her whispered "stupid kid sister" innuendos or sexy-eyed Bryce Miller when he rode up on his bike, inching along beside them, urging Tracy to hop on.

"Do you remember when we were in elementary school?" Meghan asked.

Tracy nodded. "Sure. Those were fun years . . ."

Once they started talking, the fond memories rolled out one after another. They remembered the parties, the best friends, the whispered secrets, and the stories of the early years when they'd shared a bedroom. Meghan was recalling that last year in middle school when Tracy cut in.

"We were close for so many years, then we just kind of drifted apart," she said wistfully. "What happened?"

"You went to high school," Meghan said.

"But why did that change everything?"

"You were going to a different school, you had all new friends, and I felt left out." Meghan gave an almost imperceptible shrug. "It wasn't like we were angry with one another; we just didn't do things together the way we did before."

She remembered that year all too well. It was the same year Clancy disappeared. There were endless days of walking home from school alone and knowing that alone was better than being bullied by Madison Cramer or Kevin Hurley. They'd taken to calling her "Beanpole Briggs" and found a thousand different ways to torment her. That year her heartache was greater than she'd ever dreamed possible. She filled ten tearstained composition books, because feeling the scratch of a pen beneath her fingers was easier than wondering about Clancy or listening to Madison find ways to embarrass her.

"Left out?" Tracy said as she dragged a picture into position. "That's odd, because I felt the same way. You and Daddy were so close, and you seemed to understand all the stuff he was doing."

Meghan laughed. "When Daddy first started running the *Snip 'N' Save*, I didn't understand any of it. I hung around watching because it was better than going out and running into Madison Cramer or one of the kids in her clique."

A puzzled look settled on Tracy's face. "Madison? I thought you two were close."

"Not once you were gone. She and Kevin Hurley used to make fun of me."

"Why didn't you tell me?"

Meghan wrapped her arm around her sister's shoulders and gave an affectionate squeeze. "I wanted to be more like you. I wanted to fight my own battles, not just count on you to stick up for me."

Tracy chuckled.

"Funny," she said as she clicked "Save" and moved the ad to the current week's folder. "I would have loved the thought of you needing me. I was mad that Dad treated you like you were so special. He kept saying how smart you were, and that just made me feel dumb. That's when I started hanging out with the not-so-smart kids."

Meghan hesitated a moment, thinking of how for so long she'd seen things in reverse. All those years she wanted to be like her older sister and never once considered Tracy might want what she had.

"By the time I got to high school, you were so popular I figured you didn't want to have your kid sister following you around."

"Jeez, that wasn't it at all . . ."

The years of misunderstanding seemed to fade away that afternoon as the two sisters worked together in a way they had never done before. Instead of feeling frustrated or less talented, Tracy listened to what Meghan had to say. Before the day was out, she'd learned how to resize the copy, add leading to the line height, and space out the text.

At the end of the day, when Lila called them to supper, Meghan smiled at her sister and said, "You did a great job. Much better than I did when I first started."

Tracy laughed. "Get out, you're just saying that."

"No, honestly."

Tracy gave a grin that stretched ear to ear. It had been a good day. Oddly enough, concentrating on work had taken her mind off Lucas's problem. For the moment anyway.

That evening the dinner table was abuzz with conversation. Everyone had a bit of excitement to share, Lila perhaps more than anyone else.

For years she had felt at loose ends with herself. She was a mother, a homemaker, and a woman with the ability to make meals that melted in a person's mouth. With George gone and Tracy moved out, there was little for her to do. Meghan was happy to nibble on a bag of pretzels, and, besides, cooking for two was always problematic. You could search the world and not find a pot roast small enough for two people, and fresh vegetables, sold by the pound, meant days of leftovers. Now, with both girls living at home, she had a family to feed and a baby to care for. Lucas being there changed everything.

Lila couldn't stop raving about what an absolute angel he was. He rarely cried, went down for his naps without a fuss, and although he pretty much ignored Beulah, the geriatric cat who was content to be ignored, he played with the dog and understood the need to be gentle.

She moved the high chair alongside her and handed Lucas the rubber-handled spoon that once belonged to his mama.

Tracy laughed. "I can't believe you've still got that thing."

Holding back a grin, Lila said, "Don't laugh. I'll bet when Lucas is grown up, you'll find you've hung on to his baby things also. It's part of being a mama." She placed a few pieces of minced chicken on the brightly colored *Cinderella* plate and handed it to Lucas. With his left hand, he pushed a piece of chicken onto the spoon and clumsily maneuvered it into his mouth.

Lila gave a triumphant smile. "See that! I only started teaching him to use a spoon this afternoon."

She went on to say that Tracy's worries about something being wrong were clearly unfounded.

"You didn't learn to use a spoon until . . ."

The precise time frame had escaped her mind.

Tracy left her mama's words unanswered. It was another five weeks until they'd see the pediatrician. Then she'd know for sure. With every ounce of her heart, she prayed her mama was right.

It was midmorning, and Tracy was working alongside Meghan in the *Snip 'N' Save* office when her cell phone jangled with "On the Floor" by Jennifer Lopez and Pitbull. It was Dominic.

She ignored the familiar ringtone, and in time the song stopped. Determined not to let him get into her head, Tracy tried to focus on the ad in front of her. Minutes later the song sounded again. This time it was too much to resist. She tapped the green icon.

"I wish you'd stop calling," she said. "We don't have anything more to—"

"Hey, wait a minute, okay?" he cut in. "I know you've got every right to be pissed off, and I'm sorry. I acted like an idiot. But the thought of you not coming back sent me off the deep end."

"What's done is done. There's nothing—"

"Please don't say that, babe."

His voice was different, more like it had been in the beginning. The arrogance was missing, replaced by an almost apologetic tone. He spoke quickly, and the words came rapid-fire.

"Come home," he pleaded. "I'll make it up to you, I swear. I'll quit working at the bar. Find a steady job. I already got something lined up and—"

"No," Tracy said in a flat voice filled with determination. "You're no good for me, Dom, and what's even worse is that you're no good for Lucas."

"That's not true. I love the kid. Maybe I'm no good at showing it, but I can change."

"You'll never change, Dom. You know it, and I know it."

Perhaps Tracy should have ended the call there, but she didn't.

"I can change," he argued. "I'll go back to working construction. It's good money. We can save up, get a better apartment if you want. You still love me, babe, I know you do. We'll get married, right away, no waiting."

Tracy closed her eyes and tried not to listen to his words. He was saying the things she'd once prayed to hear, but after all that had happened, the words had somehow become meaningless.

"Don't do this, Dom," she said, her voice shaky and thin.

"Don't do what, babe? Say I love you? Say I'm willing to fix things?"

"Don't ask me to come back, because I can't. I've got Lucas to think about."

"I already said I'm willing to go along with whatever you want to do for the kid. You want him to have hospitalization, then fine, I'll make sure he's got it."

She listened to Dominic's plea, but in between the promises was the same thread of insincerity that had always been there. He didn't call Lucas by name, he called him *the kid*. To Dominic, Lucas was nothing more than an obstacle to be overcome, but to Tracy, he was a reason for living. Now she knew for certain she would never go back. Never. She was not a wife and never had been, but she was a mother, and it was time for her to act like one.

"I'm not coming back," she finally said. "Not ever. I have to do what's best for Lucas."

Tracy hung up and turned back to the computer screen, but tears blurred the images. Instead of seeing the smiling face of Beverly's Beauty Shop, she saw Dominic—not angry and red-faced as he'd been for all those months, but soft and caring as he'd been when they first left Magnolia Grove.

Turning to Meghan, she said, "I need to take a walk. You mind?"

"Not at all," Meghan replied. "Do you want company?"

Tracy pushed back from the desk and shook her head. "No, thanks. I need some time alone."

When she left the house, Tracy had no specific destination in mind. She just wanted to walk off her anger and frustration. Moving ahead with long strides, she turned down Lewiston and went past the elegant two-story houses without giving them a glance, then cut across the oak-lined median to Belmont and continued. By the time she reached the bungalows on Lakeshore, her calves were aching. She crossed the street, dropped down onto the grassy bank of the lake, and sat.

Only then did it dawn on her that this was Meghan's spot. It was where she came to think and dream. Tracy had never understood the draw of such a tucked-away place, but somehow she now did. She sat there for a long while, thinking back on her life with Dominic, remembering the early days, remembering the passion and laughter they'd shared, saddened by the knowledge it would never be that way again and yet determined not to be swayed by his promises.

When she stood to leave, Tracy noticed the black-and-white composition book leaned against a tree. She picked it up and flipped open the cover. The first page read, "The Secret Thoughts of Meghan Briggs, Book 83."

Some pages were stuck together, and in places the ink was blurred. But still she flipped through the book, wondering what Meghan had been writing about on the day she encountered the storm. Near the back of the notebook she found the final entry.

It was a prayer asking for Lucas to be healthy and Tracy's heart to heal.

As she stood there reading her sister's words, she could feel the love with which they had been written. That last remaining doubt, the one picking at her brain and reminding her of how it once was with Dominic, seemed to vanish as she reread the words. There was no longer a question about it—she was where she belonged. She was where she and Lucas were truly loved.

After several weeks of doing ad layouts and organizing folders, Tracy was proficient enough to handle most of the *Snip 'N' Save* tasks without help, which gave Meghan time to make the customer calls she'd been neglecting. On Wednesday afternoon, she spent four hours on the phone and before day's end had three promising new clients.

When Bruce Prendergast suggested they meet for lunch on Friday to talk about a co-op program the Chamber of Commerce was considering, Meghan readily agreed. Not only would it be good to get out of the office for a day, but Bruce also hinted at a special edition to coincide with the holiday festival.

The thought of handling things alone made Tracy a bit nervous.

"You'll have your phone with you, right?" Tracy asked. "Just in case I have a question or there's a problem?"

Meghan laughed. "Don't worry, you'll be fine. If something comes up, just use your own judgment."

Pinching her brows together in a look of concern, Tracy asked, "Are you sure that's a good idea? I mean, I could call you or maybe—"

"There's no need," Meghan assured her. "Sheldon already has everything for next week's issue, and if anything else comes up, just do what you think I'd do."

—— ❧ ——

On Friday morning, Meghan dressed in the pale-gray business suit that had been hanging in the closet for far too long and headed off. Tracy got the urgent call from Sheldon at twenty minutes past twelve.

"I'm a half page short," he said. "What have you got for fillers?"

She hesitated a moment, then asked if it could wait until Meghan got back later in the afternoon.

"No can do," Sheldon replied. "I've got to get this to the print shop by three, or else the issue won't go out on Monday."

"Oh."

"Meghan's got a folder of fillers to use when we have extra space," he said. "Grab something out of there and send it over."

"Anything in particular?"

"Nah, just whatever you've got that can fill a half page."

When she hung up, Tracy opened the FILLERS folder and started scanning the files. She spotted the ad for FOUND DOG and clicked on it.

Tracy remembered Meghan telling their mama that she planned to put a found-dog ad for Sox in the *Snip 'N' Save*. She had said it was important to do everything she could to find Sox's owner, and she wished someone would have done the same for Clancy. Tracy moved the ad to the Dropbox folder, then shot Sheldon an e-mail saying it was there.

A minute later, the *Snip 'N' Save* line rang again.

"This is too small," Sheldon said. "Can you resize it and maybe add a photo?"

"Um, okay."

Using the skills she'd developed over the past several weeks, Tracy enlarged the nine-point type to sixteen points and added a border. The ad was still loose and empty-looking, so she used her cell phone to snap a photo of Sox, uploaded it to the computer, and dragged it into position. In this photo, he was looking straight into the lens. When she was finished, the ad looked as good as any Meghan would do.

She attached it to a second e-mail and sent it off to Sheldon.

Tracy leaned back in the chair, feeling quite good about the way she'd handled things, proud that she truly was learning the business. She could hardly wait to tell Meghan how well she'd done.

It was almost six when Meghan arrived home, and she came in bustling with news of the day's meetings.

"This thing with the chamber looks like it could go big," she said. "Bruce is talking about a quarterly shopping supplement with take-one racks in the participating stores."

With the excitement of the new venture, Tracy forgot to mention how she'd devised a solution to fix the ad. She had been eager to share the good news—that she was someone who could be counted on to handle things. But the evening flew by, and somehow the thought slipped her mind until she was ready for bed. Now, with the hour approaching midnight, she wondered if Meghan were still awake. Hoping so, Tracy climbed out of bed, padded down the hallway, and tapped lightly on Meghan's bedroom door. When there was no answer, she eased the door open and saw her sister fast asleep.

It can wait until tomorrow, she thought, but just as she began to close the door, she noticed the way Sox was curled up against Meghan's chest. He lifted his head for a moment, then tucked it back into the curve of Meghan's neck.

Seeing them together as they were, Tracy suddenly had the sick feeling that maybe she'd done the wrong thing. Meghan was in love with the dog. Maybe the reason she'd never gotten around to running that ad was because she was afraid someone *would* answer it.

In the dark of night, with only a sparse bit of moonlight to show the way, Tracy tiptoed down the stairs and returned to the office. Switching on the computer, she waited until the screen came to life, then sent Sheldon another e-mail. The subject line read, URGENT! The e-mail asked that he pull the found-dog ad and replace it with the attached Boy Scouts public service ad.

For almost a half hour Tracy sat there hoping for an answer, but there was none. It was after one when she climbed back into her bed and near dawn by the time she finally fell asleep.

The next morning, Tracy was still in her pajamas when she hurried down the stairs and powered on the computer. There were five e-mails. Sheldon's answer was third from the top.

"Sorry," he wrote. "We're already on press."

Monday's Mail

Meghan was sitting at the breakfast table when Tracy came in with her chin dropped down onto her chest. Amid feeding Lucas, Lila looked up and asked, "What's wrong?"

Tracy gave a one-shouldered shrug and lowered herself into the chair alongside her sister. With a defeated sigh, she said, "I think I made a really dumb mistake."

Lila narrowed her eyes and glared across the table. "Do not even mention going back to Philadelphia."

"Mama, this has nothing to do with Dominic."

"Well, what, then?"

Tracy turned to Meghan. "I put the wrong ad in the *Snip 'N' Save*."

Meghan chuckled and placed a comforting hand on Tracy's arm. "Trust me, it's no big deal. So one of our customers gets a free ad."

"It was the ad about finding Sox."

The lighthearted sound disappeared from Meghan's voice, and her smile faded.

"I'd planned to run the ad anyway," she said grimly. "So you just saved me from making the decision."

With her heart pounding, Tracy poured half-and-half into her coffee and sat with her hands wrapped around the mug. A tiny splatter of cream had splashed onto the table, and she focused her eyes on it as she spoke.

"It was a half-page display ad with a picture of Sox." She went on to explain how Sheldon had called at the last minute needing a half-page filler, and her first thought was that Meghan had mentioned running the ad.

Meghan pushed back her plate of eggs and tried to force a smile. "A half page? I don't understand. The ad I had in the filler file was set up for a classified listing. There wasn't any picture."

"I know," Tracy replied. "I redid the layout and took a picture with my phone. At the time, I thought I was doing something to help you, but then last night I realized . . ."

She let the words drift away. There was simply no way she could explain that after seeing the dog and Meghan curled together, she'd realized how great a love they shared.

Aware of the agony her sister was feeling, Tracy added, "I tried to get Sheldon to pull it last night, but it was too late. This morning he sent me an e-mail saying the *Snip 'N' Save* was already on press."

Meghan again touched her hand to her sister's arm, but this time her fingers were stiff.

"It's okay," she said. "I know what it feels like to lose a pet you love. If Sox belongs to someone else, it's only right that I give him back."

"I knew it!" Lila snapped. With an obvious air of annoyance, she scooped up the piece of egg that had fallen from Lucas's spoon. "I should have squashed this on day one. I should have stuck to my guns and insisted you take that dog to the shelter. Now it's going to be Clancy all over again!"

"No, it's not, Mama," Meghan replied, but her eyes were already watery and threatening to overflow.

The *Snip 'N' Save* office was almost always closed on Saturday. The magazine went to the printer on Friday, so it was usually a slow day. A leisurely day meant for errands, a visit to the lake, or reading a book.

Today was different. Although it was still early, there was a feeling of unrest bristling around them. It was like the electricity that crackled

111

through the air moments before a thunderstorm—it was there but not yet ready to make itself known.

Meghan scraped the remnants of her leftover egg into Sox's bowl, then headed for the *Snip 'N' Save* office. Tracy followed close behind, still apologizing for having done the wrong thing.

"Let's take a look at the ad you ran," Meghan said. "I'm sure it's not all that bad."

She was hopeful the picture of Sox was like so many of the others she'd snapped: an image that caught only the edge of his profile or the tip of his tail as he turned away. Tracy sat at the computer, and a few clicks later the ad was on the screen.

The picture of Sox was adorable. He was looking straight into the lens with a glimmer of expectancy in his eyes.

"I d-don't get it," Meghan stammered. "How did you get him to sit still for such a good picture?"

"I said, 'Where's Meghan?' and he looked up at me."

Meghan stared at her, then looked back at the computer.

Tracy's shoulders slumped as she stared at the screen.

"I'm so sorry," she said mournfully. "I should have realized . . ."

Sheldon was the one who did the final layout. Meghan sent him the ad files, and he paginated them, placing the individual ads so competitors were not side by side. He put the filler ads in wherever they were needed, so there was no telling where the Sox ad would be. She'd never before asked to see a prepress proof and wasn't going to make Tracy feel even worse by calling for it now.

Although the *Snip 'N' Save* wouldn't arrive in the mailboxes of the Magnolia Grove residents until Monday morning, a worrisome look was already etched on Meghan's face.

Late Saturday afternoon, the delivery service dropped a package on the front porch. It was the same thing they delivered every Saturday: thirty proof copies of the latest *Snip 'N' Save*. Meghan usually carried the package into the office and left it to be opened on Monday, but this time she tore into it immediately.

She pulled out a copy of the magazine and leafed through it page by page, searching for the ad. When she got to the last page without seeing it, she breathed a sigh of relief. But then she flipped the magazine over, and there was Sox, looking back at her and cuter than ever.

Thinking he was doing her a favor, Sheldon had placed the ad on the back cover directly above the address box. People couldn't miss it if they tried.

Meghan felt an icy tremor slide through her heart and spiral into her stomach. The only thing she could do now was wait.

Determined to make the most of what could be their last days together, Meghan took Sox for a long walk on Saturday evening. She skipped dinner, then stopped for a cup of ice cream and sat on the bench in front of Friendly's. Sox waited until she was nearly finished, then looked up and swiped his tongue across his lips. Meghan set the cup on the sidewalk and watched as he lapped up the last of their summertime treat.

On the way home, they walked past the lake. Something drew her to the spot where she had been sitting the day she saw him in the water. Meghan lowered herself onto the grass, and the dog squatted beside her. For a long while there was only the faint chirp of crickets and the occasional splash of a bass jumping in the water.

As Meghan tried to remember that afternoon, darkness settled into the late-evening sky. She could recall the storm, how it had come up so suddenly, and how, as she tried to reach Sox, he disappeared from view, then bobbed to the surface again. Her heart began to pound as she recalled the blinding rain and the desperation of those last few minutes. Even now she could not remember climbing out of the lake.

She searched her thoughts but could find only snatches of fear and the sting of rain against her skin.

Almost as if he, too, could sense the memory, Sox scooted closer and began licking her arm.

They sat that way for a long while, Meghan trying to remember the moment she stepped from the lake and Sox reminding her of how he'd been there when she opened her eyes. When she could find no other answers, she looked into the sky and saw one star blinking brighter than the others.

"Daddy," she said, "were you there for me that day?"

The star blinked again, but there was no answer, just the rustle of a breeze stirring the oaks and the far-off call of a cricket.

By Monday, Meghan's nerves were worn to a frazzle. She startled at the slightest sound and found it impossible to focus on a simple task. Three times she tried to line up the text for the Tots 'n' Tykes ad and mistakenly hit "Delete."

When Bruce Prendergast called to ask if she'd like to attend the upcoming Chamber of Commerce meeting, she asked why, forgetting the project they'd discussed.

"Why?" Bruce echoed with an air of annoyance. "Well, I would have thought the holiday festival was as important to you as it is to the chamber."

Meghan quickly came to her senses.

"It absolutely is," she said, then brushed the issue aside, claiming she'd been distracted by a family problem.

"I certainly hope nothing is wrong with your mama," Bruce replied. "She's a fine woman. A sweetheart if ever there was one." After a brief moment of hesitation, he added, "You tell Lila that if she needs help of any sort to give me a call. You be sure to do that now. Tell her Bruce Prendergast was asking for her."

Ignoring the way Bruce seemed to have more than a passing interest in her mama, Meghan said, "I'll do that," and hung up.

Although he'd not mentioned it, earlier in the week Bruce had run into Lila as she was taking Sox for his afternoon walk. They'd stood and talked for a good thirty minutes, and the whole time he kept remembering how it was when they'd dated back in high school. All those years ago, he'd thought they might one day marry, but then George happened along, and that was the end of their relationship. The sweetness of Lila's kisses was something he had never quite forgotten.

All day long whenever the *Snip 'N' Save* phone rang, Meghan's heart rose up into her throat. She answered in a voice so emotionally charged, customers assumed they had reached a wrong number. Eloise Hempstead hung up and called back twice before she realized it was Meghan, and Jack Campbell apologized, saying, "Sorry, wrong number. I was calling the *Snip 'N' Save*."

By dinnertime Meghan's stomach was twisted into a knot. When Lila set a plate of meatloaf smothered in gravy in front of her, she just sat and stared at it. Lila, worried that they would go through months of turmoil like they had with Clancy, insisted Meghan eat.

"I won't have you getting sick again," she said.

"I'm not getting sick," Meghan replied, but after a spoonful of mashed potatoes, she pushed her plate back. "I need some air," she said, and stood.

With Sox at her heels, she grabbed the yellow tennis ball and headed for the backyard. Sitting on the steps, she tossed the ball across the yard. Sox eagerly chased it, then carried it back and dropped it at her feet. They did this over and over again until the ball rolled under the mulberry bush. By then Sox had wearied of the game anyway.

The moon was high in the sky when Meghan finally came inside. One last time she checked both the phone and website for messages. There were a few, but not one of them mentioned the dog. She had made it through the day, and Sox was still hers to keep.

The knot in her stomach loosened, and she grabbed a chocolate chip cookie on her way upstairs.

That night when Meghan climbed into bed with Sox snuggled next to her, she allowed herself to believe their finding one another was something that was meant to be.

"It's possible Daddy did send you to me," she whispered affectionately.

As she drifted off to sleep, Meghan could have sworn she heard a voice say, "Probably."

——— ೦ক৵৹ ———

The call came in shortly after ten on Tuesday morning.

"I'm calling about the dog you found," the man said.

Meghan's breath caught in her lungs, and several seconds ticked by before she could answer.

"Did you see the picture in the *Snip 'N' Save*?" she finally asked. It seemed obvious that he did, but she couldn't bring herself to ask if Sox were actually his dog.

"Yes, I did," he answered. "It looks a lot like Missy but not exactly. Missy is a border collie pup. She's wearing a pink collar and—"

"Missy?" Meghan cut in. "The dog you're looking for is a female?"

"Yes. She got out of the yard on Saturday—"

"This past Saturday? Three days ago?"

"Yes. The boys were playing, and they left the gate open."

Meghan's heart started to beat again.

"I'm sorry," she said, "but this dog isn't Missy. This one's a male, and I fished him out of the lake almost three weeks ago."

The man gave a sigh of disappointment. "Darn. I thought maybe you'd found her."

"Have you checked with the ASPCA?"

"Yes. No luck there, either. She's got a microchip, and we're offering a one-hundred-dollar reward. I take it the dog you found didn't have a chip, huh?"

Meghan swallowed down the lump rising in her throat. "I hadn't thought of having him checked for that."

"Please do," the man said. "If a family goes to the expense of having a microchip implanted, that means they love the dog. It's almost guaranteed there'll be a reward for returning him. Why, I'd pay anything to get Missy back. Our boys are sick over losing her, and my wife is beside herself."

"I know what you mean," Meghan said grimly. "I lost a dog I loved, too."

"Well, then, you understand."

Feeling his pain tug at her own heart, Meghan offered to run a free ad with Missy's picture in the *Snip 'N' Save*.

"Maybe that will help you find her," she said.

He thanked her and promised to send Missy's picture that afternoon.

You might think Meghan would be happy after dodging another bullet, but she wasn't. The thought of Sox possibly having a microchip implanted by a family who loved him settled in her brain and refused to let go.

She looked down at the dog lying beside her desk and said, "This isn't something I want to do, but I won't be able to live with myself if I don't."

The dog whined and dropped his head down between his paws.

Meghan

There is an almost invisible line between doing what is right and doing what is right for you. At this moment, I'm standing with one foot on each side of that line. I figured my conscience would force me to do what's right, but doing so means risking the one thing I love more than I can possibly say. The thought of having Sox checked for a microchip has become a battle of wills between my conscience and my heart.

I thought if I didn't give him a real name I wouldn't be so likely to fall in love with him, but I was only fooling myself. The truth is I started loving him that day at the lake. We survived the storm together. I needed him as much as he needed me. He was my reason to keep swimming.

I think about that, and it's easy to rationalize that my having him was meant to be. I console myself with the thought that at least I tried to find his owner; I made an effort. Then when I'm just about convinced it would be okay to stop looking, I remember how I felt when Clancy disappeared.

Night after night I cried myself to sleep wondering where he was. Every night I got down on my knees and prayed somebody with a kind heart had found Clancy, somebody who would love him and take good care of him.

That's what love is—wanting something good for somebody else more than what you want for yourself.

Yes, the thought of doing this tears my heart apart, but I love Sox too much to leave this last stone unturned. Tomorrow I am taking him to the vet and having him scanned for a microchip.

It'll take every ounce of resolve I have to go through with this, but I've got to do it whether I want to or not.

The Vet Visit

On Wednesday morning, Meghan dressed in a way that reflected her mood: gray T-shirt and jeans frayed at the bottom. She twisted her hair back in a hair claw and dabbed on a bit of lip gloss, but that was it. Her only thought was to get this ordeal over with as quickly as possible.

She fed Sox and filled his water bowl, then sat down at the table with nothing but a cup of black coffee. In the center of the table there was a platter of pancakes and sausages, but Meghan made no move toward them.

Lila looked at her with a disapproving frown. "Is that all you're having?"

Meghan nodded. "I don't have much of an appetite this morning. I'll grab something at lunchtime."

"Starving yourself is not going to solve anything," Lila grumbled. "Since last Saturday you've barely picked at your food because of that dog! If you're so set on having a pet, go buy one you don't have to worry about losing."

"Sox is special, Mama. He reminds me of—"

"I know, Clancy." Lila took a plate from the cupboard, plopped a single pancake on it, and set it in front of Meghan. "You're not leaving this house until you eat!"

Without bothering to pour syrup over it as she usually did, Meghan dutifully cut off a bite of pancake and stuffed it into her mouth. "If I get an all clear from Dr. Anderson, I'll treat everybody to a celebratory lunch. How's that?"

Lila couldn't shake loose the thoughts of what had happened when Clancy went missing. "And what if the dog does have a chip? What if he belongs to somebody else?"

Meghan narrowed her eyes. In an embittered voice, she replied, "Then I'll have to give him back." Leaving most of the pancake on the plate, she pushed back from the table and clicked the leash onto Sox's collar.

"We'll be back in an hour or so," she said, and hurried out the door.

The drive to the Anderson Animal Clinic was seven miles, but with morning traffic it took almost twenty minutes. By the time they arrived, the parking lot was already crowded.

Meghan could still remember the last time she was here. It was with Clancy, eight, maybe nine years ago. Dr. Walter Anderson was the family vet. He took care of both Clancy and Beulah, Lila's cat. If bad news were coming, Dr. Anderson was the kind of man who could break it gently. He not only cared for pets but also cared about their owners.

When Meghan opened the car door, Sox jumped out and trotted toward the front of the clinic, almost as if it were a place he was familiar with.

"You act like you've been here before," Meghan said.

Sox put his nose to the ground and followed a scent along the walkway.

She reined in his leash, and they entered the clinic together. Everything was exactly the same as she remembered. The row of leatherette chairs, the jar of treats on the counter—even Emily, the receptionist she'd known for years, was still there. The only difference seemed to be that Emily had gained a few pounds, and her hair was now streaked with silver.

She looked up. "Well, goodness gracious, we haven't seen you for years." She smiled, then came from behind the counter, hugged Meghan, and bent to pet Sox. "Now who is this cute little fellow?"

"I'm calling him Sox for now," Meghan replied. "He's a rescue I found at the lake. I wanted to check and see if maybe he has a microchip."

"No problem. I know you usually see Dr. Anderson, but he's in surgery this morning. Would it be okay if I put you in with Dr. Whitely?"

Meghan gave a reluctant nod. "Sure."

"Have a seat. I'll take you back as soon as there's a room available."

After a twenty-minute wait, Meghan and Sox were led back to one of the small examination rooms.

"Make yourself comfy," Emily said. "Dr. Whitely will be with you shortly."

Another five minutes ticked by before the door swung open and the most gorgeous man Meghan had ever seen stepped into the room. He was tall like her daddy, with light-brown hair that had streaks of sunlit gold running through it.

He stuck out his hand. "Good morning. I'm Dr. Tom Whitely."

Meghan automatically extended her arm, but when they shook hands she held on to his for a time that was longer than necessary. He had bright hazel-colored eyes, the kind that captured her gaze and wouldn't allow her to look anywhere else. She found it almost impossible to tear hers away from them.

"I'm Meghan Briggs," she finally said, "and this, Dr. Whitely, is Sox."

A faint smile played at his mouth when she used the formal version of his name. "Please, call me Tom." He squatted in front of Sox and scratched behind the dog's ear.

Tom Whitely's touch was gentle, and Sox responded by licking his arm. The dog quite obviously liked him. So did Meghan.

As if it were expected to be a shared examination, she squatted alongside the dog. "Sox is a rescue I found at the lake. I need to know if he has a microchip with his owner's name."

Feeling good about the ear scratching, Sox rolled over on his back. Tom Whitely laughed, gave the dog's belly a rub, then stood. Meghan rose when he did.

"Are you working with Dr. Anderson now?"

"For the next month I will be," he said. "Dr. Anderson is retiring, and I've bought the practice." He allowed his eyes to meet Meghan's. "I hope I can continue to keep your business."

Suddenly Meghan regretted she hadn't taken more time with her makeup or worn something with an edgier look. Designer jeans maybe, or boots and her short black skirt with a top more colorful than the faded gray T-shirt.

"Of course you will," she said. "Definitely." Sputtering and trying to pull her thoughts together, she casually swished back a curl that had fallen loose of the clip, then added, "I can see Sox already likes you. And you seem to have a wonderful way with animals."

He smiled, and there was a certain shyness in the smile that made it all the more appealing. Lifting Sox onto the examination table, he pulled a small handheld scanner from the drawer.

"Okay, now, let's see what we have here."

When he turned the scanner on and began sliding it along Sox's back, Meghan's heart stopped beating. It didn't start up again until he looked at her and said, "Sorry."

"For what?" she asked nervously.

"I can't help you. There's nothing here. Sox doesn't have a chip."

He'd heard the fearfulness woven through her words and mistakenly believed it was because she couldn't locate the owner. "If you want, I can give you the address of a shelter where you can drop him off."

Meghan gasped. "Drop him off? Why would I do that?" She explained how Clancy had gone missing, and they'd searched for months without finding him.

"As much as I wanted to keep Sox, I felt if he had an owner, I needed to try to find him or her," she said, then went on to explain she'd called the police department and the ASPCA and run an ad in the *Snip 'N' Save*.

"So far no one has come forward to claim him."

Tom Whitely looked at her with that smile. The one she'd liked from the first moment she saw it; the one where the glimmer in his eyes was a giveaway of his thoughts.

"Well, it sounds like you've done everything there is to do. I think you can safely consider him yours."

A warm flood of happiness rushed through Meghan, and, without stopping to think, she flung her arms around Tom's neck and kissed his cheek.

"Thank you!" she said. "A million times over!"

He made no move to step back but stood there with a silly-looking grin stretched across his face. Meghan moved on to hugging the dog.

He watched for a moment, then said, "If you're planning on keeping Sox, you might want to bring him in for a checkup. He's probably going to need a rabies shot and vaccinations."

"Sure. Absolutely. Can you do it right now?"

"We're booked solid today," he said. "Could you possibly come back on Friday at five thirty or six?"

Tom's voice was a bit tentative as he spoke. He hoped he wasn't being too obvious. He wanted to see her again, and having her bring the dog back was the best way to do it. With her as the last visitor on a Friday evening, he could spend plenty of time with the dog and get to know his mistress, maybe even go for a cup of coffee afterward.

"Sure," Meghan said. "That time works well for me."

"Okay, it's a date." The words slipped out before he had time to rethink them, and as they reached his ears he realized the implication. He gave an embarrassed chuckle.

"I didn't mean date like *date*; I meant appointment. You know, veterinary consultation."

Meghan laughed. "Of course."

"Oh. Okay, then, I'll see you on Friday."

He didn't turn and disappear out the back door as Dr. Anderson usually did. He just stood there with that goofy grin while he watched her clip the leash onto Sox's collar and retrieve the keys from her bag.

As she started toward the reception area, Meghan glanced back and gave him one last smile. It wasn't until she got to the parking lot that she realized he'd given her that time without checking his appointment book.

Hmm.

She stopped for a moment and eyed the sign on the building: OFFICE HOURS 9:00 A.M. TO 5:30 P.M., MONDAY–FRIDAY. A grin, similar to the one Dr. Tom Whitely had been wearing, settled on her face.

Apparently he liked her as much as she liked him.

Celebratory Lunch

True to her promise, Meghan took everyone out to lunch that afternoon. She turned the *Snip 'N' Save* answering machine on and said for once business could wait. After more than three weeks of wondering whether or not she would get to keep the dog she'd come to love, she could at long last breathe a sigh of relief.

"Sox is now mine to keep," she said happily.

Lila eyed her with a look of skepticism. "And what if a year from now somebody comes up to you and says he's their dog?"

"I doubt that's going to happen, and if it does it will be too late. I'm having a chip put in Sox. A chip that says I'm his owner. Then that's the end of that."

Lila raised her eyebrows and stretched her mouth into a look emphasizing her skepticism.

"Don't worry, Mama. Dr. Whitely says I've done everything possible to find Sox's owner, and since no one has come forth by now, it's safe to say he's mine to keep."

"Who's Dr. Whitely?" Lila asked.

Meghan went on to explain that Dr. Anderson was retiring, and Tom Whitely would be the new vet. The corners of Lila's mouth turned down in disappointment at the news.

"Walter's retiring? Now? When Beulah is getting to the age where she needs a reliable vet?"

"Don't worry. You'll love Tom. He's really good with animals. Sox liked him right away. He's got the softest hands and a very likable personality . . ."

Although Meghan skipped over saying how a lock of his hair tumbled onto his forehead at just the right angle and his eyes were a greenish gray with a magic all their own, it became obvious that she had taken more than just a passing interest in the new vet.

Tracy and Lila both spoke at once.

"How old is he?" Lila asked.

"Is he single?" Tracy wondered aloud.

Meghan laughed. "Mama, don't start making this into something more than it is. He's just a nice man who has a way with animals. I certainly didn't ask his age, and it doesn't matter whether or not he's married."

The truth was Meghan did notice he wasn't wearing a ring, and if she went by the way he'd smiled at her, she'd also guess he was single. Hopefully she was right.

Since Lucas and Sox were joining them for lunch, they bypassed the Italian restaurant with great veal scaloppini and headed for the McDonald's on Grove Street. With outdoor seating and a fenced-in playground, it was a perfect place to eat.

They carried trays piled high with cheeseburgers, chicken nuggets, and fries and settled at the outdoor table. Since no one else was around, Meghan let Sox off his leash, and he started sniffing his way across the playground. Lucas toddled along behind him.

Lila watched for a few moments, then called out for Lucas to slow down and be careful. He ignored her completely and did neither. Instead of fussing at him, she laughed.

"How can you be angry with the little rascal when the way he plays with that dog is so cute?"

What she said was true. Lucas and Sox looked like they belonged together. They chased one another back and forth across the playground, circling around the jungle gym and tables to somehow come out on the other side at the same time. Hearing the child laugh as he played with the dog made it obvious that Sox connected with the boy in a way no one else had.

"In times like this, Lucas seems like such a normal little boy," Tracy said wistfully. "If only . . ."

Meghan reached over and squeezed her sister's knee. "Don't worry. It's only a few more weeks, then we'll see what the pediatrician has to say."

Tracy said nothing, but a range of ridges settled on her forehead, and she moved on to talking of other things. She told how Dominic had called and pleaded for her to come back to Philadelphia.

"He said he wants to be a daddy to Lucas, and he's truly sorry for what's happened." She hesitated a moment, then added, "I'd like to believe he's changed and that he could—"

"Don't be foolish," Lila cut in before Tracy could finish the thought. "You know men like Dominic don't change. They use people and—"

"Save your breath, Mama," Tracy said, tired of hearing about Dominic's bad qualities over and over again. "I'm not going back. I was just saying . . ."

Her words drifted off, but in them Meghan sensed the weight of longing, the heaviness of wanting something not yours to have. It was the same feeling she'd had when she missed out on going to the Grady College of Journalism. That first year, the thought of all those wonderful classes moving on without her was like a stone lodged in her heart. At times she could actually feel herself hunched over from the sheer weight of it.

She scooted closer and touched her hand to Tracy's arm.

"I understand what you're going through," she whispered. "But in time, it gets better."

Tracy turned with a grim smile. "I know. But right now . . ." Then she sighed and just shook her head.

Once the food was gone, Lila left, saying she had books that needed to be returned to the library. Tracy and Meghan stayed behind, soaking up the warm sun and enjoying the mellowness of the day. It was nearly three when Meghan began gathering up the empty wrappers and cardboard containers.

"Let me take those to the trash bin," Tracy said. "You can stay here and keep an eye on Lucas."

With that, Tracy disappeared into the restaurant.

As Meghan sat watching Lucas toddle across the playground with Sox following along, she heard the familiar call of a blue jay. The bird swooped down, settled beside a fallen French fry, and sat pecking at it for nearly half a minute before Lucas noticed. Once he did, he stopped and stood there, obviously interested in this new thing. Not quite ready to quit the game, Sox came up behind Lucas and barked.

The sound was loud and energetic. It was the bark of a dog that wanted to play. Lucas always responded to that kind of bark, but this time he didn't budge. He didn't turn or acknowledge Sox in any way.

Strange, Meghan thought.

For him to do that to Grandma Lila or his mama was one thing, but ignoring Sox was something else entirely. He was crazy about the dog, loved him enough to leave a new toy or offer up the last chunk of cookie.

What's different this time?

Lucas was almost impossible to understand. One moment he would be laughing and playful, then he'd turn away and nothing anyone said mattered. Sox was the singular exception. When Sox barked, Lucas always squealed with delight.

Meghan sat there, thinking back on the countless times she'd seen Lucas turn and squeal when Sox yapped that same playful bark. She'd seen him do it in the kitchen, in the living room, even upstairs in what was now his room. Two days earlier, Lucas had been in the backyard when she and Sox came home from their run. The dog darted out into the yard and gave that yappy bark, but Meghan couldn't remember if Lucas had responded to Sox because he'd seen him or because he'd heard him.

Still behind Lucas, Sox barked again.

Lucas didn't turn.

Did he not hear the dog when they were outside? And if that were the case, then why? What was different?

At home they were in a room with walls and a ceiling. It boxed the sound in. Noises seemed louder and caused a bit of a vibration in the air; at times she herself had felt it. Here in the open-air playground there was no vibration, and sounds, loud or small, were swallowed up by the cement or carried off on a breeze.

A question began to pick at Meghan's mind. Was it possible Lucas didn't hear Sox's bark but felt it?

Life was full of possibilities, but probabilities were a lot harder to come by. Still, there was always a chance . . .

The thought that she might have discovered the reason for Lucas not talking was settling into her head when Tracy reappeared.

"I heard the commotion," she said. "What was Sox barking about?"

"I'm not sure," Meghan replied. "Could be he was trying to tell me something."

"Oh. So now you understand dog language?"

"No," Meghan said, laughing. "But I wish I did."

Meghan made no mention of what she suspected. How could she when all she had was a hunch? Tracy had enough worry on her plate. Before Meghan added anything more, she'd have to be certain.

For the remainder of the afternoon, Meghan couldn't stop thinking about the way the dog stayed behind Lucas and barked. When Lucas didn't respond, the normal thing would have been for Sox to paw his back or circle around to the front for attention, but he didn't.

Was he trying to show me something?

Meghan had known for years that dogs sense things people don't. Their power of smell was a million times stronger than a person's. They could follow a trail days old or smell smoke in the air when the fire was miles away. And their hearing was so sharp that from the far end of the house they could catch a baby's whimper or the crinkle of a potato-chip bag. Although she'd never experienced it herself, Meghan had even heard stories of dogs that could tell beforehand when an earthquake was coming or an epileptic patient was going to have a seizure.

If all that's true, couldn't it be possible that Sox knows Lucas can't hear? And if he does know, isn't it also possible he's trying to tell me?

Possible, maybe even probable.

A Book of Thoughts

At the dinner table that evening, Meghan was quieter than usual. She had a million thoughts bubbling through her brain, but they were cloudy and mixed up, not something she was ready to talk about. Shortly after they'd left McDonald's, she'd remembered something their former classmate Gabriel Hawke had once said, and now she couldn't get it out of her mind.

Gabriel had been born almost completely deaf but played the guitar as if his fingers had their own special magic. One summer evening when the smell of jasmine was in the air and a light breeze carried a whisper for miles in any direction, she'd heard the sound of Gabriel's guitar. He was strumming a country song about a lost love. She followed the sound of that song to Claremont Street and found him sitting on the front porch.

When she stopped to listen, Gabriel invited her to sit. That evening she listened to him play for nearly an hour, song after song, with each one sounding more beautiful than the one before.

Everyone considered Gabriel deaf, but that evening, as Meghan watched his expression, she could have sworn he actually heard the music.

Later on, when he set the guitar aside, she stayed, and they talked for a long while. She asked him how it was possible to play an instrument so beautifully when he couldn't hear the sound of his own music.

He gave a broad smile and said, "I don't have to hear it. I can feel it."

As they were clearing away the supper dishes, Meghan said, "Mama, do you remember the Hawke family who used to live over on Claremont?"

Lila glanced across with a puzzled expression. "Hawke?"

"They had a boy named Gabriel."

Lila's face brightened. "Oh, Miriam and Frank. Yes, I do remember. Their boy played guitar in a group at church."

"They moved away a while back, and I was wondering if maybe you knew where they went."

Lila wrinkled her nose and shook her head. "That was six or seven years ago, and I didn't know Miriam all that well. I believe she was close with Sally Smith, so if you're looking to find Miriam, you might try asking Sally." She slid the container of leftover chicken into the refrigerator, then asked, "Why are you so interested in the Hawkes?"

"No reason," Meghan said nonchalantly. "I passed by their house the other day and was just thinking about them."

Lila laughed. "I swear, Meghan, you come up with the strangest things."

After the counter was wiped clean and the plates loaded into the dishwasher, Meghan grabbed the leash and whistled for Sox. In the four short weeks he'd been with her, the after-dinner walk had become a ritual just as it had been with Clancy. Most evenings Meghan walked the same route she'd taken with Clancy, but tonight she turned right at the corner of Elk Lane instead of going straight.

Five blocks later, she made a left onto Claremont. When she came to the house where Gabriel Hawke had once lived, she stood for a moment and listened. She foolishly hoped to hear the sweet strains of Gabriel's guitar, but there was only the sound of a squirrel scurrying through the bushes and laughter from a nearby television.

On the walk home, Meghan found herself wishing she could hear Gabriel play just one more song or again hear him tell of how he could feel the music in different parts of his body.

As she turned left onto Elk Lane, Meghan picked up the pace. Tonight she was anxious to sit down with her black-and-white composition book. There were nights when she felt compelled to write, and this was just such a night.

Her head was filled with thoughts, but thoughts were like dandelion puffs. They could drift away and be forgotten. Written words were different. They were solid and long-lasting. She could touch her finger to them and recall the emotion with which they had been penned. Written words remained in place, and she could revisit them time and time again until their meaning became clear. Tonight clarity was what she was searching for.

That night, when Meghan opened her journal to a fresh new page, she began with thoughts of Sox and how she was certain he had been trying to show her Lucas couldn't hear him bark. After she detailed the events of the afternoon, she moved on to wondering why Sox had chosen to show her instead of Lucas's mama. Before she got to the end to add a question mark, she knew the answer. Tracy would never see what she didn't want to see.

It had taken her two years to see the flaws in Dominic's character, and even now, after all that had happened, there was still a part of her mind that doubted the truth of what she knew.

Even as Meghan penned words of hope, she was almost certain this time she could not count on either her mama or Tracy. They both wanted to believe Lucas was simply a late talker and were not likely to change their minds without something more than her suspicion.

"Whatever has to be done," she wrote, "I must do by myself."

When there was nothing more to say about the situation, she moved on to writing about the new vet but stopped short of telling all her thoughts. It was too soon. She would wait. Perhaps after she met with him on Friday, there would be a story worth telling.

With only a scant half page about Dr. Tom Whitely, Meghan went back to thinking about Gabriel Hawke.

Recalling the evening they had sat together and talked, she pulled the box of journals from beneath her bed and dug through them. She scanned three other books before she found the one she was looking for. In it there were four pages about Gabriel and how he'd described feeling the pitch and tone of a song in his body, the low sounds in the large muscles of his legs, the higher notes in his face and neck, and the thunderous melody in his chest. There was also the story of how his deafness had gone undetected for more than two years. In loopy letters stretched across the page, it told how after two years of nothing but babble, Gabriel's parents discovered his deafness and taught him to talk.

Meghan reread the entry three times. Once the details were settled in her mind, she retied the green ribbon around the book, placed it on top of the others, and slid the box back under the bed.

It was well after midnight when she climbed into bed, but still sleep wouldn't come. Even though Sox was snuggled next to her, Gabriel Hawke was at the forefront of her mind. She kept remembering the story of how his mama placed his hand on her throat to teach him the vibration of words.

The pale gray of morning was filtering into the sky when Meghan finally drifted off, and by then she had made a decision.

Finding Gabriel

Over the years, Meghan had learned it was always wise to have an answer at hand before she told her mama about a problem. So on Thursday morning when they sat down to breakfast, she avoided any mention of Gabriel. Later on when she and Tracy were alone in the *Snip 'N' Save* office, she asked, "Do you remember a guy named Gabriel Hawke?"

Tracy turned with a puzzled look. "From where?"

"He was a year or two ahead of you in high school. Tall, dark hair, good-looking, played the guitar."

"Oh, yeah, I remember. He hung out with the Jackson twins, right?"

Only vaguely remembering that part of his life, Meghan answered, "Possibly. Did you know Gabriel was deaf?"

Tracy thought for a moment, then gave a barely perceptible nod and turned back to the computer. "It wasn't all that obvious."

Meghan couldn't have asked for a better lead-in. "That's because his mama taught him how to talk. He was two years old before he said a word, then they found out he couldn't hear."

Tracy's neck stiffened. With her brows pinched together and her eyes narrowed, she turned back to Meghan.

"Why are you telling me this?"

"I thought because of Lucas it might be worthwhile—"

"Good grief, Meghan! Don't I have enough to worry about without you trying to scare me over something like this?"

"I'm not trying to scare you, but if Lucas does have a problem hearing, it's better to—"

"He doesn't have a problem hearing!" Tracy snapped. "He has a problem paying attention. It's got nothing to do with his hearing."

"You don't know that for sure."

"Yes, I do! The day before yesterday, Mama was making breakfast, and the cast-iron skillet slid out of her hands. When it hit the floor, Lucas looked like he was going to jump out of his skin. There's no question he heard that crash."

"Okay, he reacted. But that doesn't mean he actually heard the sound. He may have reacted to the vibration of the skillet hitting the floor."

Meghan started to explain what Gabriel had said about the vibrations of sound, but Tracy cut her off with a thunderous huff and turned back to the computer.

Not taking her eyes off the screen, she grumbled, "If you don't mind, I don't want to talk about it."

Meghan knew that was that. She'd heard Tracy say those same words countless times before, and once she'd said them, it was the end of the discussion.

"I just thought maybe . . ."

Meghan sighed and turned back to her laptop. Although nothing more was said, you could almost see lightninglike sparks of tension bouncing off Tracy. It was as if an invisible wall had suddenly sprung up in the narrow space between the two desks in the *Snip 'N' Save* office.

That afternoon, Meghan angled her laptop so only she could see the screen and began her search for Gabriel Hawke. After going down a few blind alleys, she found him on a site for hearing-impaired children. Gabriel was the author of the blog. His profile said he ran a specialized training facility based in Barrington, Georgia, a town less than forty minutes away.

In the "About the Author" section, Gabriel told the story of how he himself had been found deaf at the age of two and how his mother had taught him his first few words by passing his hand over her throat and mouth to let him feel the movement of her lips and tongue as she repeated the word over and over again.

The website went on to say that most children diagnosed with a hearing disability prior to the age of two often achieve perfect speech with the aid of a cochlear implant. It explained the medical procedure and the challenge of teaching a child to talk once the implant was in position.

The website illustrated a number of tips to get started. Meghan studied them carefully, made notes on scraps of paper, then tucked the papers into her pocket and cleared the browsing history on her computer. Even if Tracy suspected something and tried snooping, she'd find nothing.

Now all Meghan could do was wait for an opportunity to present itself.

———— ❧ ————

Sister love is an odd thing; it runs hot and cold, sometimes changing in less than the blink of an eye. It was something that boggled Lila's mind. When she and her daughters sat down to lunch on Thursday, she noticed the way the girls barely spoke to one another, and she asked what was wrong.

"Wrong?" Meghan replied, as if she had no inkling what her mama meant.

Tracy simply said, "Nothing," and chomped down on her sandwich.

Given the iciness between them, you'd think it was an issue that could roll into days or even weeks, but by Friday morning they were back to normal. Meghan reminded Tracy that she would be taking a part of the afternoon off.

"Sox has an appointment with Dr. Whitely," she said. "Would you mind covering the *Snip 'N' Save* this afternoon?"

"No problem," Tracy said. "In fact, I was going to ask if you could babysit Lucas tomorrow. Mama's busy, and I was hoping to join Kelly MacPharland and the girls for lunch."

"Sure," Meghan said. "Take the whole day if you want. I have no plans for Saturday."

It was the opportunity Meghan had been hoping for, and if she'd had plans, she would have readily canceled them.

"If it's a nice day, maybe I'll take Sox and Lucas to the lake for a picnic."

"That would be great, but keep a close eye on Lucas," Tracy warned. "I don't think he knows not to wander off into the water."

"Oh, I will," Meghan promised. "A very close eye."

Though the appointment with Dr. Whitely wasn't until five thirty, Meghan powered off her laptop shortly after three and trotted upstairs to her room. That afternoon she painted her toenails the rose color of sunset and twisted her hair into curls that cascaded down her back. Gathering a handful of hair at each temple, she crisscrossed the small clusters into two narrow braids and pinned them up so they circled the back of her head.

It was after five when she came downstairs wearing the short black skirt, a cold shoulder top, and strappy sandals.

"Wow!" Tracy exclaimed. "You look fantastic!"

Lila raised an eyebrow. "Aren't you kind of dressed up for a visit to the vet?"

"It's just a denim skirt," Meghan said.

True, it was a casual skirt, but it wasn't just the skirt. There was the glowing look of Meghan's complexion, the touch of mascara she'd brushed onto her lashes, and the curls that replaced a rubber-banded ponytail. She looked every bit as pretty as she did when Trent Gallagher had taken her to the Elks Club dance the previous month, the only difference being she'd worn a silk dress that evening.

Before Lila could go deeper into questioning her intent, Meghan whistled for Sox, grabbed his leash, and headed out the door. Just as she was leaving, she hollered back, "Don't wait on dinner for me!" Then she was gone.

Lila stood there for a moment, then glanced at Tracy with her nose scrunched. "Why did she say don't wait on dinner?"

Tracy laughed. "I think maybe she likes the new vet."

Meghan anticipated a few red lights and a bit of traffic, but she encountered neither and arrived at the Anderson Animal Clinic at twenty minutes past five. Hopefully it wouldn't make her seem overanxious or, heaven forbid, desperate.

Figuring it was the end of the day and no one else would be in the reception room, Meghan allowed Sox to walk beside her and didn't bother with a leash. When they pushed through the door, she was surprised to see a silver-haired woman with a pet carrier sitting alongside her feet.

Emily, the receptionist, was already pulling her car keys from her purse.

"We had a last-minute emergency, so Dr. Whitely is running late," she said. "I don't like to run off and leave you, but tonight is book club, and it's at my house. I've got to get ready."

"Don't give it a second thought."

As Emily hurried out the door, Meghan settled into the chair across from the silver-haired woman. Sox sat next to her for a moment, then began sniffing beneath the chairs.

"Would you prefer I put my dog on his leash?" Meghan asked.

"No need," the woman replied. "He's not bothering Winnie."

Sitting opposite each other as they were, Meghan couldn't help but notice the look of anguish on the woman's face. Her shoulders were slumped, and her fingers continuously plucked invisible bits of lint from her skirt. Trying to ease the tension in the room, Meghan smiled and gave a nod to the carrier.

"Dog or cat?" she asked.

"Winnie's a cat." The woman glanced down at the carrier and then looked back to Meghan. "She's seventeen years old."

"Oh, my, that's quite . . ." Meghan was going to say "old" but thought better of it and substituted, "Astonishing."

The woman gave a solemn nod. "Yes, it is astonishing, and up until now she's been very healthy."

The woman introduced herself as Agatha Wilton, and one word followed another until the two women found themselves deep in a conversation about the love of pets. As they chatted, neither of them noticed Sox edging closer and closer to the carrier.

Agatha was in the middle of telling how she'd gotten Winnie as a tiny kitten when they heard a gagging noise followed by something that sounded like a cross between a baby's cry and an old man's moan.

"Oh, dear," Agatha said. She bent down and whispered into the cage, "Try to be patient, Winnie dear."

She looked back to Meghan and said, "Poor Winnie has been sick to her stomach for the past two days. She's fussy because she's not feeling well."

Meghan noticed Sox had now backed away from the carrier. "Is it possible the dog coming so close upset her?"

"I don't think so. She's just cranky because she's sick."

"Poor thing." Meghan got out of her chair, crossed over to the carrier, and squatted in front of it. She peered in at the silver-haired cat with eyes the color of the Caribbean Sea.

"Winnie's a Persian," Agatha said. "They have wonderful dispositions. It's unlike her to be so irritable."

"Hi there, Winnie," Meghan said gently.

The cat moved into a lunge position, flattened her ears, and spewed a nasty hiss.

"Winnie, shame on you making such a ruckus!" Agatha said. "This lovely young lady is just being friendly."

Without saying another word, the cat turned herself so she was facing the back end of the carrier and all they could see was the bushy tail.

Agatha gave an apologetic shrug. "That's the problem with cats. They're fiercely independent."

Moments later, Tom Whitely came into the reception room.

"I'm sorry for the delay," he said. "We had an emergency—"

"We know," Agatha cut in, obviously anxious to have him see Winnie. "Emily already told us."

By then she had the carrier in her hand and was headed toward the examination room.

Tom looked back at Meghan, smiled, and mouthed the words *I won't be long.*

Seeing the glint in his eye, Meghan knew wearing the skirt had been a good move.

After Agatha

Agatha was in and out in less than fifteen minutes. As she passed through the reception room, Meghan asked, "Was Dr. Whitely able to help Winnie?"

"I believe so. He gave her something to soothe her tummy."

Meghan smiled. "Good. Hopefully she'll be back to herself in no time."

"Yes, hopefully." Agatha gave a goodbye nod as she carried Winnie out the door.

Seconds later, Tom Whitely came from the back office.

"It's good to see you again." He smiled at Meghan, then squatted to greet Sox. "You too, young fellow," he said, and lowered his hand for Sox to sniff.

Sox skipped past the sniffing part and went directly to licking.

"He obviously likes you," Meghan said.

"It must be my bedside manner."

She smiled and gave a soft chuckle.

Tom looked up at her. She was even prettier than he remembered.

"I'm glad you could make it," he said. "I hope my running late hasn't interfered with whatever plans you had for this evening."

"Not at all," she replied. "I have no other plans."

"Good. I mean, good that I'm not keeping you from anything else."

He stood, gave a nod toward the hallway, and suggested they head back to the examination room. Stepping aside, he allowed Meghan to go in front of him. As she passed by, he caught the scent of something light and fresh, flowery but not overly so. Last time he'd thought she looked great in jeans; now he thought she looked even better in the skirt.

"First door on the right," he said. From behind her, he pushed the door open and accidentally brushed his arm across her shoulder.

Both of them felt it. Neither of them mentioned it.

Meghan knew she was smiling way more than was appropriate. It was unlike her. She wanted to appear friendly and open, not giddy.

"If I seem extraordinarily happy today, it's because of knowing Sox is finally mine," she said. "I know how terrible it feels to lose a dog, so I'd never keep one that belonged to someone else, but if Sox's previous owner can't be found or doesn't come forward . . ."

Tom lifted the dog onto the table, then looked at Meghan and smiled.

"Happy looks great on you," he said, "and I know exactly what you mean. It's obvious that you and Sox were meant for each other."

As he continued talking, he probed Sox's mouth, checked his gums and teeth, then felt around his ribs and hips.

"The problem is people sometimes pick out a pet the way they pick out a suit or a sofa. They just think about what looks good, but there's more to it than that. Having a dog, cat, hamster, or any other pet is a commitment, and not everyone is emotionally prepared for it."

"I have no problem with commitment," Meghan said emphatically. Then, realizing what she'd implied, a spot of color rose up in her cheeks, and she added, "You know . . . a commitment like taking care of Sox."

He laughed. "I can see that."

As he moved through the process of taking the dog's temperature, checking both ears, and parting the fur to where he could see Sox's freckled skin, Tom flitted his eyes back and forth from the dog to Meghan.

The examination could have been done in ten minutes, but it was more than a half hour before Tom said, "Well, Sox certainly seems healthy enough, so let's get a blood sample and then . . ."

Determined to see Meghan again, Tom said, "Perhaps you could bring Sox back for his follow-up next Friday at about the same time. By then I'll have his blood analysis, and we can map out a health-care plan."

"Sure, next Friday is good."

It seemed he'd finished more rapidly than intended, so they stood there, him on one side of the examination table, her on the other, neither of them eager to leave.

"Emily told me you've been bringing the family pets to Dr. Anderson for a while," he said. "Have you lived in Magnolia Grove long?"

"Only all my life," Meghan replied with a grin. "My family owns the *Snip 'N' Save*, and I manage the magazine."

"Really?" Tom was impressed. "What a coincidence. With Walter retiring, I've been thinking I should do some advertising to introduce myself to the townspeople."

In reality he'd seen only one copy of the *Snip 'N' Save* and taken no more than a minute flipping through the pages, but now he saw this as an opportunity to spend more time with Meghan.

"Let's get together and talk about setting up a campaign," he said.

"Sure. Anytime. We've got a Preferred Services section where a number of doctors and lawyers run business card ads."

"That sounds perfect. Since Sox was my last patient of the day, I have some time now. If you're available, why don't we discuss it over a cup of coffee or maybe a glass of wine?"

Meghan lifted her lashes and looked directly into his beautiful hazel eyes.

"Wine sounds great."

The clinic was on the far edge of town, but a few miles away was a restaurant called the Garden. He followed her there in his car, and when she pulled into the parking lot, he pulled in right beside her.

The building was fairly small. Behind it was a grassy courtyard strung with tiny white lights and a scattering of tables, only half of them taken. Tom couldn't have asked for a better place; the outdoor dining area was casual yet still romantic.

As they settled at a table, he said, "This place is great. How'd you find it?"

Meghan laughed. "The *Snip 'N' Save*. Mrs. Bonucci advertises with us." She looped Sox's leash over the knob of the chair, then sat and told of how Anna Bonucci opened the restaurant after her husband was killed in Iraq.

"It gave her a reason for living. Anna cooks for the restaurant almost like she's cooking for family. It's a fairly limited menu, but no one cares because the food is so great."

"It's nice that you know so much about the town," Tom said. "I've never lived in any one place long enough to get to that point." He fingered his chin and gave a soft chuckle. "Or maybe it's just that I never really made time. I've been here almost a month and haven't seen much other than my apartment and the clinic."

"If you want, I could show you around or maybe take you to one of our Chamber of Commerce meetings."

"That would be great," Tom replied. He gave a smile of satisfaction and ordered two glasses of pinot noir. Conversation came easily and flowed across the table, bubbling and cascading like the rush of water in a brook. One subject inevitably led to another, and as they sat talking, the sky turned crimson, then darkened.

The shadows of tall pines fell across the yard, and as she told about losing Clancy, Tom leaned in so far it seemed as though their noses might touch. The whole time, he kept his eyes fixed on her face, seeing not only the blue but also the passion of her eyes.

When they finished the first glass of wine, he ordered a second and suggested they stay for dinner. Meghan agreed. There was nothing about Tom Whitely she didn't like. He had a soft, easy laugh and a way of making even the tiniest fact interesting.

He told of how from the age of six he'd wanted to be a veterinarian. Laughing at his own memories, he spoke of bringing home strays and bandaging legs that had no injuries.

"After Dad's death, Mom and I moved to a small apartment," he said. "The building didn't allow pets, but that didn't stop me from carting them home. On Saturday mornings, Mom and I would get up early and spend most of the day looking to find homes for whatever animals I'd carried back to the apartment that week." He laughed and told how the building superintendent knew they had animals coming and going but looked the other way.

"Mr. Sullivan," he mused fondly. "He was a good man."

"Were you really young when your dad died?" Meghan asked.

Tom nodded sadly. "It was fourteen years ago. I was twelve at the time."

In that single moment, Meghan knew he'd loved his daddy the way she'd loved hers.

"I lost my dad, too," she said. "Almost four years ago. It was the summer before I was supposed to start college. That's when I took over running the *Snip 'N' Save*."

"That's quite a responsibility for someone so young . . ." The solemn sound of understanding was threaded through his words.

She nodded. "It wasn't what I'd planned to do with my life, but at the time, I felt keeping the *Snip 'N' Save* up and running was kind of like keeping my dad with me."

As she recounted the sadness of that time, he stretched his arm across the table and touched his hand to hers. His fingers were warm and gentle; he folded them across hers in a way that was caring but not possessive. As they moved on to talking of Tracy and Lucas, his hand remained in place, and she made no effort to move hers.

When Anna Bonucci passed by, they ordered the daily special, which was chicken tetrazzini. After only a second bite, Tom smiled and said he could see why she thought the restaurant was so special.

Once the dinner dishes were cleared away, they ordered cappuccinos and continued to talk, not about the clinic or the *Snip 'N' Save* but of the things in life that gave them pleasure. Meghan told about her love of writing, and Tom spoke of running.

"That's the only time my mind is clear of everything else," he said.

Even as the words came from his lips, he knew running would not clear the image of her ocean-blue eyes from his mind. He took a sip of his cappuccino, then set the cup back in place. Each sip was a thing to be savored because he wanted to make it last. Draining the cup could possibly bring the evening to a close.

It was nearly eleven when Meghan realized they were the last people left in the courtyard.

"Oh, my goodness," she said, laughing. "I didn't realize it was so late."

"Neither did I," Tom replied. "And we never even got around to talking about my doing an ad in the *Snip 'N' Save*."

When she took Sox's leash in her hand, Tom casually looped his arm through hers. "If you're free tomorrow afternoon . . ."

"I'm not," she replied, sounding regretful. "I promised I'd take Lucas for the day."

Seeing the disappointment on his face brought out a boldness she did not normally have. She stopped and turned to him. "I could do any evening next week."

They settled on Tuesday, and he suggested he'd pick her up at the house.

"Plan on dinner," he added.

After Meghan loaded Sox into the car, Tom circled around and opened the driver's side door for her. She climbed in, looked up, and allowed her gaze to linger on his face.

"It's been a wonderful night," she said.

"Yes, it certainly has been." He leaned down, touched his fingers to her lips, and whispered, "Until Tuesday." Then he closed the car door.

If he had asked her to stay or suggested they sit by the lake and look up at the moon, Meghan would have gladly done it, because Tom stirred something inside her. Something she thought she'd forgotten.

On the drive home, Sox slept on the seat beside her, and Meghan hummed the melody of a song she'd heard coming from inside the Garden. She couldn't remember the lyrics but believed it to be a love song, one that in time she might come to know.

Probably.

Meghan

I keep telling myself it's ridiculous to feel so smitten after a single date, especially since it wasn't even a real date. Tom is new in town, and it's possible he was just looking for company, but honestly, it didn't feel that way.

Aunt Phoebe claims there's no such thing as love at first sight, and only fools believe in it. Show me a person who falls in love after a single kiss, and I'll show you a person headed for heartbreak, *she says.*

Daddy didn't feel that way at all. He claimed Aunt Phoebe not believing in love was why she never got married; that, plus the way she could talk a man into the madhouse. One time he told her, Phoebe, if you can't trust your own heart, how can you ever hope to trust anyone else's?

I'm certain Daddy knew what he was talking about, because he said the first time he met Mama he knew right then and there that he would marry her one day. Now if that's not love at first sight, I don't know what is.

Given my druthers, I'd prefer to think like Daddy.

I'm not saying this thing with Tom is flat-out love, but we've definitely got a strong attraction to one another.

He reminds me of Daddy, so how can I not like him? It's not so much a physical resemblance but his mannerisms. Tom has Daddy's way of making people feel special, and not just people but animals, too.

Sox took to him right away, which goes to prove what I'm saying. It's easy enough for someone to put on a good show and fool other people, but it's not so easy to fool a dog. Dogs have a sixth sense that people don't have. They can smell trouble even when it's covered with a layer of cologne.

For now I'm going to trust Sox's judgment and follow my heart.

We'll see what happens.

Saturday

On Saturday morning Meghan was awake before anyone in the house had stirred. She rose from the bed, pulled out the notes she'd copied from Gabriel Hawke's website, and sat in the chair to study them. After she'd read them over three times, she stood in front of the mirror and began practicing an overemphasized version of the word *mama*.

All she needed to convince Tracy was a word, a single word. Gabriel Hawke's mother had taught him how to speak fluently. Surely she could teach Lucas one word.

It was close to eight when Tracy rapped on Meghan's door asking to borrow her yellow sweater. Meghan hurriedly stuffed the packet of notes in the top bureau drawer and called out, "Sure, come on in."

Tracy was wearing an ivory top with trousers that looked as if she'd been poured into them.

"Wow," Meghan exclaimed. "You look fantastic!"

Tracy gave an embarrassed grin. "These pants are actually a bit snug. I haven't worn them since I worked at the bank."

"No, they look good." Meghan pulled the yellow sweater from the closet and handed it to Tracy. "What time are you leaving?"

"Ten thirty, if that's okay with you. Kelly and I are going for coffee before we meet the others." Tracy hesitated a minute, then said, "It's funny. Back in school I thought Kelly was a scatterbrain, but it turns out she's really smart. She's the one who invited me to come along today.

Once a month Kelly and the other moms get together and leave their husbands to watch the kids."

Tracy gave a disheartened sigh as she turned away and said, "Needless to say, that doesn't work for everybody."

She wasn't usually a person to feel sorry for herself. When the worst that could happen ended up on her plate, she straightened her back and dealt with it, just as she had in Philadelphia. But this time Meghan sensed a feeling of hurt bristling beneath the so-what surface.

"I know you're still missing Dominic," Meghan said, "but if he were here, you probably wouldn't be going out with the girls, and I wouldn't have one whole wonderful day to spend with my nephew."

Tracy laughed. "I guess you're right. Good thing I've got you to remind me of how lucky I am."

Later, as soon as they finished the breakfast cleanup, Meghan packed a picnic lunch with sandwiches, fruit, and two juice boxes. She tucked in several handfuls of dog treats and a baggie filled with the gingersnap cookies Lucas loved.

Twice Tracy volunteered to drive them, but Meghan insisted on walking.

"Lucas and I are out to enjoy the fresh air and sunshine," she said.

There was never a question that Meghan was the responsible sister. It had been an accepted fact since she was old enough to toddle around and gather up the toys Tracy left strewn about. But that morning it was as if the tables had suddenly turned. Over and over again Tracy reminded her to be careful of Lucas getting close to the lake, not to let him eat too many cookies or too much fruit and to make certain he wore a sweater if a breeze came up.

Meghan patiently nodded to each of these commands, then she folded a quilt across the handle of Lucas's stroller and slid him into the seat. Off they went, Meghan, Lucas, Sox, a cooler full of food, an extra sweater, and a comfy quilt, but when they turned the corner to wave goodbye, Tracy stood on the front porch with her face scrunched into the worried look of a fearful mother.

It was more than a mile to the lake, but this was a good day for walking. The sun was warm on Meghan's shoulders, and a gentle breeze ruffled her hair. The motion of the stroller thumping along the walkways lulled Lucas into an easy, relaxed mood.

As she walked, she ran through the instructions on Hawke's website again. Choose a calming environment: check. Select a time when the child is neither overtired nor overstimulated: check. Eliminate unnecessary distractions: check. Make learning sessions a one-on-one experience without the interference of others: check.

They arrived at the lake, and Meghan unfolded the quilt and spread it beneath the umbrella of a leafy oak. When the sun rose high in the sky and the afternoon grew hot, the tree would provide a cooling shade. She lifted Lucas from the stroller and plunked him down in the center of the quilt. Leaving Sox attached to his leash, she looped the handle over her wrist. Today there was to be no running and chasing; today was to be a day for feeling and hearing.

Dropping down beside Lucas, Meghan lifted him into her lap and turned him to face her. Unaccustomed to this position, the boy's head turned one way and then the other, perhaps looking for some unknown something or possibly searching for a way to pull free. Sensing his impatience, Meghan tented her knees and locked him in position.

He sat motionlessly for a few moments, then listed to the side and stretched his arm toward Sox.

Taking his small hands in hers, Meghan held them to her cheeks with his fingertips touching the corners of her mouth. Giving the word a sound that was large and round, she said, "No." The word rolled out slowly and with enough growl to be felt in her jawbone and cheeks.

Although his eyes had been focused on the dog, Lucas's head snapped back, and he looked up with an expression of surprise. Meghan knew he had felt the word.

She repeated it twice more in that same overly round way, and as the rumble rose in her throat, Lucas laughed and stretched his fingers toward her mouth. With the look of a newfound pleasure sparkling in his eyes, he rocked his body back and forth, a sign he wanted more.

She sounded the word over and over again, shaking her head side to side and adding a motion significant to the word. She moved his hands from her cheeks and mouth to the spot just below her jaw where sound vibrated through the bone.

After she'd lost count of the number of times she'd said the word, she took his hands from her face and moved them to his own. She positioned his chubby little hands alongside the curve of his mouth and held them in place with the light touch of her finger. Looking deep into his eyes, she shook her head as she had before and used overexaggerated lip movements to repeat the word with the same deep-throated growl. Lucas didn't take his eyes from her face, but neither did he make any attempt to mimic her sound. After a long while, he tired of the game and looked away.

Taking the package of cookies from her bag, she pulled it open and handed him one. She hoped that after a break, Lucas would be more responsive. Meghan sat gazing out at the lake, wondering if she'd somehow missed a step, wondering if she'd positioned his hands too high or too low. She heard the crinkle of paper and turned. Sox was sniffing his way into the cookie package.

"No!" she called loudly, and shook her head. It was a knee-jerk reaction, certainly not planned, but as she reached to grab the package, Lucas shook his head and repeated the word. The *N* was missing, and it had the sound of a single letter *O*, but it was a clear and distinct effort to mimic what she'd been trying to teach him.

Meghan's eyes filled with tears as she lifted Lucas to her chest, and she hugged him until he squiggled to get free. After whispering that he was the sweetest little boy God ever put on this green earth, she sat him back between her tented legs, pulled a box of jelly beans from her pocket, and gave him two. He squealed with delight.

As soon as the two jelly beans were gone, he held out his hand for more. Meghan shook her head and again growled out another no.

He again mimicked her. It was doubtful that he'd heard her or felt the vibration of the word, but he'd associated the movement of her head with the sound.

Now more than ever, Meghan felt the courage of her conviction. Reaching into her tote, she pulled out the photo of Tracy she'd taken from atop the dresser. It was years old, but there was no mistaking Tracy's smile.

She took Lucas's fingers, positioned them on her lower lip, then said, "Mama," in the overemphasized way she'd practiced.

He studied her face quizzically, then repeated, "O."

Meghan repositioned his hands, with his fingertips touching her upper lip and his palm resting on the lower one. Pressing her lips together, she let him feel the grumble of the *M* rolling out and then parted her lips and allowed the *ah* to follow. After she'd done this a dozen or so times, she held Lucas's hand to her face, repeated "Mama" again, and pointed to Tracy's picture.

Lucas laughed merrily and smacked a hand against the image of his mother.

Meghan knew she was on the right track but was unclear as to where he'd feel the strongest vibrations, so she moved his hands from her lips to her jawbone and then to the front of her throat where the *M* came up like a roll of thunder. In time, he seemed to understand the connection between that vibration and the picture, but still he made no attempt to mimic the word. She lowered her legs, and he scrambled across, reaching for Sox.

With the sun already high in the sky, Meghan knew she had only a few hours left. She thought back and remembered the worried look on Tracy's face. If they weren't home by five, she would come in search of them.

Unwrapping the lunch pack, she handed Lucas a strip of string cheese. He gobbled it down and after that another one and a third. When the cheese was gone, Meghan carved off thin slices of apple and handed them to him one by one. He ate the apple down to the core, then emptied a juice box and crawled into Meghan's lap. With his eyelids drooping, he leaned his head against her chest, and seconds later he was asleep.

Precious minutes sped by as Lucas dozed, and Meghan tried to recall some step of Gabriel Hawke's instructions she might have missed. She'd meant to bring the notes with her, but when Tracy came into the room asking about the sweater, Meghan had gotten flustered and shoved the notes into the drawer instead of putting them back in her tote where they belonged.

Meghan closed her eyes and imagined herself writing in her journal. The words of a prayer came to mind, and she pleaded that Lucas speak one word.

"Enable him to say his mama's name," she murmured, but before she'd finished the thought, two black-bellied ducks skittered across the lake, calling *Waa-choo, waa-choo*. The sound startled Sox, and he jumped up, barking. The dog's movement jostled Lucas and woke him.

For a moment he sat there looking sleepy, then he spied the picture of Tracy lying next to him. He leaned over, reaching for it, and squealed, "Maaaaaa."

It wasn't exactly a word, but it was the sound of a word, and it settled in Meghan's heart like a Fourth of July explosion. Pronunciation meant nothing; he had associated the word with Tracy, so it was only a matter of time.

Bristling with renewed confidence, Meghan rewarded him with more jelly beans, and they went back to work. All afternoon they sat face-to-face with his small hands feeling the vibrations of speech in her mouth and in her jawbone and in the rumble of her throat as she repeated the word over and over again.

By the time the sun began its descent toward the rooftops at the far end of the lake, he could say three words clearly. Well, at least clearly enough to be understood. His vocabulary consisted of *mama*, *Sox*, and *no*. Of the three, *Sox* was the least understandable, since it came out sounding like *Sah*.

It was more than Meghan had hoped for. How he said a word was unimportant. He'd attached names to objects, not because he'd heard the words but because he'd felt the vibrations. He was smart, and he wanted to learn. Already she could imagine the smile on Tracy's face when he called her mama.

Bundling Lucas back into the stroller and packing away the quilt, Meghan started for home. She had not gone three full blocks when a car pulled alongside of them and screeched to a stop.

Tracy jumped out. "Where on earth have you been? I've been calling your cell all afternoon, worried sick that something horrible could have happened!"

Lucas raised his arms in the air and said, "Maaaa."

Appearing dumbstruck, Tracy turned to Meghan. "Did he just—"

"Say mama?" Meghan answered with a nod.

"But how . . ."

"I taught him to say it. He's not autistic, but he—"

"So Mama was right after all!"

"Not exactly," Meghan said, but by then Tracy had lifted Lucas from his stroller and was no longer listening.

Knowing there was a long and difficult road ahead, Meghan decided the explanation could wait. For now she would let Tracy enjoy this moment of great happiness.

A Painful Truth

On Saturday evening, Meghan filled the better half of a composition book with her thoughts. She wrote page after page telling of the afternoon with Lucas, detailing each action, explaining her discouragement when she feared her plan might not work, and telling of the overwhelming joy she felt when at long last it did. She expressed confidence that Lucas would one day speak as clearly as Gabriel Hawke and that he would grow to be a handsome and intelligent young man. Giving a nod to the challenges that lay ahead, she swore to stand by Tracy and see that the boy got all the help he needed.

Partway through the pages, she set the book aside and tapped out a lengthy e-mail to Gabriel Hawke. In it, she said he probably wouldn't remember her but that she certainly remembered him. She told of Lucas and how because of Gabriel's story she had taught the boy to say his first three words. At the end of several paragraphs, she wrote that she was hopeful Tracy would see fit to have Lucas attend Gabriel's learning academy.

She clicked "Send," then returned to the composition book. After nearly three years of writing about her and Tracy's lives, the growth of the *Snip 'N' Save*, and loveless dates that left her uninspired and unimpressed, Meghan was now bubbling over with thoughts of Tom Whitely.

"His face is narrow," she wrote, "with hazel eyes that sometimes appear to be a mix of gray, green, and blue with flecks of copper circling the edge of the iris. Although you could say his hair is a sandy brown, it's more the color of a wheat field in the waning hours of sunlight when the stalks radiate a golden glow. He's tall like Daddy and has the same gentleness in his voice, but his shoulders are wider and his waist narrower. I look at him and can almost picture his arms around me, his lips pressed against mine.

"Last night when he walked me to my car, I thought he would try to kiss me, but he didn't. Instead he touched his fingers to my mouth and whispered, 'Tuesday.' That may not sound like much, but, truthfully, it sent a shiver up my spine. If the touch of a finger can do that, I can't begin to imagine what will happen when he actually kisses me."

When Meghan had emptied her heart of words, she pulled the box of ribbons from the closet. Choosing the strand of metallic gold she had saved for just such an occasion, she wrapped it around the composition book and looped it into a bow. This time she didn't knot the ribbon as she usually did. Already she knew this book was one she would return to, and when she did, a small tug on the end of the tie would allow it to fall open.

Meghan waited until Sunday evening to share with her mama and Tracy just how she had taught Lucas to speak the words. As they gathered at the kitchen table, she said, "There's something I need to tell you."

She began with reminding them of Gabriel Hawke and explaining the magic of his music. At first Tracy and Lila eyed her with a curious look, wondering if perhaps Gabriel was the reason for this strange new gleam in her eye.

"Are you dating this Gabriel?" Lila asked.

"No," Meghan replied, "I'm not. I'm only saying how much I admire what he's done with his life. Look at the challenges he's over-come and how he reaches out to help others."

Tracy turned her head, and she eyed her sister with a suspicious glare. "Does this have something to do with Lucas?"

"I suppose you could say that." Meghan drew in a shallow breath. "Gabriel runs a school that teaches deaf children—"

Tracy slammed the palm of her hand against the table. "I don't want to hear about it!"

Lila chimed in. "Tracy's right. I've told you a dozen times boy babies are—"

"Get real, Mama!" Meghan's voice was louder now, more emphatic. "I taught Lucas to say those words the same way Gabriel's mama taught him to speak—by letting him feel the sound of the word in my mouth."

As Meghan began to explain the process, tears welled in Tracy's eyes and spilled out onto her cheeks.

"You're my sister," Tracy said. "How can you do this to me?" Her voice cracked, and when the words came out, they were raw and splintered like razor-thin shards of glass. "How can you sit there telling me my child is deaf? That he'll never hear the sound of—"

"Stop it!" Meghan shouted. "Stop feeling sorry for yourself! Denying the truth won't help Lucas."

"I'm not denying anything! I know Lucas is having a hard time adjusting, but it's only because—"

"It's because he can't hear!"

Lila watched the exchange the way one watches a tennis match, with eyes flicking back and forth from one daughter to the other.

"Girls, please!" she said, but they both ignored her.

"I can't say for sure he's deaf," Meghan argued, "and you can't say for sure he's not! But I do know his hearing is not normal. Gabriel says—"

"Gabriel, Gabriel, Gabriel! I'm sick to death of hearing what Gabriel says! He's never even laid eyes on Lucas, so how can he know?"

Meghan lowered her voice. "Maybe you're right, Tracy. Maybe Gabriel can't do anything for Lucas. Maybe nobody can, but you'll never know unless you have him tested and get the kind of help he needs."

A sob caught in Tracy's throat, and there was a moment of nothingness before she spoke.

"Don't you think I'm already trying to help him? I've got an appointment with the pediatrician. What more can I do?"

"He needs to go to a pediatric audiologist. Someone who can test a baby's hearing and tell us what steps we need to take." Meghan went on to explain Gabriel's website indicated that in most cases where the problem was caught early on, a child's hearing impairment could be corrected with either a hearing aid or surgery.

Tracy pushed back the tears and listened to Meghan's tales, not of tragedy but of success. Recounting the stories she had taken from Gabriel's website, Meghan told of children who were born deaf and before they were five years old had hearing sharp enough to catch the tick of a clock or hear the crunch of leaves beneath their feet.

Later that evening, Tracy and Lila sat in front of the large computer screen in the *Snip 'N' Save* office and watched as Meghan pulled up Gabriel Hawke's website. Reading aloud, she retold the story of how Gabriel had been born deaf and now wore hearing aids. A tear came to Tracy's eye as they watched the video of him telling how his mother struggled to teach him to feel the vibrations of sound and how he could still remember the touch of his hand to her face.

And there were other videos. A professor who spoke of the need for patience while a child learns to listen, conversations between students and teachers, pictures of children studying at the Hawke School. They watched and listened as the children called out names of animals and objects the teacher pictured.

Lila pointed at a boy who looked to be near Lucas's age. "It seems almost inconceivable that child was born with a hearing impairment," she said. "His words are completely understandable." She held back the remainder of her thought but couldn't help weighing the child's ability to talk against Lucas's shrieks and keening.

After the videos, there were testimonial letters filled with the heartfelt gratitude of parents who claimed that because of Gabriel their child could now pull words together into a sentence and differentiate a request for *soup* versus *sock*. The letters held words such as *compassion, understanding, devotion, miraculous*. There was only the muffled *whoosh* of Lila's sigh as Meghan read about how a cochlear implant placed in a toddler would last a lifetime.

It was after midnight when Meghan finally clicked off the computer and went to bed.

Tracy had leaned close to the screen and listened to every word but said nothing. At the end of it all, she'd walked away with her shoulders hunched and her eyes focused on some distant thing no one else could see.

———— ❧~❧ ————

It was hours before Meghan fell asleep, and when at long last she did, she dreamed of a baby crying, a baby she could neither find nor comfort. Throughout the night she tossed and turned, and it was near daybreak when she finally fell into a deep sleep.

She woke late, and by the time she came downstairs everyone else had already eaten breakfast. A plate of French toast was warming on the back of the stove, but she passed it by and poured herself a cup of coffee.

Standing there, she heard Tracy's voice coming from the *Snip 'N' Save* office. Although Tracy's tone was insistent, Meghan couldn't make out the words. She tiptoed toward the office and stood outside the door, listening.

"Yes, I realize you don't have any new patient openings before October, but Gabriel Hawke is a close personal friend of my sister, and he felt certain you'd be able to work us in."

The conversation went back and forth a few times, then Tracy said, "Sure, Thursday would be great. Thank you so much." After a moment of quiet, she said, "Yes, I will certainly mention it to him," and hung up.

Meghan stuck her head in the office. "Everything okay?"

Tracy turned and gave a slow nod of resignation. "As okay as it can be. I cancelled the appointment with Dr. Driscoll and got Lucas an appointment with Dr. Mallory on Thursday."

"Dr. Mallory?"

"A pediatric audiologist in Barrington." With a guilty grin tugging at the corner of her mouth, Tracy said, "I hope your Gabriel Hawke doesn't mind, but I used his name to get an earlier appointment."

The Portuguese Fisherman

By Tuesday morning there was an air of expectancy in the Briggs household, a sense of knowing something was going to happen but not knowing whether it would be good or bad.

At the breakfast table, Lila, a lifetime believer that food was the salve for everything, announced she'd be making chicken and dumplings for dinner.

"I won't be here," Meghan said. "I'm going out."

Given that Meghan didn't date all that often, and when she did it was almost always on a Saturday night, Tracy and Lila both turned with their eyebrows lifted.

"Out where?" Lila asked.

"I have a date."

"On a Tuesday?"

Meghan stirred a spoonful of sugar into her coffee and nodded.

"Is this one of those Chamber of Commerce things?" Tracy asked.

"No." The thought of seeing Tom again caused Meghan's lips to curl into a smile. "I'm having dinner with Tom Whitely, the new vet."

Hoping to hide the grin on her own face, Lila turned away.

———— ❧❧ ————

That evening, Tom arrived early, but Meghan was ready and waiting. She'd been watching from an upstairs window and recognized the blue Audi when it turned in to the driveway. It was a convertible, and tonight he had the top down.

Earlier she'd thought of pinning her hair up, doing something a bit more glamorous than her usual look. She'd pulled a narrow black sheath from the closet and slipped it over her head, then twisted her hair into a dazzling black clip. But when she'd looked in the mirror, her reflection screamed, "This is not you!" At the last minute, she'd changed her mind and was now glad of it.

She watched him climb from the car and start up the walkway. He was dressed casually: khaki trousers and a white, open-collar shirt. She breathed a sigh of relief, glad she had changed into the sundress and strappy sandals. Meghan heard the ding-dong of the doorbell, but the last thing she wanted was to seem overly eager. She waited a minute, listened as he introduced himself to Lila, then started down the stairs.

He was standing in the living room, and when he looked up, his eyes widened.

"Wow," he said. "You look fabulous!"

The way he said it caused a spot of color to rise in her cheeks.

"You too," she said. "I mean, you look good. A manly kind of good."

He laughed.

After several minutes of polite conversation with Lila and Tracy, he tactfully said they had a dinner reservation and should get going.

From the moment he backed out of the driveway, Meghan had a feeling it was going to be a good evening. Their conversation seemed to pick up almost exactly where it had left off Friday evening. He said he'd made a reservation at the Portuguese Fisherman and asked if that was okay with her.

"Doc Anderson recommended it," he said. "He claims they have a flame-grilled Chilean sea bass that's to die for. And if you don't care for fish, they have pretty good steaks."

"I love seafood," Meghan replied. In truth, she would have eaten anything or nothing at all, because the pleasure of the evening was simply being with him.

The restaurant was in the next town over, a forty-minute drive that you could make in thirty if you took the highway. Tom didn't. His GPS was set to bypass highways, and they drove leisurely along back roads rich with the smells of summer: apple orchards not yet ready for picking, fields of watermelon, and peach trees heavy with fruit.

As they drove, the breeze lifted the ends of Meghan's hair from her shoulders, and in the setting sun it appeared more golden, luminous almost. Tom cast a sideways glance and smiled. When they stopped at a crossroad, he reached across and tucked a loose tendril behind her ear.

"If the wind is too much, I can raise the top," he said, but she shook her head and told him it was perfect as it was.

The Portuguese Fisherman was a small building that looked as if it had at one time been a house. The entrance opened into a foyer that led to different rooms. The hostess, noticing the way Tom's arm circled Meghan's waist, suggested the Lareira Room. It was one with a stone fireplace along the wall and a scattering of candlelit tables circling a small dance floor. In the far corner, a man with silver hair and an easy smile strummed a guitar. Although he sang in his native language, Meghan knew these were love songs. The tenderness of his expression told the tale.

Tom held his hand to the small of her back and led Meghan to the table. Feeling the heat of his touch, she leaned closer and whispered, "This place is lovely."

He smiled and again credited Dr. Anderson for the recommendation.

Once they were seated, he asked if she would like to share a pitcher of sangria. She nodded, and he ordered the red. It was rich and fruity, the kind that had been made hours earlier and was given time to soak in the flavor of sweet orange and fleshy peach. He filled both glasses, and they lingered over the drinks for a long while before ordering appetizers.

They talked of all the things they had yet to learn about one another. He spoke of the hardships after his father had died and described how he'd worked his way through college. During the years of grad school, he'd worked at a clinic in Ohio, saving every nickel so he could one day have a practice of his own.

As Meghan listened, she could imagine the boy and then the younger man, studious and dedicated to his cause. She fell into the magic of his words while he spoke. With each thing he said, she asked for more, and he gave it freely.

"I haven't been able to stop thinking about you," he said, and stretched his arm across the table, his palm open, an invitation for her hand to be placed in his.

As she reached out to accept his offer, Meghan lowered her eyes and said, "I've been thinking about you also." The shyness of a new and still fragile relationship was in her voice. She didn't mention how at night when she closed her eyes, she could picture the soft gray-green of his eyes and the curve of his mouth as he smiled. She said nothing of how she had written pages about him in her journal. Those thoughts were too private, and it was too soon.

She blushed at the remembrance of what she'd written, then hurried past the moment by asking about Agatha and her cat, Winnie.

"Winnie is doing fine now," he said. "She had a mild trichobezoar."

"Oh. With Winnie being a Persian and coughing as she was, I thought maybe it was just a hairball."

He laughed. "That's what a trichobezoar is. Vets give it a technical name to impress people." Tom liked that she'd asked about Winnie and was impressed she'd known about hairballs. "Do you have a cat?"

"Mama does, but Beulah is strictly her cat and won't come near anyone else." With a twinkle in her eye she added, "Sox is my baby."

"Lucky for me you found him," he said. "Had you not brought Sox into the clinic, we might never have met." He looked into her eyes, feeling this was the start of something special. In a voice as soft as velvet, he whispered, "I think it was fate."

Meghan's heart fluttered, and she felt the warmth of a blush coloring her cheeks. "Maybe it was something far more powerful than fate . . . ," she said, and told him about the storm.

"For a while I thought we might not make it back, then this big wave came and pushed me ashore. The odd part is there are no waves in the lake. Not ever. There's no force to push the water one way or the other."

He raised an eyebrow, and a look of concern settled on his face. "So then what . . . ?"

"I don't know," she said, and gave an easy shrug. "I've since wondered if maybe it wasn't Daddy watching over me."

The expression of concern was still stuck to his face. "Do you realize you could have been killed?"

Although he had known her only a short time, that thought struck him like a bolt of lightning.

"Promise me you won't do anything like that again."

She laughed, even though there was nothing funny. "Finding Sox was a once-in-a-lifetime miracle. I doubt I'll ever come across another dog who needs saving."

"If you did, would you do the same thing again?" The words were out of his mouth before Tom had time to reason why he would ask such a question.

Meghan hesitated, then answered, "It's hard to say, but yeah, I probably would. Animals and babies can't always fend for themselves," she said, "so how can you not do something when they're in trouble?"

That answer was yet another thing to like about Meghan, although Tom preferred to think she'd be more cautious next time.

When he asked about her weekend, she told him of the day with Lucas. She spoke of remembering Gabriel Hawke and how she'd learned from his website the techniques for teaching a deaf child to speak.

"I can't begin to imagine how Gabriel's mother did that," she said. "I spent almost a full day teaching Lucas three words."

She explained that Tracy had finally acknowledged the problem, and they were scheduled to see a pediatric audiologist on Thursday. She hesitated a moment, drew a small breath, then added, "I pray Lucas's hearing disability is something that can be corrected."

Tom saw the heaviness of this thought in the furrows of her forehead. Her love for the boy touched his heart, and he affectionately tightened his fingers around hers.

"Lucas is fortunate to have an aunt who cares so much," he said, and in his mind he was thinking he, too, was fortunate to be sitting across the table from her.

When the sangria neared the bottom of the pitcher, Tom ordered a second one and a sharing plate of appetizers with a taste of everything: garlic shrimp, fried calamari, broiled octopus, and stuffed clams made tastier by the addition of bacon. Meghan scrunched her nose at the thought of octopus, but when he speared a small piece and held it to her mouth, she ate.

Later, after they had finished dinner, the guitarist thrummed a song so achingly beautiful it was impossible not to be swept away by it, and they danced. Feeling his hand pressed to her back, Meghan was again glad she'd switched to the sundress that bared her shoulders. When the song ended, they remained on the floor to dance again and then again.

In the dimly lit room, it seemed as though the rest of the world fell away and the music was meant only for them. They moved together, bodies swaying, her hip tight against his, his arm pressing her to his chest, so close she could feel his heartbeat. This was the magical moment when Meghan knew—not suspected but *knew*—she was madly, happily, crazily in love with Tom Whitely.

Later still, they ordered espressos and sat at the table looking dreamily into each other's eyes.

Tom

There are a dozen different things people can say about me, but the one thing no one could ever say is that I am the least bit impetuous. I'm the kind of guy you can trust to follow the rules, do exactly as expected, and be responsible all day long.

Growing up, I had no choice. After my dad passed away, Mom had a hard time making ends meet, so I had to step up to the plate and do my share. I've been working since I was fourteen, and if it wasn't for the basketball scholarship, I probably wouldn't have been able to go to college.

I've made it this far because I planned things out, planned them out to the very last detail. I saved every cent I made in Ohio for the one goal I had in mind: to have my own veterinary practice before I turned thirty. Now that I've not only done it but with three years to spare, my plan was to fully establish myself in the community over the next several years, find a nice girl, and get married a year or two later.

Then I met Meghan.

Something draws me to her. I felt it the first time she came into the office. Last Friday when we had dinner together, I came home telling myself she was a wonderful woman and would be a terrific friend. But the longer I thought about her, the more I came to realize I wanted something more than just her friendship.

Tonight, when we were dancing, she fit into my arms as if she were made to be there, and I had a feeling I've never before experienced.

I've always believed I was far too practical to fall head over heels for a woman the minute I met her, but with Meghan everything changed. Okay, she's beautiful, but there's a whole lot more than just beauty. There's something else, some intangible thing I can't even name.

We've known each other less than two weeks, but I can't get her out of my mind. Before we said good night, I'd already asked to see her again. So I guess it's safe to say the least impetuous guy in the universe has taken a huge leap and fallen in love without one ounce of forethought or planning.

That thing I once said about love at first sight being a lot of nonsense . . . well, I guess you can forget it. Meghan Briggs proved me wrong.

A Day of Testing

Four days after Meghan e-mailed Gabriel Hawke, she got a text.

Of course I remember you, he wrote. He went on to say he was sorry to hear of her nephew's problem, and if there was any way he could be of service she should feel free to get in touch.

Seconds after she read the message, Meghan texted him back.

We'll be in Barrington on Thursday. Lucas has an appointment with Dr. Mallory at ten. She clicked "Send" and waited.

His answer was immediate.

Mallory's one of the best. When you finish up, stop by and bring Lucas.

With a smile, she tapped out her response.

Will do, she wrote, **and thanks.**

On Thursday, both Meghan and Tracy were up before the sun crossed the horizon. Neither of them had slept through the night.

After almost two hours of tossing, turning, and worrying, Meghan had climbed out of bed and sat at the desk, writing page after page of jumbled thoughts in her journal. The first page was about Tracy and the hard decisions that awaited her, but there were other pages also. Pages of hopes for Lucas, that he would grow up strong and healthy and with the ability to hear.

Tracy spent endless hours staring at the ceiling. Although she'd never been a praying person, she'd prayed that night. Over and over again she asked that Lucas be found normal and if not normal at least curable. When she finally did find sleep, she was tormented by dreams of Lucas. She saw him in a high place where she feared he would come crashing down. When she woke, it was with her heart pounding and a cold sweat covering her brow.

Most mornings, Lila was downstairs long before the girls. She was in the habit of rising early and setting a pot of coffee on to brew. But on this particular morning it was Meghan who fixed the pot and waited as it dripped, plunk by plunk, into the carafe. When it was at long last finished, she poured two cups and sat opposite her sister. Stretching her arm across the table, Meghan took Tracy's hand in hers.

"Don't worry," she said. "This is the start of something good. We're finally going to get the help Lucas needs."

Tracy lifted her eyes. They were reddened, and the saddest look imaginable was stretched across her face.

"I know," she said. Her words were hollow, like the sound of a distant echo.

"I've been in touch with Gabriel, and he said when we're finished with the tests to stop by and say hello."

Tracy rolled her eyes. "Gabriel again?"

Although Tracy knew it was not so, it somehow seemed as if he and he alone were responsible for the problem.

"He's offered to help, and he'd be good for Lucas. He understands the challenges of being . . ." Meghan hesitated, searching for the right word, the word that wouldn't make Tracy more fearful than she already was. "Hearing challenged," she finally concluded.

Tracy sat silently.

"Trust me on this," Meghan pleaded. "Gabriel's a good man. You owe it to Lucas to at least listen to what he has to say."

"Okay." Tracy gave an almost imperceptible nod, but her expression didn't change.

Although Barrington was only a forty-minute drive, they left the house before nine. Meghan drove, and Tracy sat alongside her. Lucas was in the back, strapped into his car seat. At nine thirty, they pulled into the parking lot of Barrington Pediatric Audiology.

"We're too early," Tracy said. "Maybe we should just find a McDonald's and go for coffee."

She didn't come right out and say it, but she feared the thought of sitting in the dreary waiting room of the doctor's office.

Meghan ignored the comment, unbuckled Lucas's seat, and lifted him into her arms. She passed him over to Tracy and started up the walkway.

The office was as child-friendly as a McDonald's playground. The walls were painted with brightly colored animals. A tiny play table sat in one corner, and toys were scattered across the room. After only fifteen minutes, Dr. Mallory was ready to see them. By then Lucas had become attached to a stuffed lion that in an odd way resembled Sox. When Tracy tried to take it from him, he clung to it, crying, "Sah, Sah."

The grandmotherly nurse smiled. "It happens all the time. It's okay; let him take it in with him."

Dr. Mallory was a silver-haired man with a slight paunch, round face, and soft-spoken manner, the kind that put a person at ease. Even knowing it was unlikely Lucas heard his words, he squatted, welcomed him, and patted the lion's head as if it were alive. He then turned to Tracy.

"There's nothing to worry about," he said. "Most of the time you'll be holding Lucas in your lap, and the tests are just diagnostic, so there's no pain whatsoever."

He led the trio toward the first room, saying, "We'll start with a visual reinforcement audiometry and take it from there."

The first test took place in a soundproof room with a single chair in the center. Tracy sat and held Lucas on her lap. Dr. Mallory pointed out the speakers on different sides of the room.

"I'll be testing Lucas with different voices and sounds, but you need to ignore them. It's important we see what he does without your influencing his reaction."

Tracy nodded, then Dr. Mallory stepped outside and closed the door.

For the next fifteen minutes, there was a series of voices, beeps, and bongs. In the few instances when Lucas turned in the direction of the tone, he was rewarded with a colorful display of flashing lights.

When the doctor reentered the room, Tracy looked up with apprehension.

"Lucas failed the test, didn't he?"

"I don't think of it as failing or passing," Dr. Mallory replied. "I see it as a road to finding the problem and fixing it."

She gave just the slightest hint of a smile.

Next came an otoacoustic emissions test. They moved to another room where again Lucas sat on Tracy's lap. Explaining the process as he worked, Dr. Mallory placed a small device in both of Lucas's ears, then connected the wires to the computer.

"This only takes a few minutes," he said, "but you need to keep Lucas still while it's running."

He stepped over to the computer, and moments later Tracy heard a series of soft clicks coming from the device. This time there were no happy dancing lights. When Dr. Mallory removed the device, Tracy asked how Lucas did.

"The OAE just measures the sound waves in Lucas's inner ear," he said. "We'll know more when we're finished."

The final test was the auditory brainstem response, for which Lucas needed electrodes placed on his head. This was something new for Lucas, so he fussed and tried to pull the electrodes off. The technician, having been through this countless times before, offered a new toy, and in time Lucas settled down.

All three tests, including the moves from room to room, took just under two hours. Afterward they gathered in the back office, Dr. Mallory behind a large mahogany desk, Meghan and Tracy sitting across from him, and Lucas digging through the basket of toys pushed up against the back wall.

"Is it okay if he plays with those things?" Tracy asked.

Dr. Mallory nodded. "That's what they're there for."

Going slowly, and thoroughly explaining each step of the process, he reviewed the test results. At the end he said, "There's no question that Lucas has a significant hearing disability. The tests indicate he doesn't hear anything below ninety decibels. This means unless the sound is greater than that of a lawn mower or motorcycle, he can't hear it. It's impossible for him to hear someone speaking in a normal voice or even shouting. Now that we know he has a problem, the next step will be to pinpoint the cause. For that he'll need to see an ear, nose, and throat specialist."

Tracy's eyes grew teary, and her chin started to quiver.

"Don't worry," Dr. Mallory said. "Lucas is still young, and because we're catching this early, there's a good chance the problem can be corrected."

"How?" Meghan asked.

"It depends on the cause of his hearing loss. It could be something as simple as eardrum ventilation tubes or hearing aids. Or there's a chance he may need a cochlear implant." Seeing the distress on their faces, he added, "The important thing to keep in mind is that we're out in front of this problem, and we *will* correct it."

His emphasis on the word *will* held out a sliver of hope.

He went on to suggest Dr. Goldstein, who was right there in Barrington and was one of the best.

"I can have my receptionist set up an appointment if you wish."

Given no alternative, Tracy nodded.

They returned to the waiting room, and Dr. Mallory asked the woman at the desk to call Dr. Goldstein's office and book an appointment for Lucas. After nearly fifteen minutes of holding on the phone, the receptionist said the earliest available appointment was six weeks out.

"Six weeks?" Meghan said. "There's nothing sooner?"

The assistant shook her head. "Dr. Goldstein's booked solid."

With a sigh of disappointment, Meghan took the appointment card and handed it to Tracy. As they walked back to the car, she texted Gabriel.

Just finished up. Are you available?

Before they had Lucas buckled into his seat, Meghan had her answer.

Absolutely. Let's do lunch. He included the address and said to pick him up at the school.

Several minutes later, when Meghan pulled up, Gabriel was waiting in front of the building.

"There he is," she told Tracy, and beeped the horn. He caught sight of her, waved, and started toward the car.

Tracy turned, stretching her neck for a better look. She remembered Gabriel from school, and back then he had been a skinny kid slouched over with hair hanging in his face. Now she gasped.

"*That's* Gabriel Hawke?"

Before she could say anything more, he was standing beside the car with his dark eyes and squared-off jaw tilted toward her window. He wasn't skinny anymore, nor did he have long hair. In fact, it was short enough that she could see the hearing aid behind his right ear. The video she'd watched definitely did not do him justice.

After a quick hello, he said, "I'll jump in the back with Lucas," and climbed in.

Following his directions, Meghan drove nine blocks to a small vegan restaurant called the Healthy Choice. She parked in the back lot, and as soon as they were out of the car, she hugged Gabriel and told him how good it was to see him again.

"Still playing the guitar?" she asked.

He gave a wide grin. "Absolutely. It's what keeps me sane."

Meghan took Tracy's arm and tugged her into the conversation. "Gabriel, do you remember my sister, Tracy? She was a year or two behind you in school."

Gabriel shifted his eyes to Tracy and smiled as he gave a nod. "Sure I do, but I'll bet she doesn't remember me."

His playful challenge caused Tracy to blush.

"I do so," she said. "I remember the guitar you had slung over your back all the time."

He gave a hearty chuckle. "That guitar is what got me through the toughest years of my life. In high school it was my best friend."

They chatted for a few minutes, then went inside. It was easy to see why Gabriel had chosen this place; it was whisper quiet with standing plants and bits of greenery in every open space. On each table there was a small pot of herbs: basil on this table, dill on that, rosemary on yet another.

"How charming," Meghan said, sighing.

"I like it here because it's quiet, and I don't pick up a lot of background noise." In a low whisper Gabriel added, "Of course, every so often I find myself wishing they had meat on the menu."

They slid into a booth and ordered salads, bean burgers, and lentil soup. Once the waitress was gone, Gabriel asked what the audiologist had said. Tracy and Meghan went back and forth, with one of them remembering this and the other remembering that.

"Lucas can't hear anything below ninety decibels," Tracy said. "That's really bad. He had almost no reaction in the blinking light test."

Not showing any visible signs of concern, Gabriel said, "I'm assuming Dr. Mallory referred you to an ENT. Who was it?"

"Dr. Goldstein," Meghan replied. "We've got a consultation set up for mid-September."

"September? Why so long?"

"It was the earliest appointment we could get."

"Nonsense," Gabriel huffed. He pulled his cell phone from his pocket and tapped out a text.

Sorry to bother you, Herb, but a friend of mine needs a consultation for her fifteen-month-old. Can you do me a huge favor and fit them in this afternoon?

He set the phone aside, and they started eating. Halfway through the soup, the screen lit up, and he had an answer.

Will 3:00 p.m. work?

Before answering, Gabriel glanced up at Meghan and Tracy. "Is three o'clock okay?"

Tracy's jaw dropped. "Today?"

Not waiting for her sister, Meghan said, "Absolutely."

Gabriel tapped out, Perfect. Thanks. He clicked "Send," then slid the phone back in his pocket. "After lunch we'll have enough time for me to show you the school."

"That would be great," Tracy said, and gave a smile of gratitude. Any previous impression she'd had of Gabriel Hawke was long forgotten. She now saw him as a powerhouse, a man to be respected. A man who changed things with just the mention of his name. For the first time, she could imagine Lucas growing up to be much the same.

"Thank you," she said. "You can't begin to know how much I appreciate what you've done for Lucas."

With a gentle smile crinkling the corners of his eyes, he said, "I've been there, so, yes, I do know."

The Consultation

After lunch, Gabriel took them on a tour of the school. It was a two-story building with testing labs and offices on the second floor. On the main floor there were several small therapy studios, brightly colored rooms with toys scattered about and comfy overstuffed chairs. In one of the rooms, a therapist worked with a child, a toddler no taller than Lucas. A woman, the mother most likely, sat in the side chair and watched as the therapist guided the child into identifying items in pictures.

When Meghan and Gabriel began to move on, Tracy stood there with Lucas in her arms and watched as the toddler selected a picture from the table.

"Oh, my," the therapist said, "can you tell me what that is, Ella?"

"Cat," the girl replied, laughing as though the sound of such a word was the most wonderful thing in the world.

Meghan looked back. "Tracy? Are you coming?"

"Uh-huh."

Tracy stood there a moment longer, then reluctantly followed along, but the memory of the child's voice stayed with her. As they walked through the classrooms designed for play and study, she kept thinking back on the joyful sound of that single word, and she knew this was what she wanted for Lucas.

"How old does a child have to be to attend this school?" she asked.

"We've had students as young as ten months," Gabriel said. "The younger a child is, the easier it is for them to get accustomed to sound."

"Accustomed to sound?"

He nodded. "It may not be obvious, but many of these children have been living in a world of complete silence since the day they were born. The first time they hear a voice, it's a shock to their system."

Suddenly, more than she'd ever wanted anything in her entire life, Tracy wanted Lucas to say *cat* in that joyful-sounding voice. Not just *cat* but *dog, horse, girl, boy*, all the words other kids said. She wanted him to know an object and give it a name, to put words together as a sentence, to ask for a cookie or a glass of milk. She wanted him to hear her voice and one day speak as fluently as Gabriel.

"How much does it cost to go to this school?" she asked.

Gabriel looked at her with the corner of his mouth edging toward a smile.

"Don't worry about it," he said, and winked. "Not once have we turned a child away because of finances."

A feeling of hope swelled inside Tracy's chest and brought tears to her eyes. "Really?"

Gabriel nodded. "Really."

———— ❧❧ ————

The consultation with Dr. Goldstein was over in less than an hour. He reviewed the test results, examined both of Lucas's ears, then told them it appeared Lucas had sensorineural hearing loss.

"My belief is that he'd do well with a cochlear implant," Goldstein said, "but before we proceed, I'd like to get a CT scan to check for any hidden problems."

He went on to explain the surgery, saying it was a fairly simple operation but, given Lucas's age, would entail a one-night hospital stay.

"Afterward, will Lucas be able to hear?" Meghan asked.

"Not right away. You have to wait four to six weeks, make sure the implant is set and the skin completely healed, then the audiologist attaches an external device and turns on the sound."

That was that. To Dr. Goldstein it was a relatively simple procedure, something he'd done a thousand times before, but Tracy felt as if she'd been caught in an avalanche and was tumbling head over heels downhill. She could barely catch her breath.

As they walked back to the car, she was as silent as a stone.

They pulled out of the parking lot, and Meghan cast a sideways glance. "Want to talk?"

Tracy shook her head. Truthfully she did want to talk, but the words were caught in her throat, and she simply couldn't find the strength to push them out. Several minutes ticked by, then in a whispery voice she said, "I'm afraid."

"Afraid of what?"

"Everything. Lucas never speaking. The thought of him having an electronic thing in his head." She sucked in a small breath, and her voice quivered. "The doctor said with that implant voices will be translated into electronic signals and sent to Lucas's brain, but what if all he ever hears are beeps and buzzes?"

"I doubt that could happen. He said—"

"I remember what he said. Cochlear implants almost always work well. *Almost*. Not *always*."

"If you have misgivings about this, why don't you talk it over with someone who's more knowledgeable than me? If you'd like to talk to Gabriel—"

Tracy reached across and grabbed hold of Meghan's arm. "Turn around! Let's do that. Let's go back and talk to him."

Meghan pulled to the side of the road and texted Gabriel, asking if he could spare some time to talk with them again. She waited a few minutes until his answer pinged, then she made a U-turn and headed back.

Tracy brushed away the tears that threatened to overflow her eyes and whispered, "Thank you."

By the time they arrived at the school, Lucas had grown restless and was wriggling to get free. Gabriel took them to one of the empty classrooms, where there was space for him to romp around and enough toys to keep him occupied. Lucas found a yellow truck that he liked and sat on the floor pushing it back and forth as Gabriel and the sisters gathered at the table. Tracy rolled off question after question about the cochlear implant procedure, and Gabriel answered each one.

"The thing is," Tracy said tearfully, "I want Lucas to be able to speak normally, not like a computer. I want him to speak like that little girl did."

Looking puzzled, Gabriel echoed, "Little girl?"

"The girl that therapist was working with earlier."

Gabriel laughed. "Oh, you mean Ella. She has a cochlear implant—had it done before she was a year old." He went on to talk about how the audiology lab upstairs handled all of Ella's cochlear activation and mapping.

"She's doing beautifully," he said proudly.

"Can you do that for Lucas?"

"Yes, if you want us to."

Tracy breathed a sigh of relief. In a world where every moment seemed so fragile, and danger was lurking at every turn, she believed Gabriel was the one person she could trust to bring Lucas through this.

As they sat at the table and talked, Meghan stepped out into the hallway and dialed Tom's cell phone number. When he answered, the sound of his voice brought back the sweet memory of Tuesday evening. She explained all that had happened that day.

"I'm still in Barrington," she said. "Do you mind if we cancel tonight and make it tomorrow night? I think Tracy needs someone to lean on tonight."

"I understand," he said, and he did. Meghan caring about her sister and Lucas as she did was just one more thing he loved about her. He added *loyal* to the list that was growing by leaps and bounds.

They spoke for a while longer, and when they said goodbye he told her, "Drive carefully."

He could have said, "Drive carefully, because if something happened to you it would break my heart," but it was too soon. When the time was right he'd say it, and when he did, she'd understand exactly how he felt.

Tracy

I've always been a fairly independent person. For as long as I can remember, I've been able to look trouble square in the eye and say, Bring it on, *but no more. Now I cry at the drop of a hat. Weepy Wanda, that's what Meghan should call me.*

The thing is, I'm not crying for myself; I'm crying for Lucas. When you love someone as much as I love my sweet baby, seeing him hurt is way worse than hurting yourself. If it were me, I'd take my hits, then go at it again. But I can't do that when the problems are his.

He's my baby. I'm supposed to watch over him and make sure nothing bad ever happens. But I'm powerless to do so. Those doctors could tell me anything, and I wouldn't know whether to believe them or not. Okay, I think what they say is true, but there's a world of difference between thinking and knowing.

Thank God for Gabriel.

It's hard to believe he's the same kid I knew back in school, and not just because of his looks. Yeah, he's really good-looking, but I wouldn't care if he had the ugliest face on earth. The important thing is that I trust him to help me take care of Lucas.

If everything goes as planned and Lucas has this operation, I'm gonna make sure he goes to that school. If I have to work five jobs to pay for it, I'm gonna see that he gets to learn the way little Ella did.

I can almost imagine Lucas pointing to a picture and saying cat *in that happy little-kid voice.*

If the Lord Himself came down to earth and said I can have one wish, that's what I'd ask for: to see Lucas talking. I'm gonna start praying every night and asking God to make it happen. I haven't been real saintly in the way I've lived my life, but I'm hoping He's willing to forgive and forget so I can have this one wish.

A Family Affair

Friday morning dawned with a sizzling red sun bleeding across the horizon and a haze of clouds overhead. Even with the bedroom window shut tight, Meghan could smell rain in the air. Sox rolled onto his back, stretched, then offered up his tummy for some pets.

Meghan laughed. "Forget about it. We've got a busy day ahead."

She swung her feet to the floor, grabbed a bathrobe, and headed for the shower. Sox was right behind her.

In the month they'd been together, Sox had become like a shadow, trailing along wherever she went. He woke her with slobbering kisses in the morning, and at night he snuggled into the crook of her arm as she closed her eyes. When she climbed into bed, he climbed in beside her, and when she sat at a desk—whether it was in her room or in the *Snip 'N' Save* office—he was right there at her feet. A stranger could easily believe the girl and dog had been together all their lives.

Meghan splashed water on her face, wiped the sleep from her eyes, then grabbed Sox's leash.

"Let's go," she said, and headed for the door.

The truth was Sox didn't need a leash. He would have happily trotted along with only his love for her tying them together, but she wasn't willing to take chances. Not after what happened to Clancy.

With Sox charging out front, Meghan ran three blocks, then slowed to a walk. The humidity, as thick as pea soup, made it too hot to run.

When Meghan returned, Tracy and Lila were sitting at the kitchen table.

"I can't work today," Tracy said. "The hospital called, and Lucas has an appointment for a CT scan at eleven thirty. Mama's gonna go with us."

At times Lila could be excitable and blow a minor incident into a catastrophe, which wasn't necessarily good if you were edgy to start with.

"Are you okay with that?" Meghan asked.

Tracy nodded. "I've explained the situation, so she's prepared."

Meghan knew with both of them being out of the office yesterday there would be plenty of catching up to do.

"Well, if you're sure . . ."

Lucas banged his spoon against the tray of the high chair, yelling, "Sah! Sah!"

Once everyone was gone and the house quiet, Meghan whizzed through the ad scheduling and moved on to roughing in a layout for the following week's issue. As promised, she included a picture of the lost Missy and in large bold letters stated there was a $100 reward offered by the owner. By the time Tracy returned, Meghan had finished up for the day.

"Let's just take it easy for the rest of the afternoon," she said. "I'm seeing Tom this evening, so I'd like to have time to get ready."

That afternoon, the two sisters sat on the back porch, Meghan painting her toenails a peachy pink and Tracy watching as Lucas ran back and forth chasing Sox and calling out a word that had little resemblance to the dog's name. Tracy sat there for a long while. Then she sucked in a deep breath and gave a sigh.

"I'm praying this implant thing works," she said quietly.

Meghan reached across and squeezed her sister's knee. "It will. I'm absolutely positive of it."

She forced a note of conviction into her voice, but the truth was she felt as fearful as Tracy. Once she'd finished the *Snip 'N' Save* scheduling, she'd spent well over an hour searching the Internet for stories with a thread of similarity. She'd watched YouTube videos of toddlers having their cochlear implant sound turned on for the first time. Some cried, some laughed, and a few closed their eyes, pulling their faces into a fearful grimace. There was no telling what Lucas would do, but according to Dr. Goldstein, it was his best shot at a normal life.

Tom pulled into the driveway with the convertible top up. All day it had been threatening rain, and the echo of thunder was off in the distance. After he'd heard about the episode at the audiologist's office, he'd gone in search of a toy dog that looked like Sox, and he'd found one. Not a stuffed toy but a clickety-clack dog with a leash and legs that moved as he was pulled along. Tom had the toy in his hand when he rang the doorbell.

As Meghan opened the door, he grinned and said, "I found something for Lucas." He pulled the toy dog from behind his back and held it out.

Meghan's eyes beamed. "He's going to love this!" She pulled Tom inside and insisted he give Lucas the toy himself.

Tracy and Lila joined them, and within minutes the living room was alive with laughter as they watched Lucas pull his new dog around, calling out that same barely identifiable word, "Sah. Sah."

"This calls for a celebratory drink," Lila said, and disappeared into the kitchen. A few minutes later, she returned, carrying a tray with glasses of icy wine coolers, a plate of cheeses, and a basket of crackers.

As they sipped the coolers, an easy conversation circled the room. Tom told of his mother back in Ohio and how, after nine years of being a widow, she had married again.

"A history professor from the university," he said.

Lila spoke of George and claimed it was doubtful that she could ever love anyone else. As memories ran through her mind, she said, "We started dating in high school and got married a week after he graduated college."

One story led to another, and in time, even Tracy joined in the conversation. She spoke of Gabriel and how she had high hopes he was going to teach Lucas to talk. There was no mention of Dominic.

As Tom was telling of his veterinary studies at Ohio State, a roll of thunder sounded overhead.

Tracy sighed. "I wish it would just go ahead and rain. It's so blasted hot I can barely breathe."

The boom of thunder sounded again, louder this time, followed by a gusty rush of wind.

"Looks like you're going to get your wish," Tom replied.

While his words were still hanging in the air, heavy raindrops began plopping on the roof, and seconds later it turned into a downpour.

Meghan peered out the front window and saw the branches of the willow whipping back and forth. It was less than fifty feet to where the car was parked, but they'd be soaked trying to make the dash.

"Let's wait until the rain stops."

Tom agreed.

But the rain didn't stop. It continued on, lessening a bit from time to time and then roaring back with an even greater ferocity.

"It's foolish to go out in weather like this," Lila said. "Why don't you stay here, and we'll all have dinner together?"

Tom glanced across at Meghan. She smiled and gave him a nod.

Lila's face lit up. "This won't take but a few minutes," she said, and headed for the kitchen.

"Need help?" Meghan asked.

"Not at all!" Lila hollered back. "Everything's done. I'll just be putting things on the table." The clanging of pots and pans followed her words.

Tracy stood and followed in Lila's steps. "If you guys will excuse me, I'm going to check and make sure Mama's not out there roasting a pig."

Once they were alone, Tom said, "Are you sure our staying for dinner isn't putting your mom out?"

Meghan laughed. "Are you kidding? She loves it. Mama's greatest joy is feeding people. When it was just the two of us, she was miserable, because she had no one to cook for."

When Lila called them to dinner, it was in the dining room. The table was set with the good china and crystal glasses. In the center was a platter piled high with pork chops. Next to it was a large bowl of mashed potatoes and a pitcher of gravy.

"You shouldn't have gone to all this trouble," Tom said.

"Oh, pshaw," Lila said, waving the thought off. "It was nothing." But when they sat to eat and he raved about the chops being the most delicious he'd ever tasted, she took on a glow that hadn't been seen in years.

The rain continued, but no cared as they sat around the table telling stories, talking, and laughing. Watching the conversation pass comfortably from one person to the next, Meghan couldn't help but notice that just as Sox had seamlessly slid into the family, Tom was doing the same thing.

It was after nine when the rain slowed, then came to a stop.

Tom and Meghan were alone in the kitchen. Once he'd insisted on doing the cleanup, Lila retired to her room to watch a show she'd recorded earlier. Tracy, claiming it was way past Lucas's bedtime, disappeared minutes later.

After the last pot had been scrubbed and put away, Meghan lifted her arms over her head and gave a leisurely stretch. "Now that that's done . . ."

Tom turned and playfully wrapped his arms around her waist. With one hand cradling the small of her back and the other centered between her shoulder blades, he pulled her to him. All at once they were so close he could feel her heartbeat.

She lowered her arms and rested them on his shoulders, her breath warm against the side of his neck.

"I thought maybe the rain would have cooled us down a bit," she said.

"I don't feel the least bit cooled down," he replied, and covered her mouth with his. When their lips parted, he cupped his hand beneath her chin and lifted her face to his again. For a long moment he fixed his eyes on hers, and it was as if they were the last two people on earth. There was no one else, just the two of them, breathing the same air, feeling the same heat, burning with the same desire. He kissed her again and again, and she quivered beneath his touch.

Suddenly there was the thud of something beside them.

Tom's head snapped back, and he looked around. Beulah sat on the kitchen counter, her bushy tail in the air and her eyes aglow.

Meghan swished her hand across the counter, and the cat jumped down.

Tom gave a soft chuckle. "You don't suppose your mama had anything to do with that, do you?"

Meghan smiled and shook her head. "I doubt it. Beulah doesn't listen to Mama any more than she listens to anyone else."

Tom bent, brushed a tender kiss across the tip of Meghan's nose, then stepped back and sucked in a deep breath. "I think maybe we'd better go for a walk or something."

Meghan knew he was giving them some space, air enough to cool down before passion carried them off to a place they hadn't intended.

"How about we sit on the front porch swing?" she said.

"Yeah," he said, smiling. "The front porch sounds good."

They started toward the door, and Sox, who'd been sleeping beneath a kitchen chair, stood, gave a quick stretch, then followed along.

When they sat side by side in the swing, Sox jumped into the wicker chair and curled up on the cushion. Facing forward, he lowered his head onto his paws and looked at them, eyeball to eyeball.

Tom laughed. "I think we've got a chaperone."

"Obviously a smart dog," she replied.

As they sat, lazily pushing back and forth in the swing, the clouds drifted away, the sky cleared, and the stars came out. He wrapped his arm around her and eased her head onto his shoulder. Twining his fingers through hers, he began to speak softly about things like destiny, fate, and forever.

"I know it's too soon," he said, "and I don't want to scare you off, but—"

She turned her face to his and silenced him with a kiss. When she pulled back she whispered, "It's not too soon."

Sox closed his eyes and tucked his face between his paws.

August

In the days that followed, the Briggs household all but bristled with anticipation. There were times when you could sense Meghan's newfound love
floating through the air and other times when the worry Tracy carried in
her heart made the mood as grim as that of a funeral parlor.

Lila cooked constantly. She made trays of biscuits, chicken cas-
seroles, and beef stew enough to feed an army. When the refrigerator
was filled to overflowing, she carried casserole dishes to neighbors up
and down Baker Street, saying it was a sin to waste perfectly good food.

Two days after Lucas's CT scan, Dr. Goldstein's office called and
scheduled a second visit. Before Tracy hung up the telephone, Lila had
written the appointment on her calendar.

"Luckily I'm free," she said, and offered to drive.

Knowing how her mama disliked the drive to Barrington, Meghan
claimed such a thing wasn't necessary. "I can spare time enough to take
Tracy."

With an indignant pout, Lila glared across the room. "Lucas is my
only grandchild!" she said pointedly, then insisted at the very least she
would accompany them.

"I don't actually need either of you to come," Tracy said, but the
words came out thin and fragile-sounding.

"You might not think you need me," Lila replied, "but you do."

The look on Lila's face was one of determination.

When they settled in front of Dr. Goldstein's large mahogany desk, Tracy clasped her mama's hand.

"Well, the CT scan has confirmed what I expected," he said. "Lucas has enlarged vestibular aqueducts, or EVA, in both ears. The right ear is marginally worse, but both are badly damaged."

Tracy felt her heart stop. Before it was simply a hearing test. An outside measurement of the sound going through Lucas's ears. This time it was a picture, proof positive of the structural damage that prevented him from hearing. There was no longer even the slightest margin of doubt, and the reality of it was suffocating. It was as if a giant vacuum had suddenly sucked the oxygen from the air.

He kept talking. "EVA is a condition that begins in the first trimester of pregnancy."

She inhaled sharply. "Was it something I did? Could I have taken more vitamins? Maybe it was something I ate or drank—"

"Nothing you did or didn't do would have made a difference," Dr. Goldstein cut in. "This is a congenital malformation, and its cause is unknown. Some schools of thought indicate it could be genetic, but even that's debatable."

"Genetic? How can that be? No one in our family . . ."

Suddenly, Tracy realized she knew next to nothing about Dominic's family. Her eyes filled with tears, and try as she may, she couldn't stop them.

"That's only a single possibility," Dr. Goldstein said, "and there's no proof."

He continued, explaining that the vestibular aqueduct tube in the fetus's ear usually narrows to the proper width by midterm.

"But in cases such as Lucas's, it doesn't."

His voice droned on like a runaway train moving at breakneck speed, a disaster in the making with no way to stop it. He told how fluid collected in this tube and, over time, destroyed the tiny hairs that carried sound through the cochlea.

"There's no way to repair the existing damage, but fortunately, Lucas is an excellent candidate for a bilateral cochlear implant, and with it, he should have near-normal hearing."

Tracy tried to focus on the word *normal*, but it seemed impossible. How could you find even a semblance of normal in a situation such as this? She ran her hand over her forehead and closed her eyes for a moment, trying to picture what normal would look like.

It came to mind as Ella, a child thrilled to say the word *cat*. And after Ella, Gabriel Hawke, a man who loved music, ran a school for deaf children, used a cell phone, and spoke without fault. Tracy knew this was the normal she wanted for Lucas.

She lifted her eyes and looked across the desk. "Okay. What's the next step?"

Dr. Goldstein said his office would schedule an appointment with Dr. Phyllis Crawford, the implant surgeon. "She'll take over from here."

Tracy asked question after question, some about Lucas's condition and others about the possible cause.

When she ran out of questions, Lila took over, asking if certain foods would be more beneficial than others. Then, recalling how Lucas played with Sox, she asked, "What about dogs?"

"Dogs?" Dr. Goldstein repeated quizzically.

Lila nodded. "Lucas likes to play with the dog. Is that permissible? You know, because of germs?"

"A dog is no problem. It may even be a good distraction to keep Lucas's focus off the implant site, which will feel a bit strange at first."

"Will it be painful?" Tracy asked.

"No more so than any other surgery."

It seemed the questions were endless. Every answer only brought about another question, and when they finally left the office, Tracy had an overwhelming need to talk with Gabriel again. He was the one person who could truly understand what Lucas was facing.

"Mama, there's somebody I want you to meet," she said.

That afternoon, they spent two hours with Gabriel, first talking about the challenges that lay ahead and then looking down the road to a time when they might expect Lucas to begin learning to speak full sentences. After Gabriel had explained the auditory mapping process, he suggested Tracy might want to watch part of a therapy session.

"Yes, I would," she answered eagerly.

Lila gave Tracy a nod. "You go ahead," she said. "I'll stay here in the playroom with Lucas."

With his hand touching her elbow ever so lightly, Gabriel guided Tracy along the corridor to the window of a therapy room where a toddler was learning to speak. For twenty minutes they stood shoulder to shoulder watching the boy give a name to each item and connect words.

"Brown dog," he said.

The therapist asked, "Is the brown dog small?"

Shaking his head, he replied, "Brown dog big," and proudly puffed out his tiny little chest.

Tracy turned her eyes to Gabriel, and before she asked the question, he knew what was on her mind. He took her hand in his and smiled. "Yes, given time, Lucas should be able to speak just as well."

On the drive home, Lila was silent for a long while. She nervously picked at a loose thread on her jacket, crossing and uncrossing her ankles several times. They were close to Magnolia Grove when she finally asked, "Do you really think Lucas will be able to talk as well as the children we saw in the video?"

Tracy hesitated a few moments, then nodded. "That's what I'm praying for, Mama. With every breath I take, I ask God to let Lucas hear, to let him speak, to let him live a normal life." As she spoke, a tiny tear slid across the rim of Tracy's eye and rolled down her cheek.

In the sunlight slanted across the dashboard, Lila saw the glisten of its track. "I'm praying for that also," she said, then reached across and squeezed Tracy's hand.

Late that evening, after Lila had gone to bed, Tracy called Dominic. Until now, she had told him only that Lucas had a problem. Now it was something she could name, and it had a solution.

She'd barely had time to say hello before Dominic said, "You ready to come home yet?" His voice was sharp with that undertone of arrogance she'd come to expect.

"I am home," she replied. "And this isn't about us, Dominic. It's about Lucas."

She went on to tell of the visit with Dr. Goldstein, then asked, "Is there any sort of deafness in your family? Maybe an aunt or uncle?"

"No," he said with an air of agitation. "Don't try to lay this problem on my doorstep. Whatever's wrong with Lucas isn't because of me."

"I didn't say it was," she replied. "I'm only trying to figure out where—"

"So you right away suspect me? That's what your sister said, huh?"

"This has nothing to do with Meghan. I told you, it's about Lucas, so I thought maybe you—"

"Forget it. I don't have any money. As it is I'm barely making the rent."

"I wasn't asking—"

"You should have thought about how you were gonna handle things before you walked out, stuck me with the apartment, and—"

"Dominic!" she shouted. "Will you just shut up and listen? I don't want anything from you. Absolutely nothing. But since you're Lucas's daddy, I thought you deserved to know."

"Okay, now I know." His voice was flat with a rock-hard edge. "So what do you expect me to do about it?"

"Not a damn thing!" Tracy said, and slammed down the receiver.

In the back of her mind, she'd suspected something like this would happen, but she hadn't been prepared for the heartache it would bring. She sat there for several minutes letting the tears roll down her cheeks, then she got up and tiptoed down the hall. From beneath the door she could see Meghan's light was still on.

Before she had a chance to knock, Sox grumbled a warning. Meghan shushed him, then got up from her desk and opened the door.

Still red-eyed and teary, Tracy asked, "Do you have time to talk?"

"Of course," Meghan answered, and pulled Tracy into her arms.

Meghan

Last night when I opened the bedroom door and saw Tracy standing there, my heart just about broke for her. She looked like the saddest person in the entire world. After she told me what Dominic had said, I could understand why. She blames herself for Lucas not having a daddy who cares about him.

How can a man not care for a child who's his own flesh and blood? she asked.

Of course I didn't have an answer for such a question, and I doubt anyone else would, either. Behavior like that goes against nature.

I tried to console her by saying she should just forget about Dominic, that he's the kind of man she doesn't need in her life. She agreed with me, but the truth is I could see she still loves him—although I simply do not understand why. How can you love a man who brings you that much unhappiness?

Love is a two-way street where people come together and meet in the middle. If it's just one person going one way, then you know for sure it'll end up being a road to heartache.

Tracy deserves better. She's funny and smart and has a good heart. She deserves to have someone like Tom love her. The problem is she's got to get Dominic out of her heart before anyone else can get in.

When we talk, I don't say much about Tom. I feel almost guilty being happy with him when I know she's so miserable.

There are so many things I could say—like how delicious and satisfying it is when he holds me, or how he puts his thumb on my lower lip and tugs it down just before he kisses me, or how when he whispers about forever I feel his warm breath against my ear and want to give myself to him right then and there.

I have a million things to say, but I don't. I keep those thoughts in my head and then write them in my journal. Someday, when Tracy's heartache is gone and forgotten, maybe I'll read them to her. I'll say, This is the kind of love you deserve. A love that sets itself apart from everything else and makes you feel happier than you ever dreamed possible.

Once she's no longer thinking about Dominic, she'll see the truth of what I say.

Operation Day

The next two weeks flew by. Tracy drove into Barrington three times, once for Lucas's appointment with Dr. Crawford and twice just to talk with Gabriel Hawke. It seemed that he could calm her fears as no one else could. When Tracy talked of possible complications, Gabriel came back with stories of children, some younger than Lucas, who had gone through the same surgery and were now chattering like magpies.

Tears of joy ran down her face when they sat together and watched videos of toddlers hearing the sound of their mama's voice for the first time.

"Do you really believe this will happen with Lucas?" she asked.

Gabriel nodded. "I can probably guarantee it."

Tracy wanted positive, not probable. She hated probability; it was an ever-widening crack in her world, a world that could split open at any minute. When she'd left Magnolia Grove with Dominic, he'd said they would probably get married, but they didn't. At the time she'd felt positive about it, but as the months and years passed, probability widened the gap, and it never happened.

She turned to Gabriel, her brown eyes dulled with worry. "I wish you would say positively."

"There are very few absolute things in this world. The years between birth and death are filled with possibility and probability. What you make of those years is up to you." He let his eyes linger on her face and smiled. "However, I can say I'm positive you're doing the right thing for Lucas."

The slightest hint of a smile tugged at the corners of her mouth.

On the day of Lucas's surgery, Meghan arranged for Sheldon to cover the *Snip 'N' Save*. She programmed the office phone so that it would forward calls to his cell and set an auto-response e-mail on the website.

Lila, who was normally an early riser anyway, had breakfast on the table by six thirty that morning, but no one ate. Meghan picked at a piece of toast, and Tracy barely sipped the coffee that was set in front of her. Having been forewarned Lucas was not to eat or drink anything, his high chair sat empty as he followed Sox from room to room. Shortly before eight, the table was cleared, and they all climbed into the car for the trek to Barrington.

The surgery was scheduled for 10:00 a.m. They arrived at Trinity Hospital an hour early, and when Lucas was taken back for pre-op, Tracy was the only one allowed to accompany him. She remained by his side until the gurney came and they lifted him onto it. The sight of him lying there, so small, so fragile, to be facing such an ordeal alone, was terrifying. Yet there was nothing more she could do.

It was a feeling of helplessness far greater than anything Tracy had ever known. With her heart pushed up into her throat, she cupped her hand around his chubby cheek, then kissed his forehead. "You'll do just fine," she promised. In her heart she had to believe this was true.

Once the gurney disappeared down the hall, Tracy turned back to the waiting room and was surprised to see Gabriel sitting alongside Meghan and her mama.

"I thought you might need an extra shoulder," he said, smiling.

"Thank you," she replied, then crossed over and gave him an affectionate hug.

In a waiting room, time is measured differently. A second becomes a minute, and minutes turn into hours that plod along as if held back by a team of invisible horses. The minute hand of the clock barely moves, and the hour hand appears stuck in the same spot forever.

After a painfully slow hour finally ticked by, Gabriel went to the cafeteria and brought back coffee for everyone. Tracy opened the lid, dumped in two packets of sugar, then left the container sitting on the table until the coffee grew cold and the cream clotted on top.

"It seems we should have heard something by now," she said.

Gabriel shook his head. "It's usually about three hours."

He's done this before. He's guided other families through this just as he's doing for me. She nodded and gave a whisper-thin smile. "Thank you."

It was another long hour before Dr. Crawford finally came to the waiting room.

"The implant is in, and everything went well," she said. "Lucas is in recovery now."

"Oh, thank God." The stiffness in Tracy's back went soft, and she relaxed against Gabriel's shoulder. "He's all right, isn't he? There were no complications?"

Dr. Crawford gave an understanding smile. "No complications," she said. "Everything went very smoothly. As soon as Lucas is settled in his room, the nurse will be out to get you, and you'll be able to see him."

"How long will it be?" she asked anxiously.

Dr. Crawford chuckled. "Not long, fifteen or twenty minutes. But he won't be able to go home tonight. We like to keep a patient Lucas's age overnight just to make sure he's doing well."

"How long before he can go home?"

"He should be good to go tomorrow, but you'll need to keep him quiet for a few days. Bed rest if possible."

Tracy was so happy she wanted to pull Dr. Crawford into a bear hug, but she held back. Instead, she simply reached out and took the doctor's hand in both of hers.

"Thank you," she said. "Thank you so much."

When they finally got to see Lucas, Tracy was momentarily taken aback. He was paler than she'd expected and groggy from the anesthesia. A patch of hair was missing, the bandage covering it stained with blood. Tracy gently ran her fingers along the curve of his cheek, then took his tiny hand in hers. He was so small, and it seemed so wrong that he should have to go through something like this. Her eyes welled with tears.

"My poor baby," she whispered, and bent to kiss his forehead.

Even though he had been through so much, there would be no immediate reward. It would be another long month before he would be able to hear his first sound. The waiting was going to be hard, very hard.

Tears crested her eyes, and she brushed them away with the back of her hand. "You're such a brave little boy," she said. "I know you can't hear me now, but someday you will. You'll hear my voice and come to know the sound of it." Again she blinked back the tears. "Right now this is hard, baby, I realize that. But one day you'll be able to talk like all the other children. I promise, Lucas. I swear, no matter what, I'll make it happen."

As Gabriel stood beside her, he felt a lump rise in his throat.

Meghan and Lila left the hospital early that evening, but Tracy stayed, and Gabriel stayed with her. Standing together at the side of Lucas's crib, they watched him sleep, the tiny breaths causing his chest to rise and fall rhythmically.

Tracy brushed a lock of hair from his forehead and, without looking up, said, "Lucas has a lot of hard work ahead of him, doesn't he?"

Gabriel nodded and touched his hand to the small of her back. "You both do. There will be times when you may grow weary of repeating the same phrases in precisely the same way over and over again, but I promise you that in the end it will all be worthwhile."

Even though he'd gone over it several times before, he told again of how Lucas's speech would come haltingly at first with single-syllable words and repetitive sounds. In time he would be able to look at a picture and give it a name: *duck, dog, water, house*. After that he would move on to where he could connect words to one another, asking for a drink of water or saying the dog was brown and the house was big.

For years, his actual age and his hearing age would be different. Lucas was fifteen months old now, but in hearing years, he had yet to be born. His hearing birth would happen after the external sound processor was turned on and he listened to Tracy's voice for the first time.

"It's a slow process," Gabriel said, understanding the comfort it brought to hear these things again, "but I believe by the time he turns five, his hearing age and actual age will come together and be the same."

A soft smile settled on Tracy's face as she listened. And when Gabriel spoke of the day when Lucas's speech would be no different from that of a hearing person, she clasped her hand over his.

"I don't know how I would have gotten through this without you," she said.

In the dim light of Lucas's hospital room, Gabriel looked down at her face and felt a swell inside his chest. He had seen this look of gratitude on countless other faces, but somehow it looked different on Tracy. More glowing. He hoped that what he saw was something more than gratitude. He wanted to believe it was a thing that would last, a thing he could hold on to.

He stayed with her until almost midnight, and when he left it was only at Tracy's insistence. "You'll be exhausted," she'd said. "Go home and get some sleep."

Once he was gone, she sat in the chair alongside Lucas's crib. It had been a long and tiring day, but still sleep was impossible to come by. She closed her eyes and let her thoughts drift back to the years in high school, wondering why it was she'd never before noticed Gabriel Hawke.

At ten thirty the next morning, when Meghan returned to the hospital, Lucas was ready to go home.

In the Following Weeks

A week later, Lucas saw the surgeon for a checkup. By then he was back to himself, anxious to chase after Sox and almost impossible to keep still.

Dr. Crawford examined the surgical site, declared Lucas was doing beautifully, and they were out of the office in ten minutes flat. Having the surgery behind them seemed a giant step forward, but in truth, it was only the first of many such steps. The hard work was still ahead, the hardest being the long weeks of waiting. Seemingly endless days of living in limbo, wondering if in fact everything would work as it was supposed to.

Since she was already in Barrington, Tracy texted Gabriel and asked if they might stop by the school.

I'd like Lucas to get to know the place so he won't be scared when he starts therapy.

The answer came a few minutes later.

Absolutely, he replied. I'm in my office, just come on up.

That afternoon Tracy and Lucas spent two hours at the school. Instead of touring the building, they settled in one of the small class-rooms where Lucas rummaged through the toys and plucked out a favorite. It was a red dump truck that he happily rolled back and forth across the floor.

Gabriel envisioned the thoughts filling Tracy's head and gave her a knowing smile.

"Do you realize that by this time next year, Lucas will be able to ask for that toy and tell you what color it is?"

When she allowed herself to look ahead and see such achievements, it took her breath away.

"A year," she murmured. "It'll certainly be a long one."

Gabriel chuckled. "Not if you keep busy and give Lucas time to grow into the new skills he'll be learning."

Long after Tracy left the school, Gabriel's words remained in her head. She mulled the thought over during the drive home and as she was having dinner. When Lila set her homemade apple pie on the table and poured everyone a cup of coffee, Tracy spoke up.

"I'd like to work for the *Snip 'N' Save* full-time," she said.

"Full-time?" Meghan registered a look of surprise. "I hope you don't feel that you have to."

"I know I don't have to; I want to. I want to be here with Lucas so I can watch him grow and learn to speak. A year from now he'll probably be talking, and he'll need someone to constantly reinforce the things he learns in speech therapy."

"I can do that," Lila said.

"I know, but I want to be the one to do it. It'll be good for both of us." Tracy gave a playful grin and said, "After all, Mama, if a woman is on her own, she needs to have a real job."

"That's foolish," Lila replied. "Why would you think you need a full-time job? I'm fine with the way things are."

"Mama, come on. I'm a grown woman. It's time I started getting my act together. Besides, Meghan has been shouldering the responsibility for far too long." She looked over at her sister and smiled. "Maybe it's not too late for journalism school after all."

It had been years since Meghan thought of Grady, and the mention of it now seemed strangely out of place.

"I'm not sure that after all this time . . ."

"The thing is, you can go to school or not go to school; it doesn't matter. What does matter is that for the first time since Daddy died, you'll be free to do what you want to do, not what you have to do."

Meghan considered this for a moment, then gave a small laugh. She couldn't imagine not running the *Snip 'N' Save*, and yet . . .

"If you're really serious, I suppose we could give it a try."

That night Meghan pulled the box of composition books from beneath her bed and began to read back through the years. She read page after page telling how eager she was to attend Grady and how one day she hoped to be a star reporter for the *Atlanta Journal-Constitution*. Tucked inside one book she found the school brochure, dog-eared and worn thin from all the times she'd pored over it and pictured herself there in one of those classrooms. She closed her eyes and tried to remember the passion she'd felt back then, but oddly enough, it was missing.

She moved on and read about the weeks and months after her daddy had died and the heartache of losing first him and then Tracy. How could she give up the *Snip 'N' Save*? It wasn't just a job; it was her life. When everything else fell apart, she always had the *Snip 'N' Save* with its pages waiting to be filled and deadlines demanding her attention.

Without understanding how it came about, she found herself holding yet another composition book in her hand. It was the book tied with a metallic gold ribbon. She tugged the tail end of the bow, and the book fell open just as she knew it would.

These pages told a different story. It was one of falling in love. It told of that first night and how as she and Tom sat across from one another at the Garden, she'd known they were destined to be more than friends. As she read how he'd brushed his thumb across her lip, she could feel her heartbeat quicken.

Suddenly a whirlwind of thoughts came rushing at her. This had been a summer of miracles. She thought of that day at the lake: Sox in the water, the storm, and the unexplainable wave that pushed them ashore. Sox leading her to Tom. His bark telling her that Lucas couldn't hear. If she had been away at Grady, none of these things would have happened. The thought of Sox lying at the bottom of the lake sent a shudder up her spine.

When Meghan climbed into bed, he jumped in beside her. As she absently began to stroke his fur, she thought about her life. Everything she loved was here in Magnolia Grove. She didn't have to go in search of happiness; it was right under her nose.

———— ◦◦◦◦ ————

The next day, Meghan suggested she and Tracy work together at the *Snip 'N' Save.*

"There's a lot to learn," she said, "but I'm thinking in time you could take over production, and I'll work on new business development."

"Perfect! That way you can cover for me when I take Lucas to therapy, and I can cover for you whenever . . ." Tracy gave a sly grin and didn't bother finishing the thought.

———— ◦◦◦◦ ————

As August rolled into September, Meghan found days when she had little or nothing to do. In times like that, she packed a lunch basket, and she and Sox visited Tom at the clinic. On sunny days they sat outside at the picnic table, and on rainy days Tom cleared a spot on his desk and they sat opposite one another while Sox curled up beneath her chair. Emily joined them occasionally, but more often than not, she had errands to do.

"Grocery shopping," she'd say as she hung the OUT TO LUNCH sign on the door and hurried off. If it wasn't groceries, it was dry cleaning that needed to be dropped off or a prescription to be picked up at the drugstore. Emily was a bundle of efficiency who managed to keep both the office and her family running smoothly.

On the odd afternoons when Emily did get bogged down with record-keeping duties, Meghan stayed to walk the dogs and put fresh water in the bowls. One such day, she had a boxer with a wide body and disagreeable disposition out of his crate and hooked to a leash before Tom had the chance to warn her that Bruiser had to be muzzled.

"You've got to be careful with this dog," he said, hurrying over. "He doesn't like being put on the leash and will go for your arm."

Meghan rumpled the fur atop Bruiser's head. "Nonsense. He's sweet as can be." She lifted him to the floor and strolled out the door.

Tom watched the dog trotting along as if he had no trouble whatsoever with being on a leash.

"Well, I'll be darned . . ."

Later that afternoon, he asked what she'd done to calm the dog.

"Nothing special," she said, "just told him he was a good boy."

Tom shook his head. "You're really good with animals. I think you might've missed your calling."

She laughed at the thought, but a spot of color rose up in her cheeks.

The First Sound

Tracy decided to have Michelle, the audiologist at the school, do Lucas's mapping. This was perhaps the most crucial stage of the process. It was when he would be given an external processor and hear sound for what probably would be the first time.

Her nerves were stripped raw. For nearly a month she'd counted the days, marked them off one by one, waiting, anticipating this moment, but now as she buttoned Lucas's shirt, her fingers trembled. She thought back on Gabriel's words: nothing is absolute.

There were too many ways this could go wrong. If the sound were too loud, Lucas might cry or try to yank the processor off and could reject it completely. If the sound were too low, he'd hear nothing but muted murmurs.

She lifted him into the high chair and spread a handful of Cheerios on the tray. Lucas was still a baby; all of this was foreign to him. He had developed his own habits, his own way of navigating a silent world. Now, after sixteen months, they were asking him to accept the strange new noises in his head. Was such a thing even possible? In those first few moments, he wouldn't know that what he was hearing was her voice, and there was no way to explain it because he understood no words.

Tracy knew the only thing she could do was watch his face and try to gauge his reaction. If he cried or buried his head in her lap, she would try to show him this was a good thing with the touch of her hand and the feel of a few familiar words.

For nearly a week she'd been working with Lucas the way Meghan had, holding his hand to her face and letting him feel the vibrations of her throat. She'd used only two words: *mama* and *Lucas*. Two words were enough.

When Michelle turned the sound on, Tracy would touch his fingers to her throat so he would recognize the familiar vibrations as the word came to his ear. She prayed it was enough, that he would understand this strange new sound was their link to one another. Last night she'd not slept a wink, thinking of how it would be for Lucas, praying that such a small child would have the kind of acceptance that would be difficult even for an adult.

She'd told Meghan only that she was driving over to see Gabriel. She hadn't mentioned that this was to be the day. She wanted desperately to have Meghan with her, but Gabriel said fewer distractions were better, so she'd decided to go alone.

"Tracy?" Meghan repeated.

"Huh?" The sound of her name shook Tracy from her thoughts. "Sorry, I guess my mind was somewhere else."

"Is something wrong?"

Tracy shook her head. "Just tired. I didn't sleep well last night."

"Want me to drive you over to—"

"No need," she said, rejecting the thought before Meghan finished the question. She took one last sip of her coffee, then lifted Lucas from the high chair and started for the door.

"See you later," she called out, trying to sound light and breezy.

When they arrived at the school, Gabriel was waiting in the front lobby.

"Today's the big day," he said, smiling. "Michelle has everything ready." He lifted Lucas into his arms, and they started toward the audiology lab.

As she trudged along, a row of worry lines settled on Tracy's forehead.

"I hope it goes well." Her voice was shaky and thin as an eggshell.

"It'll be fine," Gabriel assured her. "I have a feeling this little guy is going to surprise you."

The audiology room was on the second floor of the school. It was a small room with a computer desk, two comfortable chairs, and a few toys atop the desk. Michelle was at the desk making some last-minute adjustments to the program when they walked in.

"Welcome," she said with a bright smile.

Tracy returned the smile and nodded. She sat in one chair with Lucas on her lap. Gabriel took the other.

Michelle pulled a box from beneath the desk and came around, carrying the two small processors. Each one was about the size of a quarter, a magnetized unit that snapped onto the back of Lucas's head. Narrow wires connected the processors to the power pack.

"Let's get you set up," she said, "then we'll turn the sound on." She adjusted the wires and then plugged the power pack into the computer.

"Can he hear now?" Tracy asked nervously.

Michelle shook her head. "The power's not on yet." Reaching over for her mouse, she made a few clicks, then smiled across the desk. "The sound is on now, but it's very low. Let's see if he reacts."

Tracy held her breath for a moment, uncertain of what to expect. She could feel the thumping inside her chest. It seemed her heart had somehow risen into her throat. She called his name, praying he would respond. "Lucas?"

There was no reaction. He reached for the plastic truck on the desk, grabbed onto it, and started rolling it back and forth.

"Lucas," she repeated, this time a bit louder.

Michelle watched Lucas, and when there was no reaction, she turned back to the screen and clicked through a few adjustments.

"Try now," she said, keeping her eye on the screen.

Tracy leaned around him so she could watch his face. "Lucas, do you hear me? This is Mama."

He looked at the truck in his hand, then threw it on the floor.

Tracy's eyes filled with tears. "Does he not hear me?"

"It could be that the volume is still too low." She made another adjustment. "Try again."

A tear rolled down Tracy's cheek as she called Lucas's name in a quivering voice. Still there was no response. He wriggled forward and reached for another toy.

"Hmm." Michelle left the computer, came around, checked the wires, then went back to her seat. She looked at the screen and scrunched her nose. "He should be hearing now. Try speaking a bit louder."

Gabriel noticed the panic taking hold of Tracy's face. With no warning to anyone, he clapped his hands. Not a polite clap of applause but one hand smacking hard against the other: *SLAP-SLAP*.

Lucas snapped his head up and turned with a startled look.

Gabriel laughed. "He can hear."

"He can?" Tracy broke into a smile, and her eyes glistened with tears of happiness.

"He just doesn't know what to make of the sound. It's not unusual. Turn him around so that he's facing you, and try talking to him again."

Tracy reached over to the desk, pushed the toys back from his reach, then turned him to face her. She took his hand in hers and placed it at the base of her neck, just as Meghan had instructed. In a deep-throated voice, the kind she'd used to try and teach him the word, she said his name. This time she stretched it into two long syllables.

"Lu-cas."

He looked up, wide-eyed.

Now certain he had heard her, she pulled her voice back to a more normal register and said, "Mama loves you, Lucas."

As she spoke, he lifted both hands to her face and began searching for where the words were coming from. He held his fingers to her mouth and throat and the spot just below her jaw where sound bounces off bone.

Never before had Tracy known such happiness. Even the sweetest moments of loving Dominic paled in comparison to what her heart now felt. As Lucas's tiny hands continued to explore her face, she spoke, saying the things she had waited so long to say, hoping that even though he had no understanding of the words, he would recognize the tenderness in her voice and feel the love she had for him. Lucas, still looking bewildered, moved his tiny hands across her face, feeling for the source of this new thing that had suddenly come into his head.

Michelle gave a grin of satisfaction.

"Okay," she said. "Now I'm going to turn the sound off for a moment, make a few adjustments, then turn it back on."

When the sound stopped, Lucas looked as confused as he had when it started. He put his fingers to Tracy's mouth and pulled it open.

"Well, I'll be," Gabriel said, laughing. "He knows that's where your voice came from, and he's looking for it."

"Is this good or bad?" Tracy asked.

"Good. Very good. He's going to be a fast learner."

Michelle looked up from the computer. "Okay, I'm ready to turn the sound on again. Three. Two. One." She clicked the mouse. "It's on."

Looking square into his face, Tracy said, "Lucas, baby, Mama loves you."

This time he waved his arms in the air and gave a happy squeal.

For almost three hours, this was how it went: on again, off again. One by one, Michelle tested each of the electrodes in his processors and made minute adjustments. At times Lucas responded with grunts, squeals, and babbling as if he were talking back, but he said no words. Not even the few he'd learned. It would take time—months, possibly years—before he would speak with understanding of the words' meaning. In hearing age, he was a newborn.

For a long while, Lucas seemed excited and happy with the new sound in his head. When Michelle turned it off for an adjustment, he looked around as if it were something he'd misplaced, and when it came on again he looked at the person talking and babbled happily.

In time, Lucas tired of this new game. He reached up, grabbed one of the processors, and pulled it off.

"No," Tracy said firmly. "Leave it." She eased the processor back into position.

By then he'd grown fussy. When Gabriel spoke to him, he whined and buried his head in Tracy's lap.

"He's had enough for today," Michelle said. "Let him get used to this, and tomorrow we can fine-tune a few more things."

Tracy nodded. "He's tired. It's way past his naptime. That's why he's cranky." She lifted him into her arms, and he laid a sleepy head on her shoulder.

Michelle suggested Tracy leave the processors off for a while, put them on for an hour or so after dinner, and then take them off when he went to bed.

"It takes a little bit of time for a child to get used to this, so bear that in mind, and let him work through these changes at his own speed. For the next week or so, you may occasionally need to take the processors off and give him a rest. Don't be afraid to do it."

"How will I know when it's time?"

Michelle laughed. "You're his mama. You'll know."

Afterward, Gabriel walked with them to the car, and before Tracy had finished buckling Lucas into his seat, he was fast asleep.

As she climbed behind the wheel, Gabriel said, "It was a good day. I think Lucas will do very well."

Tracy looked up. "Is that a guarantee?"

"A ninety-nine percent guarantee," Gabriel replied, his eyes twinkling.

Tracy

It's funny. Your head can understand the logic of something, but that doesn't keep your heart from wishing for more. Gabriel and I have talked a lot about what to expect, and I knew after the sound was turned on, Lucas wasn't just going to suddenly start talking, but I was wishing he'd maybe repeat one word: mama. *That's all I was hoping to hear.*

No one expects an infant to pop out of his mama's belly and say, Hi, Mom, *so right now I've got to remember Lucas's hearing and speaking abilities are at the same stage as an infant's.* Have patience, *Gabriel said to me. I'm trying.*

Lucas will start speech therapy soon. Nothing hard, just easy stuff. Mostly differentiating sounds. Gabriel claims that once he understands the process of associating a word sound with a given object, he'll start talking in his own sweet time. I know this is good advice, but it's hard to be patient when your heart feels like it's so full it could explode. There are a thousand things I want to tell Lucas, but until he understands the meaning of words, it'll be nothing but babble to him.

Maybe Meghan has the right idea. I should write what I'm feeling in one of those composition books and then read it to him once he's old enough to understand.

I haven't always appreciated Meghan, but the truth is she's good for me. She pushes me to be more than I am. I remember when she first started talking about Gabriel. She spoke about him like he was some kind of superhuman god, and it annoyed me to no end. But once she decided Lucas needed her help, she was like a dog with a bone—determined not to let go.

Now I'm glad she didn't.

It's a shame that Dominic, Lucas's own daddy, doesn't show one bit of interest in him, but Gabriel, who's practically a stranger, cares.

I think that says a lot about both men.

Sharing the News

Lucas was still asleep when Tracy arrived home. She unbuckled him, hefted him onto her shoulder, and carried him up to his crib.

Lila spotted her coming down the stairs and asked, "Is Lucas napping?"

Grinning ear to ear, Tracy gave a nod, then walked over and linked her arm through Lila's.

"Come on, Mama, let's go have a cup of coffee in the kitchen. Is there any of that fudge cake left?"

Lila gave a suspicious-looking sideways glance. "Fudge cake? An hour before dinner?"

"Yeah, we're celebrating."

"Celebrating what?" Barely taking time for a breath, she added, "If this has anything to do with Dominic—"

"Relax, Mama, this isn't about him." On the way back to the kitchen, Tracy poked her head into the *Snip 'N' Save* office and asked Meghan to join them.

When they were finally settled at the table, Tracy gave them her news. "I couldn't say anything earlier, but I have something great to tell you."

Lila and Meghan looked across with wide-eyed anticipation.

"Today Lucas's sound was turned on." Tracy had a look of happiness they hadn't seen in a very long time. "I would have told you sooner, but the audiologist thought that for this first time, less distraction would be better."

"Oh, how I wish I could have been there." Lila sighed.

Tracy gave a happy grin. "It just so happens we've got another appointment tomorrow, and Gabriel told me it's okay if the family comes."

Equally bright grins lit Meghan's and Lila's faces.

"I'll get Sheldon to handle the *Snip 'N' Save*," Meghan suggested, "and we can go to that lovely little café for lunch afterward."

"Sounds good," Tracy said. "Mind if I invite Gabriel to join us for lunch?"

The corners of Meghan's mouth curled. "Of course not."

"So what happened?" Lila asked.

As Tracy told of how Lucas fingered her face in search of the sound, Meghan laughed. "He's a smart little rascal. He remembered us teaching him to feel the words in our throat."

Lila brushed back the tear that crested the rim of her eye. "He'll be talking in no time. I just know he will." She looked down at her hands for a brief moment, then lifted her eyes and met Tracy's. "I know this hasn't been easy, but you've handled it beautifully. I'm so proud of you, Tracy, proud of the woman you've become and the kind of mother you are to Lucas." She hesitated a moment and shifted her eyes to Meghan. "I'm proud of both my girls. When your daddy died, I didn't know how it would be possible for me to carry on and hold this family together, but the two of you have shown me what real courage is like. I couldn't have done it without—"

Before Lila could finish her statement, Tracy and Meghan were out of their seats, around the table, and wrapping her in a family hug.

There were several minutes of heartfelt embraces and tears of happiness, and for the first time in almost four years, Lila could imagine George smiling down on them.

———— ❧⁓❧ ————

Later that evening, Tracy reconnected Lucas's processors, and he toddled around as if nothing had changed. She'd hoped for more of a reaction, something to indicate he was hearing her voice and becoming familiar with it. Granted, it was too soon for him to understand her words, but was it too much to hope he'd recognize her voice?

Although he no longer tried to pull the processors off, he also paid almost no attention to the voices calling him.

"Lucas, come to Mama," Tracy called, but he ignored her.

The only way she knew for certain he heard the sounds was because of Sox. Whenever the dog barked, Lucas squealed with delight, jiggling up and down on his chubby little legs and excitedly waving his arms in the air.

"Sah, Sah!" he called, and lumbered toward the dog.

———— ❧⁓❧ ————

The following day, Gabriel greeted them at the door but did not join them in the audiology studio.

"Today should be about family," he said.

Bristling with anticipation, the Briggs family crowded into the small room, Meghan standing behind the chairs and Lila beside Tracy. Lucas was again in her lap. Although they expected something miraculous to happen, it turned out to be much the same as the previous day. Michelle adjusted the sound on each electrode, then waited for Lucas's reaction, which was slow in coming.

On the one occasion when Lucas did react to the sound, Meghan elbowed Lila and turned to see her mama's face wearing a smile as broad as her own. "Can you believe . . . ," she whispered gleefully.

After an hour of checks and balances, Michelle said, "That's it for now. Let's see how he does, and I'll reevaluate his mapping in thirty days."

As Tracy stood and gathered her things, Michelle added, "Oh, and before you go, Gabriel wants Lucas to meet his therapist." She buzzed his office and told him they would be down shortly.

Remembering the day she'd stood at the window and watched the therapist working with a child who spoke words and identified objects by name, Tracy nervously asked, "Is Lucas ready for that?"

"Absolutely," Michelle said.

Lila pinched her brows together. "You do realize Lucas is only sixteen months old, don't you? It would seem that's rather young."

"We have children as young as ten and eleven months in therapy classes," Michelle said. "Not only will Lucas learn faster with a structured program, but more important, we'll teach the family how to work with him and accelerate his learning."

As they left the room, Tracy looked back and gave a nod of appreciation.

When they arrived in the lobby, she spotted Gabriel at the end of the hall. It was too far to see his face, but Tracy had come to know his stance and walk, the way he stood with his back straight and his shoulders squared. She knew the cut of his chin and the casual way a lock of hair dropped down onto his forehead. As he drew closer, she saw the familiar smile, warm and welcoming, and when he stood next to her, she caught the scent of his aftershave, a woodsy fragrance reminiscent of the trees after a spring rain.

Tracy smiled. "I didn't realize we were going to start Lucas's therapy so soon."

"The sooner we start, the faster he'll learn," Gabriel replied. "Besides, I found an opening with a therapist I think you'll like."

They moved along the hall and stopped in front of a door with a nameplate reading DR. H. BRANDON. When Gabriel pushed it open, Tracy saw the therapist sitting behind the desk. She was a woman with silver hair, violet eyes, and a face that made you feel good to be looking at it.

"Good morning, Helene," he said, then turned to Tracy. "I want you to meet Dr. Helene Brandon. Helene will be working with Lucas."

As he continued the introductions, the woman rose from her chair and started toward them.

"It's a pleasure," she said, and offered her hand.

"Holy cow!" Tracy exclaimed. "You're the therapist who was teaching Ella!"

Dr. Brandon raised an eyebrow. "Have we met before?"

"No," Tracy replied, "but when Gabriel took us on a tour of the school, I saw you working with Ella, and I was so impressed. I thought, 'If only Lucas could work with her.'"

Giving a soft chuckle, Helene said, "Thank you, but I'm just doing my job. The ones who are truly impressive are the children." She bent and squatted face-to-face with Lucas.

"Hello, Lucas."

In clear distinctive tones, she went on to say she'd be working with him and they were going to have a lot of fun together. She spoke as if he could understand every word, and as she was talking, he reached out and touched her mouth.

Helene laughed. "I can see Lucas will learn quickly. He's already figured out where my words are coming from."

They spent several minutes talking, then scheduled Lucas's first therapy session for the following week.

"I'd like you or a member of your family here," Helene said. "The most important part of Lucas's therapy will be understanding how we feed words into his brain."

"I'll be here," Tracy said.

"I'm available also," Lila volunteered.

When they left Dr. Brandon's office, Tracy turned to Gabriel. "We're going to celebrate today with lunch at that little café. Would you like to join us?"

"Not today, unfortunately," he said. "I've got a busy schedule."

"Oh. Okay." Tracy felt an unexpected sense of disappointment wash over her.

A Temp Job

By early October, the Briggs household had settled into a completely different routine. Tracy worked full-time at the *Snip 'N' Save*, except on Thursdays when she took Lucas for his therapy. More often than not, they went to lunch with Gabriel afterward. Although not a word was mentioned, you could almost see something special in the way they looked at one another. Dr. Brandon just happened to schedule Lucas's therapy sessions for 10:15, which meant they'd finish up in time for lunch, and coincidentally Thelma, the waitress at the café, began asking Gabriel if they'd like a dessert to share.

Dominic called a number of times. In September it was to ask how Lucas's surgery had gone and if Tracy was ready to come back to Philadelphia.

"I told you I'm not coming back," she said. "Not ever, so you can stop asking."

Another call came later in the month. He said if she wasn't coming back, he was giving up the apartment and would be staying in a room above the bar.

"If you come to your senses and decide to return home where you belong, we can get another place," he said, "but I'm tired of paying for something I don't use."

Tracy assured him she'd already come to her senses and was precisely where she belonged. When he said, "Suit yourself," and hung up, she thought that would be the last of him, but it wasn't. Despite her rejection, he continued to call, and each time he warned that this would be his last offer to take her back.

"Good," she inevitably replied, and hung up.

That fall everyone in the Briggs household seemed happier. For the first time in well over twenty years Lila had a toddler to fuss over, and she was cooking up a storm. Following Dr. Brandon's instructions, she talked to Lucas all day long, giving a specific word to each task as she performed it.

"See?" she'd say. "Grammy is baking cookies. Lucas likes cookies."

A dozen or more times, Tracy told her, "Mama, if you don't quit fussing over Lucas like that, you are gonna spoil him silly."

More often than not, Lila gave that same so-what shrug Tracy had once given her and continued on with whatever she was doing.

"Grandmas are supposed to spoil their grandbabies," she'd say, and laugh.

In addition to her trips to Barrington, Tracy found that she actually enjoyed doing ad layouts for the *Snip 'N' Save*. She'd somehow developed quite a flair for design, and at times Meghan would find her changing a perfectly acceptable ad just to make the border a bit wider or add some small flourish.

"Well, it does look better," Meghan would have to admit, then she'd scurry off to a client meeting or head out with a picnic lunch for Tom.

No longer burdened by the day-to-day work of the *Snip 'N' Save*, Meghan and Sox began visiting the clinic more often. Some weeks she'd stop by as often as every other day, and once she got there she was in no hurry to leave. While Tom was with patients, she'd check the water bowls, walk the dogs, and fill the treat jars with dog biscuits or kitty treats. If she ran out of things to do, she'd ask if Emily needed a hand mailing out appointment cards or tidying up the reception room.

In the middle of November when the leaves were starting to turn, Emily came down with the flu. She called in Monday morning sounding like a foghorn.

"I'm too sick to even get out of bed," she said through a moan. "You'll have to get someone to fill in this week."

"There isn't anyone," Tom said. "It's November, and the temps are all working at the department stores."

"Ask Meghan." Emily sneezed into the phone, then hung up.

Tom mulled it over for several minutes, stuck on the thought that visiting for a few hours was quite different from spending the entire day behind a desk. Then he hit on the idea of not asking *her* to do it but simply asking if she knew anyone who might be willing to fill the spot for a week.

He dialed the office number, and she answered.

"Good morning, this is the *Snip 'N' Save*," she said. "How may I help you?"

"Meghan?"

"Oh, hi, Tom. I thought it was a customer call, so I used my *Snip 'N' Save* voice."

"Oh, you're working," he said, sounding disappointed.

"Not right at the minute," she replied. "I have time to talk. What's up?"

The way he'd had the speech all planned out suddenly felt wrong. It seemed conniving, and he cared too much for Meghan to go through with it.

"It's nothing," he said. "I'll talk to you later. I've got to make a few phone calls."

She heard the hesitation in his voice.

"Is something wrong?" she asked, but by then he'd hung up. When she called back, the line was busy.

After fifteen minutes of getting a busy signal, an edgy feeling began to settle in Meghan's stomach, and she decided to go to the clinic and check on Tom. She whistled for Sox, then jumped in the car and took off. She made it in eight minutes, which was a near record.

The reception room was empty, other than the perturbed-looking Francine Birnbaum and her schnauzer.

"Where's Emily?" Meghan asked.

Francine scrunched her nose in a look of annoyance.

"You're asking me?" she snipped. "We had a nine-fifteen appointment. It is now twenty-five past, and no one has even checked in Bailey."

Meghan slid her tote bag under Emily's desk as Sox bolted toward the back office.

"I'm so sorry," she said. "Give me a minute, and I'll try to get Dr. Whitely for you."

With her heart now thumping hard against her chest, she turned and headed toward the back of the clinic. Something was wrong, drastically wrong. Picturing Tom in the operating room with the victim of some terrible accident, she almost flew by his office and would have kept going had she not heard the sound of his voice.

"I'll pay time and a half," he pleaded.

"Tom?" Meghan stuck her head through the doorway. "Mrs. Birnbaum's in the reception room, and Emily's not there."

He covered the phone with his hand. "Emily's out sick. Would you tell Mrs. Birnbaum I'll be with her in a few minutes?"

"Sure, but—"

He turned back to the phone. "Friday is no good. I need someone all week."

"What are you doing?" Meghan whispered.

"Yes, I'll hold." He covered the phone again. "Trying to get a temp to sub for Emily."

She took the phone from his hand and said, "Go see Mrs. Birnbaum; I'll take care of this."

When the Reliable Temps representative came back on the line, Meghan said, "The position has been filled. We won't be needing anyone after all."

She then made a quick phone call to Tracy saying she'd be helping Tom for the rest of the week, and settled in behind Emily's desk feeling perfectly at home.

Meghan had been around the clinic long enough to know what to do. She powered on the computer and checked the appointment log, then moved the credit card reader to the counter where it belonged. Without skipping a beat, she became Emily. Not an Emily who just booked appointments and validated credit cards, she turned into an Emily who came from behind the desk to greet the animals.

The hours flew by, and in what seemed like the blink of an eye, the day was gone. Tom insisted he wanted to pay her, but Meghan flatly refused.

"You can, however, take me out to dinner," she said.

Once the office was closed and the clinic's patients all cared for, she clicked the leash onto Sox's collar and the three of them went back to the Garden and sat at an outside table. After the crimson glow of sunset disappeared and the candles on the tables were lit, a crisp breeze came up. Seeing Meghan shiver, Tom draped his jacket over her shoulders and scooted close enough to press his thigh against hers.

Meghan turned and let her eyes linger on his. "It was a good day."

"Very," he replied.

They ordered two cappuccinos and sat looking up at the stars for yet another hour. Sitting with his arm curled around her shoulders, Tom never noticed the chill, even though the temperature had plummeted and he was without a jacket.

It was close to midnight when he finally dropped her off at the house. Rather than going back for her car, he suggested he'd pick her up on the way in the next morning.

"That sounds good," she answered dreamily.

On Tuesday morning, Henry Mosley came in with Chelsea, a collie with a gray muzzle who appeared almost as old as her octogenarian owner. When Meghan noticed the dog limping, she came from behind the counter and squatted down to take a look at the paw.

She inhaled sharply. "Good grief, there's something stuck in there." Before you could bat an eyelash, she'd reached in and plucked out a rusty nail.

"Well, if that ain't something," Henry said. "I looked and didn't see a thing."

"It was stuck between the pads," Meghan explained. "She should be okay, but I think you need to clean her paw with peroxide and put some Neosporin on it." She thought a moment, then added, "It would help if you had something to cover that paw and keep it clean. A baby sock maybe."

"Baby sock? Where am I gonna get such a thing?"

"Let's see if I can get one for you." She lifted the phone and punched in her home number. When her mama answered, Meghan asked if Lila could come over with one of Lucas's baby socks.

In the middle of watching her TV show and only half listening, Lila replied, "Lucas is napping, and I thought Sox was with you."

"Sox is with me, but what I need is a *baby sock*." She explained the situation, and Lila agreed to come.

"My show's over in five minutes. Can he wait?"

Meghan covered the mouthpiece and turned to Henry. "Mama can be here in twenty minutes. Can you wait?"

He bobbed his head and settled back into the chair.

Henry was still waiting when Mildred Washington emerged from the back office with her cat carrier and stepped to the desk. As Meghan was processing Mildred's payment, Tom came out. He greeted Henry, then squatted to pet the dog.

"So what's wrong with Chelsea today?" he asked.

"Nothing now," Henry replied. "Your nurse took care of it."

"My nurse?"

Henry waggled a finger toward Meghan. "Pulled a nail out of Chelsea's paw, good as you could've done. I don't need peroxide or Neosporin; I've got those at home. I'm just waiting for the sock."

"Sock?"

Henry nodded. "Her mama's bringing it over." He went on to say using a baby sock was the cleverest thing he'd ever heard of. "It beats trying to bandage a paw, that's for certain."

After Lila had come and gone and only Meghan was left in the reception room, Tom came up behind her and kissed the back of her neck.

"So how's my favorite nurse?" he teased.

She swiveled the chair and came face-to-face with him. "I'm sorry. I didn't mean to jump in ahead of you. I saw the nail in Chelsea's paw, and I just—"

He laughed. "There's nothing to be sorry about." He touched his fingers to her chin, tilted her face up toward his, and then added, "Other than how you've missed your calling."

Before she could answer, he covered her mouth with his. He would have lingered there and let the moment lead to something more were it not for the sound of a car door slamming.

With the kiss still warm on her lips, she whispered, "I think your three o'clock is here."

"Later, then," he said, and gave her a quick peck before he turned away.

For days Tom had been noticing Meghan's way with animals. Not only Sox but just about every animal that came into the office. Twice before he'd said something—not an out-and-out suggestion, simply a hint at one—but she'd not picked up on it.

Tonight, he thought. Tonight he was having dinner at the Briggs house, but afterward he and Meghan would most likely sit on the front porch or take a stroll down to the lake, and that's when he would ask her. Now that Lucas was doing so well and Tracy content to stay put, there was no reason for her not to consider it.

The Question

After work, Tom went back to his apartment to change and freshen up before dinner. He and Meghan left the office together. As she climbed into her car, he kissed her cheek and said, "See you this evening."

Seconds later, they pulled out of the parking lot, one behind the other. She turned left; he turned right.

On the drive to his apartment, Tom thought through how he would broach the subject. He couldn't just come at it out of the blue. There had to be some kind of groundwork, something to spark the conversation.

An opportunity for a better future?

He didn't waste a lot of time thinking that one over, because positioning it in such a way could imply he held the *Snip 'N' Save* in low regard. Definitely not a good idea.

An opportunity to do something she loves?

Not a good enough argument. She'd loved working at the *Snip 'N' Save*. It's possible she still did.

After a certain amount of consideration, he settled on starting with the story of how she'd plucked a rusty nail from Chelsea's paw and how without anyone telling her to do so, she'd come up with the idea of bandaging the paw in a baby sock. He'd tell the story as they were gathered at the dinner table and then move on to saying such a talent was a God-given gift. Later on when they were alone, pushing back and forth on the porch swing or maybe sitting on the grassy bank of the lake, he would return to the subject and ask the question.

Confident he'd hit upon the perfect plan, he pulled a soft blue shirt from the closet and finished dressing. On the drive over, he stopped and bought a potted chrysanthemum. He'd give it to Tracy and say it was a token of his appreciation for her covering work at the *Snip 'N' Save* this week so Meghan could sub for Emily.

It was a fifteen-minute drive, and by the time he turned down Baker Street, he was certain he'd covered all the bases, but when he pulled into the driveway, there was an unfamiliar car parked there.

Could it be Dominic? Tom had never met him. Still, he'd heard enough about the angry phone calls to know that his showing up would not be a good thing. Tom climbed out of the car, drew a deep breath, then grabbed the chrysanthemum and started for the door. Meghan answered his knock and didn't look the least bit upset. Tom brushed a kiss across her lips, wrapped his free arm around her, and leaned toward her ear.

"Whose car is in the driveway?" he whispered.

"Aunt Phoebe came with a gentleman friend tonight," she said in a hushed voice. "But don't let on that it's anything out of the ordinary, or you'll embarrass her."

"Why? Doesn't she—"

Meghan hushed him as they rounded the corner and stepped into the living room. A silver-haired man in a navy blazer and gray slacks stood and looked across with a broad smile.

"Ah, so this is the young veterinarian Phoebe has been telling me about." Without waiting for anyone to do the introductions, he stretched his arm out and started toward them. Pumping Tom's hand up and down, he said, "Charles Franklin, Esquire. Retired."

"A pleasure to meet you," Tom replied.

Seconds later, Lila came in carrying a tray of glasses and bottles of both white and red wine. Setting the tray on the coffee table, she turned to Meghan.

"Dear, will you pour the drinks while I fetch the hors d'oeuvres from the oven?"

"Certainly," she said, then asked Charles what he'd prefer.

"Is that a French or Italian pinot noir?" he asked.

Meghan checked the label. "French."

"Ah, well then, my decision is made." When Meghan handed him the glass of wine, he held it up and eyed the color.

"Beautiful," he said. Then, bringing the glass to his nose, he sniffed the aroma. "Ah, the earthy fragrance of mushrooms and fresh-picked cherries. Delightfully familiar." Before she'd filled the remaining glasses, Charles launched into a story of traveling through the south of France on a wine-tasting excursion.

He'd barely finished the story when Phoebe jumped in and told how Charles was organizing a wine-tasting group at the apartment complex.

"We'll meet once a month, and everyone will bring a bottle of their favorite. Charles says the secret to a successful wine tasting is to serve a small savory between each sampling. A French cheese, like a Boursin or a Camembert."

After everyone had a glass of wine in hand, Charles proposed a toast and felt compelled to say it in French.

"À votre bonheur et à votre santé."

Charles continued on, telling of first one exploit and then another until at long last Lila announced dinner was on the table.

They stood and started toward the dining room. Tom, hoping to divert the topic of conversation from Charles's travels, said, "Well, it's been nice hearing about those adventures. I know you probably have hundreds more, and maybe sometime in the future—"

"He most certainly does," Phoebe said. "Although Charles is modest to a fault, I can tell you he's extremely well read and very involved at the library. That's how we met. He's going to chair next year's lecture series."

Charles reached over and patted her hand. "My dear, you flatter me."

He then seized the opportunity to segue into a lengthy description of the plans he had for the series.

Throughout the salad, leg of lamb, garlic smashed potatoes, and string beans, there was not a single opening for Tom to bring up the subject of Meghan's skill with animals. When Charles launched into a story of cattle grazing on the hillside, Tom thought there might be a slim chance, but that story led to the description of a centuries-old farmhouse. By the time Lila brought out dessert, Lucas, who'd been sitting in his high chair for way too long, started banging on the tray. Anxious to finish dinner and get him off to bed, Tracy jumped up and started for the kitchen.

"I'll get the coffee, Mama," she said.

Lucas screeched, then held out his arms and cried, "Ma-ma!"

Tracy whirled around on her heel. "Did you hear that? He said mama."

"He surely did," Lila agreed. "Clear as a bell!"

For the first time that evening, Charles leaned back in his chair and stopped talking.

"Say it again, baby," Tracy urged. "Mama. Come on, one more time."

Lucas impatiently bucked back and forth with his arms held out for her to pick him up, then cried, "Ma-ma."

Tracy lifted him from the high chair and turned to the group.

"It's his first word," she said proudly.

At that point, the conversation turned to Lucas and all that had happened. Tracy told of how Sox barking had caused Meghan to suspect Lucas wasn't hearing.

Thinking this could be an opportunity, Tom said, "Yes, Meghan is wonderful with animals. Why, just today—"

Before he could even get started, Tracy moved on to telling how Meghan had introduced them to Gabriel Hawke.

Tom resigned himself to the thought that later, when he and Meghan were alone, he would talk to her about it. Even if he hadn't been able to bring it up at dinner and get some support from Lila and Tracy, the incident was still fresh in Meghan's mind. She'd have to see the value of such an idea.

After the table was cleared and the dishwasher loaded, everyone except Tracy moved toward the living room. She headed upstairs with Lucas.

Not wanting to give Charles the chance to start another long-winded story, Tom said, "I hope you'll excuse us. Meghan and I were planning to take a walk down to the lake. You know, stretch our legs after sitting for so long."

"By George, that sounds like a splendid idea." Charles patted his stomach as if it were a drum. "Work off a few calories after that meal."

"Do you mind if Charles and I join you?" Phoebe asked.

Noticing the look of disappointment on Tom's face, Meghan gave a polite smile. It was obvious that he wanted some alone time with her as much as she wanted it with him, but the situation had no easy exit.

"Why, of course not," she said. "We'd love to have you."

"Count me out," Lila volunteered. "I'm bushed. Lucas is an early riser, and I like to be there when he wakes up."

They slipped on sweaters and started down the block. Before they were halfway to the corner, Charles began telling of a trip to Germany where, before the wall came down, he'd seen barbed-wire fences. In the middle of his describing how the soldiers stood ready to shoot, Meghan suggested it might be a bit nippy for the lake.

"Let's just go to the far end of Baker Street and back," she said.

Tom gave a weary nod of agreement.

For the remainder of that week, Meghan worked at the clinic. While there were a few instances where she calmed a nervous animal or weighed a dog that refused to step onto the scale, there was nothing quite as notable as what she'd done with Chelsea. Had there been another such incident, Tom would have brought up the issue right then and there.

Thinking perhaps he might have missed something while he was with a patient, on Thursday afternoon he asked, "Anything unusual happen yesterday or today?"

She shook her head. "Nothing worth telling about."

"No more rusty nails?"

Meghan gave him a playful nudge.

"Come on," she said, laughing. "I know you're just teasing me."

"No, I'm not," Tom replied, suppressing a sigh.

On Friday, Emily called to say she was feeling quite a bit better and would be returning to work on Monday.

"Glad to hear it," Tom replied in a flat, rather unenthusiastic voice.

Spurred on by the knowledge that this would be their last afternoon of working together, Tom waited until Meghan was settled in her spot at the reception desk, then suggested they commemorate the week with dinner at the Starlight Lounge.

"Not many people could have stepped in and taken over as you did," he said. "Pulling that nail out of Chelsea's paw showed real skill."

Meghan laughed. "Are you gonna keep teasing me about that forever? I've already said I was sorry."

"No, no. There's nothing to be sorry about. Caring for an animal that way is a God-given gift. It's something to celebrate, not be sorry about."

He'd planned to wait until they were at the Starlight Lounge, maybe start with a glass of wine, relax with a plate of canapés, and then creep up on the subject. But now here he was, smack in the middle of what he'd planned to say. He had to continue.

"You have a way with animals. They trust you. Not everybody has that. Look at the way Sox follows you place to place."

"Well, of course he does; he's my dog."

"It's not just Sox. What about Bruiser? If anybody else tried to walk him on a leash, he'd be snapping and snarling, but he let you do it because he trusted you. And that day with Agatha's cat. You knew right off she had a hairball."

Meghan scrunched her nose and eyed him with a look of bewilderment. "I don't see what—"

"I'm planning to grow the business," he continued on, "and before long I'm going to need a full-time assistant."

"You've got Emily. She's coming back on Monday."

"Emily's a receptionist. She's great with the customers but has no interest whatsoever in working with animals. I need someone to assist me, somebody who can step in for surgeries."

"So you're planning to hire another vet?"

"Dammit, no, Meghan, I'm asking you to do it."

She gasped. "Me? I don't know one end of a scalpel from the other. Pulling a nail out of a dog's paw is one thing, but—"

He took her by the shoulders and held her at arm's length. "Stop talking and let me explain. I'd like to sponsor you to become certified as a veterinary technician. You can do most of the course work online and get the necessary hands-on experience here working with me."

She looked at him with her eyes wide.

"What about the *Snip 'N' Save*?" she said.

Tom cringed. It was the one answer he feared.

"I know how much the *Snip 'N' Save* has meant to you, but Tracy seems happy doing it, and she's got Sheldon."

"What if Tracy leaves? What if after Lucas finishes his therapy, she decides to go back to Philadelphia? Daddy built the *Snip 'N' Save*. I can't just walk off and let it die."

He pulled her into his arms and held her close.

"I know you can't," he said solemnly. "I would never ask you to, but maybe you could talk to Tracy, ask if she's planning to stay, and see if she'd be interested in taking over."

"What if she says yes now and then two or three years from now—"

"If that happens and you want to go back, I won't stop you."

"You won't be angry or disappointed?"

He gave a small, almost regretful-sounding laugh.

"I can't swear I won't be disappointed," he said. "But I can promise you I won't be angry. Even though I believe you have a unique gift for working with animals, your happiness is far more important than my keeping or losing an assistant."

Meghan hesitated. "This is so sudden; I need time to think it over. I've got the *Snip 'N' Save* to consider. I can't just walk away. I have to make certain Tracy is ready to handle the magazine alone and is really going to stay." Even as Meghan spoke of these concerns, the idea of working at the clinic, day after day, week after week, was filling her heart with a warm glow.

That evening they didn't go to the Starlight Lounge. Meghan suggested they save such an extravagance for when they were in more of a celebratory mood. Even though there was a chill in the air, they went back to the Garden. As they sat beneath the stars and drank hot cider spiced with cinnamon sticks, she thought back on that first night and how over the months they had come to mean so much to each other.

Meghan didn't doubt her fondness for Tom, and it was true she had a soft spot in her heart for animals. But how could she leave the *Snip 'N' Save*? Over the years, the magazine had come to be a part of her. Walking away would be like tearing loose an arm or a leg.

Besides, it was the only piece of her daddy she had left.

Finding an Answer

That night, Meghan found it impossible to sleep. Even with Sox curled up beside her, she felt restless. For hours she lay there stroking his tummy and wondering what to do. This week she'd loved every minute of being at the clinic—so much so that it hardly seemed like work. But was it because of the animals or simply being near Tom?

And she couldn't just dismiss the issue of the *Snip 'N' Save*. Thinking back over the years, Tracy had proven herself to be flighty—passionate about something one minute and ready to drop it like a hot potato the next. What if she agreed to stay and then next year or the year after, Dominic came to the door asking her to come back to Philadelphia? Would she stay or go? It was possible either could happen.

Granted, she'd said she was never going back, but Meghan couldn't count the number of times she'd heard muffled sobs coming from Tracy's room late at night. Saying something and believing it yourself were sometimes two entirely different things.

If not for the *Snip 'N' Save*, she would say yes to Tom in a heartbeat, but as things stood now, she felt doing so would be disloyal to her daddy.

Maybe it was just a question of time. It was possible that after Tracy had stayed for two or three years, Meghan could be more certain of her dependability. Then such a decision would be easier.

Opportunity doesn't wait forever, though.

After hours of running through these thoughts, Meghan became so tired she could no longer hold her eyes open and drifted off to sleep.

It was early morning when Meghan heard her daddy's laugh and caught the fragrance of his pipe tobacco. He was back, right here in the house. She hurried down the stairs and into the office. He was at the desk with Tracy beside him.

"Hi, sweetheart," he said, and smiled.

"Daddy, I thought you were . . ." The word *dead* felt strange in Meghan's mouth, so she substituted, "Gone."

"I am," he replied. "But before I leave here, I thought I'd give Tracy a few pointers."

Tracy turned with a proud grin. "Daddy says I'm a really good designer, good enough to take over the magazine."

"Daddy!" Meghan felt a swell of resentment rising in her chest. "Don't you realize Tracy might not stay? Dominic has called her a dozen times or more. She could easily enough decide to go back to him. I'm the one who's supposed to take care of the *Snip 'N' Save*. You know I'm the one; I've always been the one."

He eyed her with a stern look.

"No, Meghan, you're not," he said. "That thought is yours, not mine. The only thing I want you to do is find yourself some real happiness and take care of the dog I gave you. Now don't you think it's high time you got started?" His stern expression morphed into a soft smile.

A tear came to Meghan's eye. "But, Daddy, what if Tracy leaves?"

Using the old familiar phrase, he said, "The probability is she won't, but if she does, so what?"

"Your *Snip 'N' Save*," Meghan said, her throat feeling tight. "I've got to keep it alive because—"

"Nonsense," he said. "This is just a business. It's not me. The *Snip 'N' Save* was a way for me to earn a living and still spend time with Lila and you girls. I never considered that either of you would step into my shoes. I never envisioned my girls spending their life squinting at a computer screen rearranging coupons. I want you and Tracy to follow your heart. I want you to experience a love like your mama and I had." He gave a soft chortle, then added, "This is your time, Meghan. Be happy and enjoy it. Don't worry—wherever you go or whatever you do, I'll still be with you. I'm your daddy, and that's never going to change."

The phone rang, and Meghan woke with a start.

The first light of morning was creeping into the sky. She sat up and rubbed her eyes, remembering the dream. Even now it seemed so real that she wondered if she hurried downstairs, would she actually find her daddy sitting at the computer? Dropping back onto the pillow, she tried to recapture the dream, but it was gone.

That morning, after the breakfast dishes were cleared from the table and Lucas was napping in his crib, Meghan took Tracy aside.

"We need to talk about the *Snip 'N' Save*," she said. Her words were small and fluttery, like a baby bird learning to fly.

Tracy's eyes narrowed, and she pinched her brows together. "Is this because I redid the *Golf World* ad? That illustration they were using was not good."

"This has nothing to do with an ad. It's about management of the magazine."

"Jeez . . ." Tracy gave a sigh of discouragement. "Now that I've got the hang of it and I'm enjoying myself, you wanna take it back?"

"Take it back? No. Absolutely not." Meghan laughed. "So you really do like doing the *Snip 'N' Save*?"

"Yeah." Tracy gave a sheepish grin. "The guy at *Golf World* said I've got an eye for design, and I've gotta admit I feel good doing it."

"You enjoy the design element, but how would you feel about taking over management of the magazine?"

Tracy's eyes widened. "Management? But isn't that *your* job?"

"Now it is, but I'd like to try my hand at something new."

Meghan told her about Tom's offer and how working with animals was something she really wanted to do.

"The thing is, I'd have to know you're not going back to Dominic, that you'll stay here and love the *Snip 'N' Save* as I have."

Even as her words still hung in the air, Meghan heard her daddy's voice repeating what he'd said in the dream.

This is just a business. It's not me.

"Don't worry, I'm not going back to Dominic," Tracy replied. "I absolutely am not. And I swear I'll take care of the *Snip 'N' Save*, just like you have."

Meghan's smile was wide, and they hugged.

"Of course," Meghan added, "in the future, if your heart takes you somewhere else, I think Daddy would understand."

When Tom rang the doorbell that evening, Meghan wore a silk dress that matched the blue of her eyes and bared her shoulders. Her hair was an upsweep of curls pinned in a sparkling clip. He eyed her head to toe and gave a grin of approval.

"You look amazing," he said. "Are we celebrating a special occasion?"

She nodded. "I thought maybe we'd go to the Starlight Lounge."

The previous day she'd sounded rather doubtful about taking his offer, so Tom was almost afraid to ask.

"Does this mean . . ." He left the remainder of the question unspoken.

Her mouth curled into a smile as she grabbed her shawl and hooked her arm through his.

"It means you've got yourself a new assistant."

The Starlight Lounge was a dinner club with a glass ceiling over the dance floor and tables lit only by candlelight. It was a place where waiters appeared and disappeared without a sound and music floated through the air soft as a cloud. They sat side by side at a banquette with Tom's thigh against hers and his fingers cupping her hand as she told of the dream.

When the waiter appeared, Tom ordered a bottle of champagne and a plate of appetizers. They toasted the new venture and then danced. He pressed his hand to the small of her back and held her so close the thump of her heart felt as if it were part of his own.

Meghan, too, felt their heartbeats, perfectly matched, synchronized, a symphony that was meant to be. As they danced, she nuzzled her head against his shoulder, and their bodies moved as one, swaying to the music, falling deeper and deeper in love. Later, after they'd had their fill of Chateaubriand and roasted vegetables, she tilted her head back against the leather upholstery, drew a deep breath, and gave a soft sensuous sigh.

"This has been the most wonderful evening."

He traced his finger along the curve of her cheek and down her throat.

"Yes, it has," he said. Then he leaned close and kissed her neck in that tender spot just below her jawbone.

She felt the warmth of his kiss slide down her chest and come to rest in her heart.

It was the smallest hour of the morning when they returned home, and by the time Tom kissed her good night, any reservations Meghan once had about following her heart were gone. Vanished like a missing button or a forgotten thought. There was only the future.

Thanksgiving

Lila began cooking a week ahead of time, and by Thanksgiving morning she had four pies, a chocolate cake, ginger cookies, and so many side dishes the buffet groaned beneath the weight. That morning she was up before the crack of dawn, sliding a twenty-six-pound turkey into the oven and adding watermelon-rind pickles to the relish tray. After the coffee was turned to brew, she hollered up the stairs for the girls to get moving.

"We've got a lot to do," she said, "and our guests will be here by noon."

Lila was certain this was going to be the best Thanksgiving they'd had in years. Tracy was back home, Lucas was starting to talk, and Meghan was about to begin a new adventure. And if all that weren't enough to be thankful for, there would be twelve people at the table. In addition to Lila and the girls, Tom would be there and Phoebe was coming with Charles.

Earlier in the week, after Tracy had learned Lila had invited the Harpers from three doors down, Ida Wentworth, and Fred Cummings, she'd decided to invite Gabriel.

On Tuesday afternoon as they were finishing lunch at the café, she'd said, "I don't know if you're up for this or not, but Mama has a slew of people coming for Thanksgiving, and Lucas would love it if you could join us."

She lifted the coffee cup to her mouth, took a tiny sip, and then, peeking over the rim of the cup, added, "I'd like it, too."

His mouth pulled to the side as if he were thinking it over, then it eased into a smile.

"I'd be honored," he said.

Tracy smiled. At first, she'd been hesitant about inviting him, afraid that he'd think her too forward and be forced into making some clumsy excuse about having previous plans. Now she was glad she had. "You won't be sorry. My mama's a real good cook."

"It wouldn't matter if she wasn't," he'd replied.

For the remainder of the afternoon, Tracy had wondered about the meaning of his remark. Was it a way of being polite, or was he telling her something? Although she never did come to a conclusion, when Gabriel knocked at the door, she was wearing a russet-colored top and a brand-new smoky brown eye shadow that made her eyes sparkle.

Tom arrived just minutes after Gabriel. He kissed Meghan, then shook hands with Gabriel.

"I've heard a lot about you," he said. "Awesome work you're doing with children."

Lila came into the living room with a tray of hors d'oeuvres and smiled when she saw the two young couples standing in a group talking as they were. Gabriel and Tracy weren't really a couple—they were merely friends—but for the moment Lila chose to see it differently. To her, the group looked exactly as she'd imagined her family would be one day: close to one another and home for the holidays.

Before long, the room was filled. In one corner, the Harpers were talking about how fortunate they'd been to land on Baker Street. Over by the fireplace, Charles was pontificating on the treasures of the Louvre.

"You absolutely must see it," he told Phoebe, but he said nothing of how she was to get there.

Giddy with delight, Lila scurried back and forth to the kitchen delivering platter after platter of canapés and hors d'oeuvres, filling wineglasses, and chatting with the guests as she breezed by. Handing Meghan a tray of crab puffs to be passed from guest to guest, she whispered, "Your daddy would have loved this."

There was a note of melancholy in her voice, but it came from deep down and was not obvious in the smile she wore.

By two o'clock, the aroma wafting through the house was enough to make a person ravenous.

"Dinner will be served in five minutes, so please come to the dining room and find a seat at the table." She turned to Meghan. "Will you refill the wineglasses, dear?"

After the wine was poured and the guests were seated, after they'd said grace and thanked the Lord for their bounty, after Lila had begun to carve the turkey, there was a knock at the door.

With everyone chatting back and forth, Lila was the only one who heard it.

"Oh, dear," she murmured, fearful it was an unexpected guest. She'd already used the entire set of dinnerware, and there wasn't another chair to be had. She herself was sitting on the rolling chair from Meghan's desk. Still, on a day when there was so much to be thankful for, she couldn't leave a hungry guest standing on the doorstep.

Looking across the table, she said, "Tracy, I believe there's someone at the door. Will you get it, please?"

"Sure." Tracy jumped up and hurried off.

Moments later, everyone at the table heard the sound of angry voices. Lila handed Phoebe the long knife and said, "I've got to go check on Tracy. Finish carving and pass this around." She got up and trotted toward the door.

Meghan was right behind her. The driveway was filled with cars, but through the large window in the living room, Meghan saw the car with one blue fender parked alongside the curb.

"Oh, no," she said with a groan.

When they got to the door, Tracy was blocking the entranceway, and Dominic was standing out on the porch.

He was drunk—not a little tipsy, but so drunk he was listing to one side like a bent flagpole. "What do you want from me?" he whined. "I already said I'm willing to get married."

Even from a distance, the smell of whiskey on his breath was overpowering. "I don't want anything! Just get out of here and leave me alone."

He took a step forward and steadied himself against the porch rail. "Forget about it. I'm not leaving. I drove down here to be with my family for the holiday, and that's what I'm gonna do. I'm not taking no for an answer."

"You didn't come for us, Dominic. You came to see your grandma. Go back to her house. She's your family. The only family you've got!"

"Wrong, wrong, wrong!" he slurred. "I got you and Lucas."

"No, you don't. You turned your back on us a long time ago, and now we're doing the same to you. We've got our own lives, and they don't include you!"

"The hell they don't! Lucas is my kid! I got rights!" He let go of the railing and staggered toward Tracy. "I'm here to see him, and I'm gonna."

"No, you're not." She stepped forward, blocking his path and forcing him to back away from the door.

As Lila peered from behind her daughter, her face became stiff and almost colorless. "I think it would be best if you just leave, Dominic. If you want to discuss this with Tracy, come back some other time. Right now we've got a houseful of company."

"Butt out!" he yelled. "I don't give a crap about you or your company! I'm here to get what's mine, and I'm not leaving!"

"We're not yours!" Tracy said angrily. "We stopped being yours when you canceled that insurance without caring what happened to Lucas."

Dominic reached out and grabbed hold of Tracy's shoulder. "Jeez, Tracy, gimme a break! You know I didn't do it to hurt him. I was just trying to make you see you needed me."

She jerked loose of him, stiffened her arm, and slammed her hand flat against his chest, forcing him to move back another step. "What's done is done! The only thing you can do now is get out of here and leave us alone!"

"Honey babe, don't act this way. All I want is to be with my family."

"We're not your family! We never were! I tried to make us one because I loved you and wanted Lucas to have a home, but that's over and done with."

"It doesn't have to be. Just come back to Philadelphia. I swear it will be different this time. We'll get married, find a nice little apartment, and give the kid a home."

Hearing him call Lucas *the kid* rankled Tracy even more. "No way, Dominic. It's too little, too late."

Tom came up behind Meghan and whispered, "Do you need help?"

She turned to him with a look of concern. "Tracy is having trouble getting Dominic to leave."

Tom listened to the exchange for a moment, then edged past Meghan and eyed Dominic. "Do we have a problem here?"

"We?" Dominic replied with a sardonic laugh. "You've got nothing to do with this, buddy boy, so get your sorry ass back inside and leave us alone. This is between my wife and me."

"I'm not your wife!" Tracy shouted. "Not now and not ever!"

A tear glinted in Dominic's eye, and his voice turned mellow, more pleading than demanding. "Aw, don't say that, babe. You know we belong together."

"No, we don't, Dominic. It's over. There is no *we*."

"But if you'd come home—"

"I'm not going back to Philadelphia. Not ever. The only thing I want is for you to leave me alone. Let me raise Lucas in a place where he's loved." Her tone was level and resolute.

"I'm not buying that crap!" he said, his voice angrier, louder, and more aggressive. "He's my kid, too. I got rights! Either you get your ass home, or I tell the cops you kidnapped him and sue for custody! We'll see how much you like it when they come and cart him off!"

The thought of his taking Lucas came at Tracy like a tidal wave. She fisted her hands and pounded them furiously against his chest. "If you ever do anything to hurt him, I'll—"

Dominic grabbed her arms, pinned them back, pulled her body to his, and lowered his mouth toward hers.

"No!" she screamed, and turned her face.

In the blink of an eye, Tom bolted past everyone else and pulled Dominic away from Tracy. In what seemed a singular movement, he had Dominic's right arm twisted behind his back.

"No means no!" he said, and keeping Dominic's arm pinned, he edged him toward the steps. "I think you'd better leave now."

Given no alternative, Dominic lowered his right foot down onto the top step. As soon as his arm was freed, he turned back and lunged at Tom.

Tom instinctively swung, and his fist smashed hard against the right side of Dominic's jaw.

For a brief moment, Dominic wobbled, then staggered backward, missed the step, and fell spread eagle on the front lawn. The side of his face had already begun to swell.

Looking up at both Tom and Tracy, he narrowed his eyes and swore. "This ain't over. Not by a long shot." His words had a menacing tone, and Tracy feared that he'd spoken the truth.

Tom wrapped a protective arm around her shoulders and turned toward the doorway. Just before they stepped inside, Tom looked back and warned, "Don't say things you'll come to regret."

As the door clicked shut, they heard Dominic yell, "Screw you!"

Standing there on one side of the door with Dominic still screaming obscenities on the other, Tracy began to tremble, and tears cascaded down her cheeks.

"It's okay now," Tom said, and squeezed her shoulder. "That was just the whiskey talking. I'm sure when Dominic sobers up, he'll feel terrible about the things he said."

Tracy wanted to believe that, but a small niggling doubt remained in her mind. "Let's hope so," she replied wearily.

Meghan wrapped her arms around her sister and held her close. "Tomorrow we'll get a restraining order to make sure he doesn't show up here again."

Turning to Lila, Meghan said, "Go see to dinner, Mama. Tom and I will stay with Tracy for a while."

As Lila returned to the dining room and slid into her seat, she noticed the anxious faces around the table and realized they had heard everything. "I'm sorry about the ruckus," she said. "But there's nothing to worry about. Everything is okay now." She scooped a ball of mashed potatoes onto her plate, then passed the bowl to Phoebe. "You must try these. They're made with sour cream."

Despite the air of nonchalance, Phoebe saw how Lila's brows were knitted together and her face paled to a ghastly white. "You sure everything is okay?"

"Absolutely," Lila answered, and gave a stiff smile.

It was almost ten minutes before Tracy was composed enough to rejoin the others. She'd stood there listening for the sound of Dominic's car roaring off, but it didn't happen. When she finally turned away, she glanced out the side window and saw his car still parked in front of the house. She felt a strange new ache settling into her heart, partly because of the family they had never been and partly because of what she feared might happen in the days to come.

As they returned to the dining room and settled at the table, Meghan gave a lighthearted shrug and offered up a feeble explanation. "Just an angry ex looking to crash the party."

After a few minutes of stilted conversation, she segued to the subject of Charles's wine-tasting tour, and, as suspected, he took it from there. Before long, the guests were back to chatting as they had previously.

Later on, while Meghan helped Lila set pies and cakes on the table, Tracy went back to the living room and again peeked from the side of the window. Dominic's car was gone. She breathed a sigh of relief and returned to the table.

Sitting next to her, Gabriel folded his hand over hers and asked, "Are you all right?"

She gave a thin smile and nodded.

Late in the day, it turned chilly, so Tom and Gabriel gathered kindling and lit the fire pit in the backyard. Claiming it was much too cold to be sitting outside, Phoebe and Charles plopped down on the sofa and remained in the living room, as did Lila and several other guests.

"I think it's refreshing," Tracy said. She shrugged on a wool sweater and bundled Lucas into a jacket. When they pulled the Adirondack chairs close to the pit, she sat him in her lap.

For a short while, Sox chased squirrels around the yard, then he settled alongside Meghan's feet. As the sun slowly slipped from the sky, most of those in the outside group left and returned to the warmth of the house. By the time the stars appeared, it was only the sisters, Gabriel, and Tom. Meghan went into the house and returned with four mugs of hot cider, and they sat there talking long after the other guests were gone. Tracy said because of the school, Lucas was learning new things every day. She laughed.

"With all the baking Mama's been doing, she's taught him to say pie."

This was only partially true. While he made an attempt at the word, it came out sounding like "eye."

"None of this would have happened if Meghan hadn't reached out to Gabriel," she added.

Meghan described the first time she'd met Gabriel and how she'd sat and listened to his music for almost two hours.

"I was in high school then, and yet I still remember how I could hear the sound of his guitar almost two blocks away." She looked at Gabriel with a smile that lit her eyes. "It was almost a magical experience."

"Magical?" Gabriel said, and gave a shy grin.

With only the slightest bit of persuasion, he got his guitar from the car and began to play. In an odd way—a way she couldn't quite put a name to—that evening also seemed magical, and it would remain in Meghan's heart for a long time.

Secret Santa

On the Monday after Thanksgiving, Meghan began work at the clinic. That morning she carried her laptop into Tom's office and sat at the opposite side of the desk as she signed on and registered for the ACT Veterinary Assistant Training Course. After ten sessions of study and ninety hours of hands-on training with Tom, she would receive her certification.

By lunchtime, she was halfway through the first section on office etiquette and hospital procedures.

That same afternoon, she donned one of the colorful new smocks Emily had ordered from the laundry service and stepped in to calm Clara Albright's cat so that Tom could inspect a suspicious growth in the animal's ear. Afterward she walked the dogs and put clean bowls of water in every cage.

One day rolled into another, and this new routine quickly became a way of life for both Meghan and Sox. In the early part of the day, as she sat at the laptop and studied, he curled up beneath the desk and napped. In the afternoon when she worked alongside Tom, Sox explored the clinic and entertained the customers by sniffing out loose treats that had fallen to the floor.

On Wednesday, Meghan moved on to section two, which covered animal restraint and handling. That day she trimmed Biscuit's nails and applied a salve to the hot spot poor Hershey had chewed raw.

She'd taken an extra few minutes to scratch his ears and hug his neck, and afterward the large brown Labrador stood quietly, allowing her to disinfect the area and bandage his leg.

"Sweet baby," she cooed, talking to the dog in much the same way she did Lucas. The soothing sound of her voice seemed to have a calming effect on both.

Tom shook his head and smiled. "You've got the touch. No question about it."

Meghan glanced over at him.

"You were right," she said, smiling. "I love working with animals." She rolled the gauze around Hershey's hind leg another time and sighed. "I can't imagine why it took me all these years to realize it."

On the first day of December, Meghan came into the office carrying a large poinsettia and a shopping bag filled with holly garland and pinecones. Sox trotted along behind her, a bright-red bow tied to his collar.

"'Tis the season," she said gaily, placing the poinsettia on Emily's desk as she breezed by. Before the first customer arrived, there was a jar of candy canes on the counter and a festive garland strung across the back wall. Once everything was in place, Meghan eyed the reception room and noticed a bare spot on the wall behind Emily's desk.

"That wall needs a wreath," she said.

Emily, who had never in all her years of working for Dr. Anderson considered the wall behind her, turned, and looked.

"Golly, you're right. I'll pick one up at lunchtime."

That afternoon, Councilman Dolan came in and asked if he might put a sign about the tree lighting in the front window.

"Sure," Tom said, "and if you've got extras I'll stand one on the reception desk."

Councilman Dolan, of course, had extras. The Christmas tree lighting was one of Magnolia Grove's biggest events. Bigger even than the Fourth of July parade.

"You'll be there, won't you? Doc Anderson is this year's Santa."

Tom eyed the date of the lighting. December fifteenth. "So Doc Anderson's Santa, huh?"

Dolan nodded. "Yeah, he's gonna be great. After we do the community sing-along and light the tree, he'll go around passing out candy and toys to the kids."

Tom grinned, knowing this would be the perfect time and place for his next plan.

"I'll be there," he said. "We all will."

After Dolan left, Tom went into his office, closed the door, and made several phone calls. The first was to Doc Anderson.

"I've got this idea," he said, "but I'm going to need your help . . ." He went on to explain everything.

"That's a good one," Anderson said, chuckling. "I'd be happy to do it."

Tom made a few more calls, then went out and whispered something in Emily's ear.

She laughed. "You think she's really gonna believe that?"

Tom nodded. "I'm hoping."

Before the day ended, Emily announced that she was getting ready to place another order for surgical gloves and asked if Meghan knew her size.

"Small, I guess," Meghan replied.

Emily looked up, trying to keep a straight face. "They don't come small, medium, large. These are *surgical* gloves. You need a specific size." Turning back to the computer, she said, "Ask Tom to measure your hand."

"Okay."

Meghan turned down the hallway and popped her head through the doorway to Tom's office. "Emily said you need to measure me for surgical gloves."

With his face deadpan, Tom pulled a length of twine and a ruler from his desk. He started with her wrist, then measured the width of her palm and lastly all four fingers one by one. When he'd finished he said, "That's it," and smiled.

The surgical gloves were not mentioned again, but the following Monday, a carpenter came and framed out a small office directly across the hall from Tom's. By Wednesday the walls were up. It was painted on Thursday, and on Friday, a new desk was delivered. By then Meghan had plowed through emergency room procedures and was partway through pharmacy and pharmacology.

As the tree lighting drew closer, an aura of excitement seemed to settle over the whole town. Shopkeepers decorated their front windows with oversize wreaths, blinking lights, and spray-on snow, and passersby who throughout most of the year gave only a nod stopped to shake hands and say Merry Christmas.

On the eighth of the month, ladders went up around the Virginia pine in the center of the square, and for two days a volunteer team worked at weaving strands of lights through the branches, hanging colored globes, and draping countless yards of sparkly gold garland.

Lila baked six trays of sprinkled cookies for Santa to hand out at the tree lighting, and Tracy wrapped each one in festive holiday paper. The cover of that week's *Snip 'N' Save* was a photo of Lucas dressed in a pointy green hat and elf suit. Below his picture was a banner that read: DON'T FORGET THE TREE LIGHTING . . . 6:00 P.M., DECEMBER FIFTEENTH.

The Wednesday of the tree lighting, the Anderson Animal Clinic closed an hour early, and everyone went home to get ready for the big event.

"I'll finish up and meet you there," Tom said as Meghan flew by his office.

As soon as she was out the door, he called Doc Anderson.

"We're all set," he said. "I'm bringing it over now."

Anderson laughed. "Well, hurry it up! I'm dressed and ready to go."

The weather in Magnolia Grove could be iffy in December. There had been years when onlookers bundled themselves in wool mufflers and hurried off minutes after the last song was sung. But this year was pleasantly warm.

Meghan changed into a colorful Christmas sweater and winter-white slacks, and Tracy dressed Lucas in the elf suit he'd worn for the picture.

"Hurry up, girls," Lila called up the stairs.

"What's the rush?" Meghan said. "It's early. The tree lighting doesn't start for another hour."

"I want to get a spot in the front row." Lila shrugged on a sweater and jingled her car keys.

"I agree," Tracy chimed in. "Lucas won't see a thing if we get stuck in the back row. Remember that Christmas when Daddy stopped at the gas station and—"

"Okay, okay. Spare me the details." Meghan trailed out the door behind her mama and Tracy.

When they arrived at the square, Tom was already there. So were Phoebe and Charles. Over by the bandstand, Bruce Prendergast was glad-handing a few businessmen, but once he spotted Lila, he gave a wide grin and hurried across to greet her. Only a handful of other spectators circled the square.

Tom greeted Meghan with a kiss, then led everyone to a spot he deemed perfect. It was directly across from the stand where the dignitaries and newspaper reporters sat. From there you could see the tree perfectly and in the distance the steeple of the Good Shepherd Church.

Emily and her husband arrived a few minutes later, and Tom waved them over. Behind Emily were several families from Baker Street, and before long, the square was ringed with onlookers standing three and four deep.

"See," Lila whispered. "It's a good thing we got here early."

They had barely finished greeting friends and neighbors when the choir from Saint Michael's arrived. By then every seat on the dignitaries' platform was occupied. Councilman Hennessy stood and stepped to the microphone.

"Ladies, gentlemen, children of all ages, welcome to the annual Magnolia Grove Christmas tree lighting . . ."

He rambled on for a few minutes, saying it had been an honor to serve as chairman of this year's tree committee and thanking everyone who made the event possible. With a wave of his hand, he gave the signal, and the Saint Michael's choir broke into song.

After a medley of "Joy to the World," "Jingle Bells," and a number of other songs, the mayor stepped to the microphone. As he spoke about the town's growth and a bright future for its businesses, Tom nervously shifted his weight from one foot to the other. It seemed an interminably long time, but finally the mayor threw the switch, and the tree came alive with colored lights.

"Y'all be sure to stay around now," he said, "because there's more music, and Santa is on his way."

In the distance, they could already hear Doc Anderson clanging his bell and hollering, "Ho, ho, ho." When he rounded the corner and came into view, the Saint Michael's choir broke into their rendition of "Santa Claus Is Coming to Town." The kids grew wide-eyed, and everyone cheered.

Well-padded and outfitted in the traditional red suit, Anderson made his way through the crowd, handing out candy canes and small toys. When he got to the spot where Meghan was standing, he gave an exceptionally jovial "Ho, ho, ho!"

"Let's see now, missy," he said. "I think I just might have something in here for you . . ."

Meghan chuckled as he stood there rummaging through the pillowcase sack.

"Ah, here it is." He handed her a small package wrapped in shiny gold paper and tied with a red bow.

Meghan took the box and turned it in her hand. There was no tag, no marking to show who it was from, or even whether it was actually meant for her. "Are you certain this is for me?" she asked.

Doc Anderson gave a broad grin. "Oh, I'm very certain." Placing a hand on his pillowed stomach, he gave a jolly laugh. "One of my elves made sure this gift was at the top of Santa's list!"

Meghan tugged the end of the bow, loosened the ribbon, and began to peel back the gold paper. Inside was a small square box, and atop the box a tiny label written in a familiar hand. It said, "To Meghan, with love, Tom."

She drew in a quick breath and turned to him.

"Open it," he said, grinning ear to ear.

The crowd suddenly became silent, and it seemed all eyes were on Meghan. She lifted the lid, and a note folded over several times dropped into her palm. Beneath the folded paper, she saw the sparkle of a diamond.

Her hand trembled as she unfolded the note, and as she began to read, a lump rose in her throat.

"Read it aloud," somebody shouted.

She glanced up at Tom, and when he nodded his encouragement, she began to speak.

"Meghan Briggs, I love you more than anything in this entire world. Please say you'll marry me and be my partner for life. I will love you always, Tom."

Tears filled her eyes, and she lifted her face to his.

"Yes," she said in a whisper-thin voice.

"What'd she say?" another voice shouted.

"She said yes!" Tom hollered back. Then he circled his arm around her waist and bent to kiss her. Everyone cheered, and cameras began to flash.

"I love you so very, very much," he said as he took the ring from the box and slid it onto her finger. By some odd coincidence, it was the perfect size.

The following Thursday, when the *Magnolia Grove Weekly* came out, the headline for the Living Well section read, SHE SAID YES! The article told of how Santa had delivered happiness to the town's new veterinarian.

Weeks later, when the excitement of the season had faded into sweet memories, Meghan sat on her bed leafing through the composition book that told of that marvelous night and the days that followed.

That composition book was the only one that didn't go into the box beneath her bed. It was tied with a white ribbon and kept by her bedside. In time she would add a sprig of pale-blue forget-me-nots to the ribbon and tuck it into the drawer on her side of the bed.

Once a year, on December fifteenth, she would take it from the drawer, sit propped up in bed with Tom at her side, and read the pages she'd written. Reading the words and touching her finger to the photos taken that night, she could forever remember it exactly as it had been.

Lila

In the terrible time after George's death, I wondered how I would make it from one day to the next. Back then I was certain I would never again know happiness, but here I am with my heart as full and joyous as any mother's could be.

Last summer Meghan married Tom. She'd planned a small family service at the Good Shepherd Church, but half the town showed up.

Once I realized that Tom had invited everyone he knew, I started cooking up a storm. We set up tables in the backyard, and the crowd rivaled that of the annual tree lighting. Even though Meghan didn't expect it to be such a party, that wasn't the only surprise. The last one Tom kept to himself until their wedding day.

He and Meghan walked down the aisle together, and when it came time to exchange the rings, he gave a low whistle. At first I thought maybe he'd forgotten to give Tracy the rings, but seconds later, Sox came trotting down the aisle with a little basket in his mouth. Needless to say, everyone in the church applauded.

This weekend they're off in Atlanta celebrating their anniversary and her certification. I don't need to ask if Meghan's happy working at the clinic—I can see it in her face and in the way her eyes sparkle when she talks about her patients. That's what she calls them—patients. She still writes in her journals and does a lifestyle column for the Magnolia Grove Weekly.

She claims that although she'll never follow in the footsteps of Henry W. Grady, she's happier than she could have ever dreamed possible.

Whatever worry Meghan once had about the Snip 'N' Save *is long gone. Tracy has taken over and is handling it beautifully. The odd thing is that such a responsibility doesn't keep her tied to the computer the way it did Meghan. Somehow Tracy manages to find time to take Lucas to his therapy classes and spend an occasional evening with Gabriel. She claims they're not a "thing," but I've noticed the way he looks at her, so I imagine it's only a matter of time.*

It seems that every day Lucas learns a new word. It's because of Tracy. She sits him on her lap while she's working at the computer and pulls up pictures for him to identify. When I tell her what a good job she's done teaching Lucas to talk, she laughs and says we have Meghan to thank. Of course, Meghan claims it's not her but Sox we should be thanking.

Personally I'm thankful for every single one of them—Meghan, Tom, Tracy, Gabriel, Lucas, and yes, even Sox. Together we're a wonderful family, and I don't think there's a mother in the world who can ask for anything more than that. The only piece missing is George.

Meghan claims he's not really gone, that he still watches over us. She believes George is the one who brought Sox into our lives.

Thinking back on the miracles of that summer, I'm inclined to agree.

Acknowledgments

No successful novel is the work of a single person. Even the most skilled novelist is only as good as the people who support her. I am fortunate to be working with the Lake Union team, one that I consider the best in the business.

First and foremost my heartfelt thanks go to my agent, Pamela Harty, for contacting me out of the blue and then so generously sharing her wisdom, advice, and guidance. In addition to her many virtues, she is patient beyond belief.

I also owe a huge debt of gratitude to Danielle Marshall, Lake Union editorial director, for taking time to meet with me in the midst of a hectic conference schedule and for believing in me as much as I believe in myself.

I am most fortunate to be working with Alicia Clancy, my editor. As a fellow Southerner and dog lover, she has taken this book to her heart and carefully given it all the attention I could possibly wish for. And to Lindsay Guzzardo, my developmental editor, I am extremely grateful for such insightful guidance and suggestions that helped me grow beyond myself. I could not have wished for a better partner on this journey.

My utmost thanks also goes to Stacy Abrams, my copyeditor; Nicole Pomeroy, my production manager; and Sarah Vostok, my proof-reader, for their attention to detail and thoughtful edits. And to my author relations manager, Gabriella Dumpit, for so carefully seeing this project through to completion and welcoming me as she has to the Lake Union team.

To Ekta Garg and Coral Russell, I give my heartfelt thanks for their constant support and unending friendship. I would be lost without such wonderful friends.

I also owe a huge debt of gratitude to the ladies of my BFF Clubhouse, loyal fans, friends, and followers who buy my books, share them with friends, and take time to write reviews. Without such fans, my stories would grow dusty on the shelf.

Lastly, I am thankful beyond words for my husband, Dick, who puts up with my crazy hours, irrational thinking, and late or nonexistent dinners. He is my rock, the foundation of my day-to-day existence. From the very start, he believed in me, believed that I could fly, that I could reach up and touch a star; not only did he believe but he also gave me the place and the means by which to do so. For this I will be eternally grateful. I would not be who I am without Dick, for he is and will always be my greatest blessing.

About the Author

Photo © 2017 Brian Adams Photography

Bette Lee Crosby is the *USA Today* bestselling author of eighteen novels, including *Spare Change* and the Wyattsville series. She has been the recipient of the Royal Palm Literary Award, Reviewer's Choice Award, FPA President's Book Award, International Book Award, and Next Generation Indie Award, among many others. Her 2016 novel, *Baby Girl*, was named Best Chick Lit of the Year by *Huffington Post*. She laughingly admits to being a night owl and a workaholic, claiming that her guilty pleasure is late-night chats with fans and friends on Facebook and Goodreads. To learn more about Bette Lee Crosby's work, stop by her website at www.betteleecrosby.com or visit her Amazon Author Page.